The Righ
An Adam Norcr
Yvonne R

Print ISBNs

Amazon Print 9780228625285
BWL Print 9780228625292
LSI Print 9780228625308
B&N Print 9780228625315

BWL Publishing Inc.

Books we love to write ...
Authors around the world.

http://bwlpublishing.ca

Dedication

For the readers.

*Thank you to the Saskatchewan
Archaeology Society and the
Preeceville & District Heritage Museum.*

"One shovel full of dirt can change history."

Table of Contents

Chapter One......................................7

Chapter Two.....................................26

Chapter Three 42

Chapter Four 55

Chapter Five...................................72

Chapter Six.....................................81

Chapter Seven 87

Chapter Eight 102

Chapter Nine 113

Chapter Ten 127

Chapter Eleven..............................141

Chapter Twelve 154

Chapter Thirteen...........................165

Chapter Fourteen 179

Chapter Fifteen..............................199

Chapter Sixteen.............................216

Chapter Seventeen.........................234

Chapter Eighteen...........................246

Chapter Nineteen 255

Chapter Twenty 270

Chapter Twenty-One 287

Chapter Twenty-Two 301

Chapter Twenty-Three 314

Chapter Twenty-Four 336

Chapter Twenty-Five 347

Chapter Twenty-Six 362

Chapter Twenty-Seven 373

Chapter One

Adam Norcross did not break his stride as the twenty-five-story glass and concrete building came into view. He could not allow himself the luxury. If he did, he'd just walk away. Not that it would change anything.

Instead, Adam briskly moved through the frosted glass front doors of Biggerman, Case, and Abernathy Law Offices. He paused to finish collapsing his black umbrella as the revolving door slowed behind him to a stop. This gave him a chance to look around the foyer, more from habit than from need. Stop stalling, get it done.

Resolutely, Adam lifted his head. He'd been spotted by the receptionist, so he moved forward. His encrypted mobile phone buzzed as he crossed the tiled floor to the plush carpeted area.

Adam mouth twisted in annoyance, he paused again and plucked the device out of his inside coat pocket. He glanced at the display.

Declining the call from Walter Shapiro felt a bit reckless, if completely justified. His boss was increasingly impinging on Adam's off hours. Granted, sometimes the calls were necessary as they were emergency in nature. Still, he could not shake the feeling Shapiro was leaning on him a bit too frequently.

Added to that, Adam also wasn't ready to take a tongue-lashing about his involvement in the latest situation in Libya.

Zara Dare had said she thought it was her good luck Adam was already in Tripoli dealing with the mess a Canadian engineering company had got themselves into. She'd gotten the call from her MI6 boss about the terrorist hijacking of an inbound flight with little time to plan. Zara decided it was more efficient to tap someone who had the experience she needed instead of improvising and Norcross had agreed.

Violence and threats had to be dealt with seriously. When a sister agency asked for help, of course Norcross would give it.

Five terrorists were on board a Lufthansa flight. They'd wanted Qasr bin Ghashir, the active airport, but Adam convinced Zara to reroute to the closed Tripoli facility to limit causalities.

She got a message to the pilot and Adam's idea had worked. Events proceeded swiftly once the plane was on the ground. In any event, they'd sent the tearfully grateful group of passengers to Frankfurt after Zara had done the initial sniff test, screening the passengers and crew. At least this Airbus would arrive at its scheduled destination. Libyan authorities had already dealt with what was left of the hijackers.

In Adam's mind, there was no such thing as happenstance. Still, he'd taken the opportunity to off load a bunch of whinging executives into the hands of his junior associate, Benny Mufisso. His apprentice was more than up to the challenge of extracting the CINS Engineering people. Besides, the negotiations were complete. All Mufisso had left to do was a bit of clerical mopping up.

Being the team on the ground, they all agreed the hijacking was the more important crisis. However, Norcross was not confident Shapiro would agree with that assessment.

To avoid any further interruptions, Adam changed the mobile device to 'airplane' mode with a swipe of his thumb. With that, some of his tension dissolved.

He'd delayed handling this legal task for many months. He was not proud of his procrastination. A failing Adam determined he needed to work on. Do not delay personal business or postpone things that needed to be done…or said, no matter what crisis he was tasked with.

After this meeting, he had plans to fix the latter.

With his phone tucked away in his inside suit pocket, Adam walked forward again. It was past time he dealt with the final details of his late mother's estate, but he didn't have to like it.

His black leather wingtips sank into the immaculate navy-blue carpeting. He noted the light scent of expensive perfume as he approached the glossy redwood reception desk.

"Good morning, sir, how may I help?" The sleekly groomed receptionist asked. She was mid-twenties, extremely trim, with ash blonde hair dramatically swept into an updo. The neckline of her pale blue dress was conservative, yet feminine. Her blue eyes, outlined with heavy black makeup, scanned his face and his tailored grey suit. Appreciation warmed her expression and she flashed him a smile like he'd passed some kind of test.

"Adam Norcross, I have a ten o'clock with Wu Abernathy." He managed to keep the impatience he felt out of his tone. It wasn't anyone else's fault, least of all the receptionist's he found the idea of hearing his mother's will read totally repugnant. He just needed the deed done. Once completed, this chore was one more 'to-do' item to cross off the list from last December. He'd left this second most difficult chore for near to the last. Rationally he knew delaying would not change reality. Still, dealing with this type of thing made his chest tighten.

Then there were the people he had to deal with. As a rule, Adam did not like lawyers, too many of them became politicians. Politicians were forever causing him problems. He reasoned this might be another excuse but discarded the idea almost immediately.

"Of course, Mr. Norcross. One moment, please." She glanced to her left. No doubt where the list of client appointments was kept and quickly found his name. Smoothly, she rose from her desk. "This way please. May I take your coat?"

"No, thank you." He flashed her a quick smile.

She nodded like this was nothing unusual and escorted him to a separate elevator along the back wall behind her desk. Not to one of the six stainless-steel lifts grouped together on the right. A heavy redwood door slid soundlessly open at her touch to a discreet panel.

"Geeta will greet you and take you to your meeting room." She produced a proximity card and touched it against the reader, depressed the button for the twenty-fifth floor, and then retreated.

Adam boarded the car and the door slid closed on the receptionist's lithe form as she returned to her seat.

Seconds later the mirrored doors slid open and as promised, Geeta waited for him. This woman was more formally dressed in a tailored cream suit, a perfect foil for her bronze skin and ebony-black hair, subdued into a tight bun on the back of her head. She wore no makeup to soften her angular features. Her no nonsense expression reminded Adam fleetingly of Beth Leith.

"Mr. Norcross, I'm Geeta." She nodded to him. "Please follow me. The Arbutus conference room is ready for your meeting." Geeta led the way past numerous offices and alcoves down a wide hallway. "Please have a seat. Mr. Abernathy will join you momentarily." She offered water and coffee, which he politely turned down and she left him.

The room was boasted of a glass wall along the hallway. Norcross turned his back to it. He propped his umbrella against the wall and shrugged out of his damp overcoat. Directly across from the oval dark oak conference table, was a row of floor to ceiling windows. These offered a magnificent view of Victoria Harbour.

Adam folded his coat over the back of one swivel chair and hooked the wooden handle of the umbrella on top. This umbrella was a new one he'd bought in London, along with the black trench coat and suit before flying back to Vancouver. He felt he needed to wear something more respectful for the will reading. The suit was bespoke and he was sure his mother would have approved.

Zara had not stopped to shop. The MI6 operative had proceeded straight to her connecting flight which took her back to her husband and daughter.

Adam felt a twinge of envy over his friend's eagerness to return home. It had been years since Adam had felt that pull, decades really, even when his mother was still alive. His wife, Margarita, had passed on a long time ago and that particular pain, for the most part, had faded. Still, with his mother now gone, there was the emptiness left by their absence which he'd never thought he'd be able to fill. Then along came Sergeant Beth Leith and the climate change scientist murder. Adam pondered how strange life worked sometimes.

Walking around the table he bypassed the other seats and chose to stand at the drizzle-dampened windows, hands clasped behind his back. He stared down at the bustle of seaplanes arriving and departing. Farther out, the harbour marina offered concrete docks with wooden fingers. To these were tethered various types of sail and power boats gently moving against the wind and tide. He'd always thought there was something freeing about boats.

The view did nothing to lift the heavy feeling which weighed him down since he'd made this appointment with Abernathy. Like an immense rock pressing down on his chest. He hadn't felt this down in months, not since the days after his mother's funeral. The realization made him angry with himself, he needed to push past it, get over it. He wasn't immune to grief, but he needed to learn to handle the emotion better.

"Ah, Adam, I'm so glad you made it this time." There was a gentle rebuke in the older man's tone.

Adam turned as a portly Asian man closed the hallway door. He walked into the room and over to his former client's son. Wu Abernathy's statement no doubt referred to previous appointments Adam had cancelled.

"Mr. Abernathy, nice to see you." Adam said formally and held out his right hand.

"Please call me Wu." The lawyer took it in a warm two-handed grip. "It's been a long time, I am so sorry Evelyn has passed on, she was a dear friend. I also regret not being able to attend her funeral. I was stuck in Hong Kong because, well, we don't need to get into that." He released Adam's hand.

The older man was shorter, forcing Adam to look down into eyes so dark brown they appeared black in the over-head lights. There was true sincerity there and Adam knew the lawyer meant what he said.

Adam nodded, "Thank you." He did know about the political struggles of the former British colony. He was about to let Abernathy know the legal council's lack of attendance at the funeral wasn't an issue when he was struck with a thought. "You were working on the release of some political protestors. Mom would have understood."

Abernathy frowned. "How did you know—oh yes. You work for the Foreign Affairs office."

"Global Affairs," Adam corrected gently. "Yes, I read lots of reports." He gave the man a bland smile.

No, not really, but his job was easier to explain this way. People's eyes glazed over when he mentioned the civil servant post and that was good. He encouraged the idea there was nothing more boring than an analyst's job, nothing to see here.

They each chose a chair at the table and sat. "Will Ida Hill be joining us, Mr. Abernathy?" Adam could not address the older man by his first name. It didn't feel right.

Even though over several decades Abernathy had handled every legal aspect of Evelyn Norcross' career, Adam didn't know the counsel as well as his mother had. He'd rarely come in contact with the lawyer although he knew Abernathy's relationship with his mother went back to their university days.

He also knew Abernathy specialized in international contract law, while his mother had gone into the criminal side. She'd even defended one or two high-profile cases before calling it quits. Evelyn Norcross hadn't stayed a practicing lawyer for more than a few years before Adam was born.

Wu Abernathy came back on the scene with his mother's first book contract with a British publishing house. Her friend handled every aspect of her contracts, including details like the film rights to her books and the agent contract his mother had with Ida Hill, and of course her estate.

The older man took a black leather portfolio from under his arm and placed it on the table. He chose a spot and settled into his chair, with the folder in front of him. He paused to look over at his client's son for a moment as he tugged down the gold vest under his brown suit jacket. "No, no one else will be joining us. The contract between your mother and her agent expired some time ago. Although the two continued to be friends, as I understand it." Abernathy adjusted the height of his roller chair, and then shifted his gaze back to Adam.

The lawyer's fidgety demeanour demanded closer inspection Adam decided as he took a seat. Something else was going on, Adam could feel it. As he watched Abernathy, he was struck with the familiar feeling of events falling into place. His precognitive ability flashed a scene into his mind's eye for a brief second.

Papers, stapled together, with a triangle of pale blue paper on the corner of the document. Then a simple sealed cream envelope with his name scribed across it, placed on top.

Adam blinked. He knew without a shadow of doubt the information contained within the older man's portfolio would affect him. How deeply and whether the information was positive or negative was yet to be determined.

He flexed his jaw as he gritted his teeth. Adam never liked surprises.

Adam's precognitive ability took a lot of the guesswork out of a large part of his life and that was the way he liked it.

He concentrated on the lawyer and ignored the negative feelings he was experiencing. Adam rested his forearms casually on the arms of the leather chair and folded his hands to wait. He breathed in and out slowly, a familiar calm settled over him. This was an exercise taught to him years ago for maintaining control under stress.

It was then he realized moisture beaded Abernathy's upper lip. The lawyer was tense. This made Norcross curious as he watched the older man unclasp the portfolio and removed a file folder, thick with documents.

Next, the lawyer took out a black Mount Blanc pen, opened it, and placed the pen on a yellow legal pad beside the folder. Then he extracted a sheaf of papers with the pale blue triangle stapled at the corner. Clearly this document was his mother's formal will.

Finally, he extracted a pair of gold-rimmed glasses from a case in his left breast pocket. As the older man slipped on the glasses, Adam suppressed his impatience at Abernathy's delaying tactics. He frowned. What was the reason the old boy was stalling?

It was ridiculous to dread what his mother had put in her will. He knew the house and adjacent property was already his. What else could there be? Maybe a bit of cash, but that was all.

Surely anything Abernathy was about to tell him couldn't be all that bad. They would get through the task in due time, however Adam had other business to handle. "Mr. Abernathy, could we begin, please. I have another appointment I must see to."

"Yes, of course." He gave Adam a pained smile and brought order to the papers he'd removed from the folder.

It took mere minutes for Abernathy to read out the will. The document said exactly what Adam had expected, he was his mother's sole heir. Adam's ownership of the property in Maple Bay was confirmed, he owned the house outright, and there was no mortgage. So far, no real surprises.

"Do you have any questions?"

Adam shook his head. "Not so far."

The lawyer moved this document to the right of the legal pad while he retained a stack of loose papers in front of him. These he precisely lined up beside the manila tab folder.

A ghost of a smile curved Adam's mouth at Abernathy's fussing.

"There may be one or two revelations for you in the rest of this. I hope you don't mind, could we leave questions until the end when I've gone through it all once?"

Now an unfamiliar sensation crept down Adam's spine. All right maybe there was something to dread after all. "Of course."

Abernathy settled his wire-framed glasses higher on the bridge of his nose and picked up the top sheet of paper. He took a breath and looked directly back at Adam.

"To begin with, your mother's income is derived from several sources. Firstly, her mystery novels, under her own name and that of royalties from Brown Wolf

Publishing. Secondly, there is revenue in the form of funds from the two film options. These were invested into an income trust."

Adam nodded, he knew all this, but let the older man give him some details on how and where the funds were invested. "You'll have to decide what you'd like to do with those funds, as they will need to be transferred over to you. I've made a list of options for you to review and we can develop a plan once you've made your choices."

Again he nodded. Adam did not want to speak and interrupt Abernathy now that the lawyer was getting down to business.

"The third revenue stream, well." Abernathy cleared his throat and kept his eyes focused on the sheet of paper in front of him. "These are the more substantial royalties, those coming from her second series, *Dark Scandals*, under her pen name Ivy Blackwood, also from the same publisher." He said all this in a rush and by the tight expression on the older man's face, it was plain Abernathy had some issue with the information.

Adam tipped his head to one side. "I've never heard of Dark Scandals or Ivy Blackwood for that matter." His tone was pensive as he looked at the legal counsel. "I didn't see any books from this series in her library."

"I can't say I'm surprised. How does a mother tell her son she writes, or wrote, tawdry–well, never mind." Abernathy shook his partially bald head as he shuttered.

An amused smile threatened as Adam endeavoured to keep his face blank. Even so, he was beginning to find this whole thing quite entertaining. "Go on, Mr. Abernathy."

The councillor made an erasing motion with his right hand. "Anyway yes, she did. How else do you think she could afford for you to go to Cambridge University? The film options on the first mystery novels didn't come in until much later."

"Ah," Adam nodded and lifted his eyebrows. "This explains a few things. I wonder why she never told me."

Abernathy looked over the top of his half-moon reading glasses at Adam. "If you had ever read any of the Dark Scandals books, you'd know why."

"I see, well as I said, I've never even heard of the series until now. I doubt the genre is my thing."

However from the look Abernathy was giving him, it was apparent the lawyer might have read one. The skin above his white shirt and tie darkened, and his cheeks flushed. Possibly he'd read more than a couple then?

"Mm, well, I dare say." The older man cleared his throat.

Abernathy passed a printed spreadsheet across the table. "This is the breakdown of the revenue streams." He tapped the 'royalties' column with one thick finger. "Those will continue for some time. I checked with Ian Wolf, comptroller for Brown Wolf Publishing and he assured me there is still significant interest in your mother's work and the revenue will continue for some time with the help of their marketing campaign. He feels you could leave things as they are. He'll be in touch if anything regarding the sales from your mother's novels changes."

"I see." Adam looked down at the amount of money coming in. Guilt punched him in the chest. "It's not a lot, is it? What was my mother living on?" He should have checked on her finances, asked if she needed any help.

"Oh, that side of the statement merely represents the mysteries." The lawyer reached across and turned the sheet over to display the backside. "This one is Dark Scandals."

"That's...respectable." Adam started at the total for a moment.

"It is. The amount has reduced slightly over the years but is still a solid income. The royalty revenues would spike with the release of a new title." Abernathy sat back and regarded Adam. "Evelyn had no debts." He pulled out a third printed spreadsheet.

"This is the record of investment funds from the film options. It's doing quite nicely too and afforded your mother a comfortable lifestyle."

"Yes, I see that now." The surge of guilt subsided after he saw the last income statement. Apparently his mother had not been subsisting on a tiny income. The healthy portfolio dissolved his worry completely as he viewed the yearly income number.

Abernathy then reviewed alternatives for how Adam could deal with his inheritance. "You don't have to decide anything right now, you can think over the options I've given you and get back to me at a later date. The money will merely sit where it is and gather interest. I'll have to file the final income tax return in the meantime and investigate any capital gains implications. I have account numbers from your mother. Please check them so I may transfer the monthly payments to you."

"Thank you. Yes, these are correct."

Adam then gathered the statements together. The older man slid the empty file folder over to Adam and he tucked the documents, along with the copy of the will, inside.

"Now," Abernathy once again looked over the top of his glasses at Adam "There is one last thing." His tone had turned grave.

Adam patiently waited as the older man slowly extracted an envelope from the leather folder. He immediately recognized it as his mother's stationary. She wrote to him frequently, yes, old school letters, and it was easy to identify the heavy cream parchment with her name and return address printed in bronze on the envelope flap.

His name, in thick black script from her fountain pen was on the back of the sealed missive in his mother's hand. Just as he'd 'seen' it earlier in his mind's eye.

Abernathy handed the envelope over.

"What's this?" Adam held the sealed missive carefully.

"This is a letter to you from Evelyn. Your mother told me this communication would explain about your father. I was to give it to you in person."

Adam stared at the letter as it lay in his hands. "My father?" To say he was intrigued wasn't the half of it, apprehension played a part too.

"Yes." Abernathy's tone said he'd rather be doing anything else but this.

Adam's gaze shot up to meet Abernathy's. "You knew him?"

The lawyer gave a small nod. "Your father graduated the same year your mother and I did from Simon Fraser University. While she and I took up clerking posts, your father took another path. Not terribly illustrious, but still important. He took a job with Legal Aid."

"All right, then what happened? Mom didn't stop practicing law until I was born."

"I'm afraid that's all I know."

"You were friends. You must know something of their relationship."

The older man shook his head. "You have to understand, the life of an associate is one of incredible pressure. The immense workload took up every spare moment of our time. We barely had a moment to return home for sleep let alone keep up with any kind of social life. I sincerely don't know how your mother managed it." He gestured to the envelope. "I suspect the rest of the story is in your letter."

"Can you at least tell me his name?"

"Roderick Campion."

None of this information lined up with what Adam had uncovered years ago in regard to who his father was.

Interesting, to say the least.

Chapter Two

Bethany Leith killed the all-terrain vehicle's engine. Swung one long leg over the yellow Suzuki quad and stood a couple of feet away from the hot engine. She welcomed the abrupt silence and the break in the workday.

Instantly, warblers and yellow throats filled the quiet with their song while one squirrel voiced his protest to her presence.

Heat emitted from the hard worked engine as she pulled off her one battered leather work glove and looked around the 'new' property. Her father and brother had plans for the land to be used as the extended bin yard. The farmyard across the road was full. The rest of the property would be used to run cattle. The north section had been where she'd spend the morning making fence repairs.

After two days of rain, the August sun was warm as it shone from the clear cloudless sky. Heat fell on the crown of her green Roughrider cap and white T-shirt clad shoulders, making her wish she'd chosen denim shorts instead of jeans. Even so, it was too beautiful a day to worry about it.

She'd only been home in Saskatchewan these past three days and already her skin tone had darkened nicely even with the 50 SPF sunscreen her mother firmly suggested she use. Beth's skin never burned. Something she was thankful for from her parents' mixed genes.

Beth flexed her bare hand to work feeling back into her fingers.

Vancouver Island weather wasn't as rainy as people thought. Maybe it was more work than play which had washed out her complexion. Still, she was glad to be working outside in the sun now.

Work.

She shook her head once and leaned a hip against the ATV. Now there was a complete mess. The question, was the situation salvageable? Maybe, if politics had not been involved or rather, a certain politician.

Taking a deep breath, Beth pushed thoughts about her decimated career as a RCMP sergeant away. Releasing it in a long sigh, she blocked out Inspector Taggard's advice to be patient until the situation could be sorted out. Patience wasn't one of her long suits and she knew it.

At the time, she'd grit her teeth to contain her anger and said nothing, merely nodded.

"Your police union rep will stay in touch and so will I. We have to wait for the review panel to make a decision. You know how this goes." Again she'd nodded.

Beth had a bad feeling the 'situation' would not be resolved in her favour. And worse, the feeling was more than worry, it felt like certainty. "Heh, now I'm thinking like Norcross." She dismissed this too, but a smile curved her lips just the same.

A mixture of dust, prairie grass, and the unique smell of harvest beginning scented the air. In the distance she could hear someone running an engine a few kilometres south. Probably it was her brother Dawson on the field across from the house running the swather. Tomorrow she'd be out there too, bailing if the swaths were dry enough.

Beth looked back down the dirt road she'd traveled. The route wound through sparse spruce trees and dense poplar copses. Ahead, the track curved left and a grassy plain dotted with willows teased her with a glimpse of water.

Beyond to the right, there was the lazy curve of the river and the makeshift bridge. This gave access to another seventeen acres which was part of this fifty her family recently purchased. The new property was half a kilometre from the home acre, Leith Family Farm, est. 1908.

Although the property purchase was new, Beth knew the land well. When she was a kid, she and her brothers helped their grandfather when he'd pastured cattle on this piece.

Back then, Seth Leith rented the land from Morris Freeborn, their neighbour. The agreement continued for several decades until her family reduced their cattle for a time due to market conditions. This year her dad felt it was time to ramp up the numbers again and move cattle on to this land to pasture.

He had explained his plan that first day she'd been back at home. "The economy is uncertain and the price of cereal and pulse crops is iffy. Your grandfather used to say, 'In hard times grab the tail of a cow and it will pull you through.'" Apparently her brother agreed as well even though Dawson's time was almost completely taken up with the grain and canola side of farming. Maybe their father wanted something of his own to do now that her brother was taking on the larger share of field work?

"We need more crop storage too," her father had explained over breakfast. "I've ordered six new bins. When they arrive, we'll assemble them on Morris Freeborn's old property. I contacted his son Vic, about buying the property outright last month. No more of this rental crap, I want to own that land."

Even now Beth sensed there was something more to her dad's sudden desire to lay claim to the fifty acres but at the time only said, "So you've made an offer?" She merely sipped her coffee as she watched her father.

A self-satisfied smile had slowly spread across his lined face. "Oh yeah, the deal is in the works." His hazel eyes crinkled at the corners when he was pleased with himself.

Maria Leith, Beth's mother, pursed her lips as she listened to the exchange. Biting her lip, she suddenly appeared to have found something deeply interesting to read on her propped up tablet, effectively avoiding Beth's eyes.

"Your bid is more than Rupert Honeyweld's offer?" Beth turned her attention back to her father.

When she was still working in British Columbia, Dawson sent her regular emails at least once a month with family news. She hadn't given the land purchase much thought before, but she sensed her dad was up to something more than merely expanding the family holdings.

Nick had turned an innocent face to his daughter. "Is Honeyweld looking to buy the Freeborn property?" There was her confirmation.

"You know he is." Maria's words were dry as tinder. "He's been after a piece of land along the river for years." She looked at her daughter. "I don't know why, nor did Judy. She was Rupert's wife. He still owns a perfectly good house in town."

"Still?" Beth had frowned and picked up a piece of bagel to bite into. "What does that mean?"

"Judy passed away over a month ago. She had cancer." Maria shook her head. "Sad, she was a lovely woman."

"Honeyweld is an arse and I'm not going to let that snake own any property close to me or mine."

"Nick, language." Maria had said automatically without looking up. Something Beth had heard thousands of times. She could not help herself, she'd laughed. Her parents' banter was one of the things she'd miss in her years away. Thinking about them made her smile.

Her boots and denim-clad legs were damp. Mud spatters stained her clothes from the speed at which she'd traveled. The landscape was mostly unchanged from her younger years and racing down the muddy trails felt good.

Beth removed the other leather glove and used them both to slap at the drying mess on her jeans.

This area was crisscrossed with multiple trails, there was a mud hole or two that required exploring in between getting her arms scratched up looking for the next strand of barbed wire pinned to wooden fence posts. This included assessing the state the wire was in, and if possible, fixing it, or running new wire.

This part of the country had hills, coulees, and wild over-grown forested areas. It had been over a decade since anyone had used the parcel for anything other than recreation. The trails were great for quad riding, and there was a swimming hole around the bend from the abandoned beaver dam. Down river there was a stretch of beach the local teenagers used to frequent. A ring of huge stones edged a natural fire pit. Beth and her brothers attended bonfires there in their youth.

She draped her damp gloves over the black rubber hand grips of the quad to dry in the morning sun. She thought about the rivalry between Rupert Honeyweld and her dad which grew to legendary proportions over the years, and done nothing but get nastier according to Dawson. It started with a disagreement in administration of the Lone Spruce Museum and Historical Society board. The Honeywelds and the Leiths were all members of the society. Things escalated this past December when Nick Leith was charged with assault on Rupert Honeyweld.

Remembering the frantic call she'd received while working on a murder investigation in British Columbia still unsettled her. Beth could not recall any other time her mother had been so completely freaked out like that. The judge decided it was two old guys with a difference of opinion and no injuries or witnesses could be offered into evidence, so not a criminal matter. Honeyweld threatened to sue, but so far, nothing had come of it.

The sun glanced off a stretch of Conjuring Creek, part of the Assiniboia River system. Light danced across the blue water down slope from her location and tempted her to get closer. The creek's clear water sparkled in the late summer sun. There was another trail which curved right along the water.

She knew there would be a bench made of wood a few yards down, silver-grey from the weather. Her grandfather had built it and placed it there, though it was not visible at the moment. Shoulder high grass and even taller willows obstructed her view, but she knew exactly where the bench was. She'd walked down there with Grandad countless times. They would fish for pickerel and share a lunch Grandma packed. Of her four siblings, Beth had been the only one interested in the mundane sport of fishing. "Those boys are hell raisers

33

pure and simple. It's all loud engines and cold beer with them." Then Granddad used to chuckle. "No one to blame but your father, they're all just like him. See what happens when you don't take your kids to church?"

Dutifully, she'd nod and continued to cast her hook in search of fish.

The thought triggered a warm feeling in remembrance of Grandad, now gone these past twenty-four months, predeceased by her grandmother years earlier.

The existing trail wasn't wide enough for her to ride the quad down to the bench, but she was up for the stroll anyway. She'd earned a break.

Checking fences was not easy work even if she could do the chore, for the most part, from the back of an ATV.

Thirst made her remove a water bottle from the quad's storage compartment at the rear. A spool of barbed wire, and another of number nine wire, pliers, and assorted other tools were pushed out of the way so she could access the small cooler at the bottom.

"You could stay home now, Beth." Her mother's words were triggered by seeing the lunch bag she'd prepared for her daughter's day in the field. "Dad will need help with those cows." Maria's dark brown eyes looked worried, and not for just her husband who wasn't getting any younger.

Beth was sure her mother had only made the cattle suggestion to ensure her boomerang daughter knew she was welcome to stay at home, come what may.

The venture, increasing from a handful of cattle to eighty, would give her a reason to stay. Setting the farm up for the increase in numbers, would take up a lot of her time and not allow for any pity parties.

Probably a good thing Beth allowed. So yes, it was tempting to leave her career behind to stay home and lick her wounds, but this wasn't her life. Not anymore and she would be damned if she'd let 'them' win.

Beth shied away from thinking about the events which brought her back home. They only served to make her angry. The anger and frustration at how she'd been treated was still close to the surface, even after two weeks. Still, Beth regretted nothing, she'd done nothing wrong. If the brass couldn't see that well, there was nothing she could do about it. It was all in the hands of her union rep, and the review panel.

Water bottle in hand, she approached the head of the path. She was sure the trails had not felt a mower for some time. Willows were trying to take over every open space. Cows would look after some of the mowing part. Abundant grazing augmented with daily chop, a mixture of oats, barley, and other grains ground fine for easy digestion. She agreed with her dad, this property would grow nice beef cattle for sale.

Beth turned north and took three strides down the trail before catching the sound of someone or something else moving up the trail toward her.

She frowned, came to a halt, and waited. Her right hand rested on the bear spray canister in the holster on her hip.

A bear? No, the regular pace made her think it was human. Maybe it was Garrett, the neighbour from across Conjuring Creek who also raised cattle. Maybe he was missing some of his herd or something. She glanced east at the curve of the river where the swimming hole was located. From here the beaver dam didn't look so abandoned.

It had been several years since she'd seen Garrett Blackelk. They had attended the same high school and run with the same crowd for a while. Those where the days when teenagers moved as a group. This strategy avoided the logical pairing off into couples. Especially if some people didn't want to be paired off because they had bigger plans than staying in Lone Spruce their whole lives.

Instead of Garrett, an older man appeared. He emerged slowly from the overgrown trail. His camouflage green and tan clothing helped him to blend in.

Beth studied the man as he walked up the rise in the trail to where she stood. His attention was not on her, but on something in his left hand.

She judged he was in his mid-sixties as he ambled up to where she waited. He wore rough mud-stained trousers, boots, and a cloth jacket. A tan backpack rode his shoulders and he employed a willow walking stick, confidently striking it on the ground as he advanced along the path. His wide-brimmed brown hat partially hid his features but not the steel-grey of his hair.

Definitely not Garrett and also not someone she knew on sight, but then she'd been away for a long time.

As if sensing he was being observed, the older man abruptly tipped his head up and scowled at Beth. "Who the hell are you?" He came to a stop five feet away. He planted his feet and arched his back making his gut protrude over his belt. The stranger's attitude said he had a right to be here.

Lifting dark eyebrows at the man's sharp tone, Beth slowly uncapped her metal water bottle and took a drink as she studied him. Finally she recapped the container. "I could ask you the same," she said.

By this time he was bristling. "This property belongs to the Freeborns. You are trespassing."

"And you're not?"

"I have permission—"

"I doubt that." She cocked her left hip. "By the way, this is Leith property now." Or would be soon. The paperwork, now all signed was being filed with the province for the land transfer.

Scowling now, the old man advanced on her. "What are you talking about?"

"I'm saying you are actually the trespasser. According to provincial law, you have to prove you have permission to be here and I'm pretty sure you don't."

His head came up haughtily. "Who are you to demand anything?"

"Beth Leith, Nick is my father."

His upper lip curled off his teeth.

Beth straightened her spine. She didn't like the reaction her father's name triggered.

The stranger's mouth moved like he was trying to find something to say. Finally he came out with, "Morris had no problem with me being on his land." His tone was defiant.

Beth looked at him steadily. A faint suspicion was growing into a certainty. "I understand. However, that has all changed now that the property has been sold. What's your name?"

"Morris is a good man and fair. He'd have told me if he sold. He knew I wanted first refusal. Nick Leith is underhanded and sly. A back stabber." His tone was accusatory and the sour look on his face underscored his opinion.

Beth tapped the water bottle against her leg. "You, I'm willing to bet, are Rupert Honeyweld." Bain of her dad's existence.

His eyes narrowed. No doubt transferring his anger and dislike from father to daughter Beth assumed.

Then Honeyweld tossed a glance over his shoulder instead. Slowly, he turned his head back and his eyes settled on Beth. There was something new in his expression as he again lifted his chin. "I am. I'm the man your father assaulted last winter." He gave her an ugly smirk.

"I heard it was mutual and got tossed out of court."

He ignored her statement. "Are you saying I'm not welcome to hike on your land?"

"I didn't say anything close to that. I just said you don't have permission. I doubt you've ever had permission from anyone." Not from the complaints her father made about the man. According to her dad, Rupert Honeyweld felt he had the right to wander anywhere he liked.

Her father said the neighbours said similar things. It was annoying to find undesirable people randomly on your property. People who wanted to cause trouble wherever they went. Good neighbours would give you a heads up if they needed something from you or to check something on your property.

"That's not true, Morris said—"

"Nothing." Beth paused, seeing Honeyweld blink at her assertiveness. Probably few people with the exception of her father challenged him. "Two years ago, Morris had a stroke. He is incapable of speech according to his son Vic. That's why Vic has power of attorney." Actually her father had supplied the details when she'd driven to the lawyer with him and asked why the son was handling the transaction.

Honeyweld flattened his lips into a straight line as he glanced down. He appeared angry. His left hand tightened into a fist as did his right around the walking stick.

Beth merely watched him.

"I see." Honeyweld nodded his head. He dropped his chin in an air of martyrdom. "You're right, I should have asked for permission. I was just overcome with my enthusiasm for my discovery." His tone had gone smug. "I had to check it out and find proof to make sure I was right."

"Enthusiasm for what? What discovery?" Foreboding was an understatement at this point.

He opened his eyes wide feigning innocence. "Why, the discovery of an ancient Paleo-Indian settlement located on this land." Now his eyes narrowed and his smile turned in to an edged weapon. "You won't be able to use this land for some time. Probably years. Not now that I've found this artefact on the beach, your side of the river." Honeyweld held up his left hand. With a flourish, he opened his dirt-covered fingers. "I'm sure you know what this means." He was baring his teeth at her now.

Beth glanced down. Resting on his palm was a muddy arrowhead about two inches long. She stared at the lump of stone.

Oh. Crap.

Chapter Three

"Norcross." He answered his phone and stepped to his left to avoid the noon foot traffic. White collar workers exited their office tower entrances like kids let out of school early, flooding the damp humid streets in search of food and a break from office work.

"It's about time you answered your phone." Shapiro's tone was terse. He was in a fine humour, Adam could tell.

Since the federal election in May followed by the installation of a new Prime Minister in June, Shapiro had grown increasingly difficult to deal with. Norcross suspected he knew why and reasoned his boss' bad humour was definitely tied to the new administration, so he cut the man some slack.

A new PM meant a new Public Safety Cabinet Minister. Shapiro's new boss, required he keep her informed of every aspect of the agency's movements. Minister Karin Belanger was known to be a micromanager. She preferred 'detail orientated' when a scrum reporter tried to label the minister at an impromptu press conference a day after her appointment.

However, Belanger was Shapiro's problem. It wasn't up to civil servants like Norcross to figure out what the PMO should and shouldn't know. That's why Shapiro got the 'big bucks', so to speak.

Norcross kept his tone innocent. "Sir?"

His boss overrode him. "You put your phone on airplane mode. You know I can see what status you are at all times."

"I wasn't anywhere I could have taken your call, sir." Walter Shapiro needed to be reminded there were boundaries.

Shapiro made a non-committal sound. "Never mind that now."

Obviously some crisis had occurred. Usually Norcross looked forward to these calls and the unique challenges they brought. Today however he found his boss' attitude more extreme than Shapiro's regular abrupt manner.

"I need you to contact Sergeant Bethany Leith. Is she still with the Duncan Detachment? I haven't had a free moment to look at her file."

Norcross wanted to ask how Minister Belanger was working out, but refrained from tweaking Shapiro's nose. Probably not a good career move. Instead he said, "Yes sir, I believe so." Last time he'd checked she was. That was back in early August, before the Libya trip and he could not spare any time to drop by.

Duncan, British Columbia was his next planned stop. It had been nine, no almost ten months, since he'd last seen her. September and part of October had slipped by.

"We have a bit of a situation. I need you to look into it."

Norcross frowned. "Concerning Sergeant Bethany Leith?"

"That's what I said."

"Yes, sir." He kept his tone neutral. It was best at this point in the conversation to let Shapiro unpack. Eventually his boss would get to the point, but in his own time. Norcross doubted there was another high-profile climate scientist dead in a ditch somewhere. That had been how he'd met the intrepid Sergeant Leith.

"You know who Winslow Thrust is, I trust?" He did not pause to let Norcross answer. "He's a minister for the British Columbia provincial government."

"Yes, and brother of the Attorney General for the federal government, Geoffery Thrust." Well, since the last election anyway. Politicians came and went, bureaucrats stayed constant, as did their minions, which made him a minion. Odd thought.

"Exactly, Geoffery Thrust is part of Prime Minister Marco's caucus and of course, the inner circle." Shapiro sounded slightly mollified Norcross had made the connection. "Of course you know what that means?"

Norcross narrowed his eyes as he thought. "I think so." Indeed he did. 'Witless Thrust' probably wanted a speeding ticket made to disappear, or some other such thing. Infractions like that were what the thirty-something minister was known for—throwing his weight around. 'Do you know who I am?' became a catchphrase during the last provincial election.

How the voters had not seen through Thrust's thin veneer of charisma to his real lack of substance, Norcross had no idea. But, that was what entitlement got you, and those types along with their staffers, thought they should never be held to account for their actions. Such people were masters of spin, manipulation, with bribes or threats. Sadly, a portion of mainstream politicians were much less stalwart these days.

This thought made Norcross think of Mufisso. He wondered how he'd made out with the CINS engineers.

He planned to ask after the younger man, but right now Norcross needed to get his feet moving. "Thrust the elder, is a close adviser and strategist in the PM's caucus. He wants his brother to run in the next federal election and join him in Ottawa." He turned right and strode along the sidewalk, uphill toward the parking garage entrance where he'd left the vintage Mercedes.

"Yes, that's my assumption too. I judged Geoffery Thrust to be a more sophisticated version of his younger brother. He is just as self-serving but more dangerous due to his experience on the Hill. He has some influence upon the inner circle and some agenda I have yet to ascertain."

On this side street few pedestrians were around and he could finish the call before picking up the car. Norcross paused outside the parking garage. He dropped his gaze to the sidewalk and purposefully did not roll his eyes. Even though that was exactly what Beth Leith would have done if he'd mentioned the current minister for Bear Mountain to her. Shapiro would without a doubt hear the action, his boss was like that. Sensing attitude was Shapiro's superpower.

A half smile lifted the left side of his mouth when he thought of the sergeant's dry humour. He longed to see Beth again.

This conversation needed to be moved along so Norcross took the lead. "What has Winslow Thrust done to warrant the RCMP's attention?"

"There was some dustup between Thrust the younger and Sergeant Leith.

Thrust was participating in what the media called a 'peaceful protest' back in August."

"In front of the BC Legislature? Where cars were lit on fire?" Norcross knew he sounded incredulous.

"That was one incident. I also have a report Leith was working crowd control with Victoria PD. Apparently there were some troublemakers and Winslow Thrust was, and I quote 'at the wrong place at the wrong time.'" He paused for a moment. "Or so the report says."

Images of the protest flashed in Norcross' mind. He scrolled through the current events mentally. "There was a riot and the incident was far from peaceful. Businesses were also broken into and looted. People were injured."

Shapiro made his usual noncommittal noise when not wholly agreeing with Norcross. "The outshot was Winslow was arrested and charged. The arresting officer was your Sergeant Leith. Of course, Thrust swears he was nowhere near the protest, and he had nothing to do with any thefts, looting, or assaults. He also claims he has never even heard of Solitary Diamond and Jewelry, has no knowledge of any stolen rings. All the Crown has is Leith's statement contradicting him."

"No video?"

"None I can lay my hands on." Shapiro sounded dubious.

Norcross lifted his eyebrows. "So Thrust is guilty, but someone is suppressing the evidence."

"That's not what I'm saying." Shapiro sounded annoyed. "It's not my job or yours to figure out what Winslow Thrust did or didn't do. That is the responsibility of local BC law enforcement. Our job is to keep the current administration ticking along." And out of any scandal, went unsaid.

There was more here than Shapiro was saying, Norcross could feel it. "Of course," he said neutrally instead.

"AG Thrust wants this all to go away. The charges are without merit, he says, and he's spoken to the British Columbia Attorney General. Apparently, AG DeShane agrees with AG Thrust. We have more important things to worry about than whether Winslow Thrust nicked an engagement ring for his girlfriend."

"What do you need from me?"

"I want you to talk to the Sergeant about her charges."

Her charges, not the Crown's charges. Interesting. Instead he said, "I see."

"Geoffery Thrust communicated to me it should be made clear to the Sergeant, that taking this matter any further could hurt her career." Shapiro's tone was completely flat.

Adam lifted his head abruptly. Thrust would go so far as to threaten an RCMP sergeant's career if she didn't comply?

Shapiro continued, "You *know* what this means." It was not a question.

"Yes, sir." There was definitely something more going on and Shapiro wanted to know how far it went up the tree. A minister or AG meddling in a criminal case was disturbing.

"Apparently, it's in her best interests to make a public statement with an apology regarding BC MLA Thrust and drop the complaint. Let me know if you need to involve the Crown prosecutor if you have to. I have an 'in' there. I'm sure the Crown will want to be kept informed."

"I'll look into it today." His tone was neutral.

"As I expected you would."

"Before I do, may I ask how Mufisso made out with the CINS thing?"

"Quite well, in fact. He is on his way back here as we speak. All the engineers are out of jail, and CINS just might be able to resurrect their lucrative contract."

Shapiro ended the call.

Norcross was pleased for his apprentice.

He then shifted his thought to the task at hand. It was plain to anyone who ever worked with Beth that if she deemed charges should be laid against Winslow Thrust they would stick because she would have enough evidence to ensure it. Norcross doubted there was anything he could say to change her mind. Bethany Leith was not 'malleable' like some people. She would not 'look the other way.'

Leith was ethical to the core. If anything, it would be Winslow who should look to his own legal counsel and public relations people to handle the incident instead of putting pressure on law enforcement.

The average voter had a short attention span anyway, they would forget by the next election. Sadly, this was how things were done in politics, but he didn't have to like it. Norcross avoided this type of task whenever possible. Politics always made him feel tainted. More disturbing was the fact the attorney general for the federal government thought he could influence the outcome of criminal charges, or threaten an RCMP officer's career. Geoffery Thrust was one on Norcross' radar.

He entered the garage and took the steps to the third level two at a time as his mind worked over the problem.

First were the questions this task triggered. Why would a federal MP get involved in this type of situation? Typically sitting ministers distanced themselves from troublesome siblings, making them fight their own battles and lump the results, but apparently not in this case.

He gained the third level and moved down the row of vehicles.

Whilst it was true Winslow Thrust's political career could well be over if the case went to trial, that wouldn't happen unless there was compelling evidence the MLA was guilty. Was there evidence he stole the diamond ring in question? Jewelry stores as a rule had video cameras. Where was the footage?

Unfortunately, things like this rarely got out about the ruling party's actions. In this case, it was apparent Bethany Leith was gumming up the works. He wondered who else had been charged and had they been let off the hook? Was someone keeping a lid on the riot fallout? He'd have to check social media with regard to the riot to confirm his suspicions.

Norcross found his row and strolled to his car. He used the key to open the driver's door and got in.

Possibly, and not for the first time, the media were suppressing the information pertaining to Winslow Thrust's illegal actions, burying the incident. With no video, and no news reports on the events, it was like the riot never happened. This meant there would be no negative public opinion linked to MLA Thrust. No doubt it was only Sergeant Leith's statement holding the man accountable. It wasn't hard to figure out what was going on.

Shapiro's annoyance, his flippant tone, this all told Norcross someone was putting pressure on Norcross' boss, someone with more power and authority.

So, was it Attorney General Thrust, Minister Belanger, or even the PM? It would take someone at Marco's level to make Shapiro twitch. Even then Norcross found that doubtful. People like his boss spent their careers staying out of elected official's crosshairs. He was a master at it. Before this, Adam would never have thought there was anyone who could make Shapiro flinch. Could Geoffery Thrust have something on Walter Shapiro? Now there was a disturbing thought.

What was even more disturbing was his boss asking him to speak to Beth Leith with regard to the Thrust charges. The implied task, have him get Beth to drop the charges, although Shapiro hadn't exactly put that request into words.

Sure, that would happen, Adam thought derisively.

Then he blinked. Ah, now that made sense. This task required more digging. He sucked air through his teeth as he thought about it. He was owed a favour or two.

He started the car to get the heater going. He felt the damp more today for some reason.

Norcross scrolled through his phone contacts and dialed Leith's mobile number. It rang several times, and then clicked over.

The call was being forwarded. One more ring and a male voice answered.

"North Cowichan Duncan Detachment, Constable Bighetty."

Norcross' eyebrows rose. "Hello Constable Bighetty, Adam Norcross."

"Mr. Norcross, it's been a while."

Adam could hear a car engine, the constable must be on patrol."That it has. Why are you answering Sergeant Leith's phone, Constable?"

There was a pause at the other end of the call. Norcross adjusted the temperature of his heated seat, turning it to high as he waited for Collin Bighetty to respond.

"I think you might want to speak to Inspector Taggard about any inquiries regarding the sergeant."

"Thank you, Constable, I'll do that. In the meantime, can you please tell me where I might reach Sergeant Bethany Leith?"

"Yeah, I can." Bighetty's tone changed as he rattled off a phone number.

"That's a Saskatchewan area code."

"It is she's at her parents' farm."

"On leave for a bit?"

Again the pause. Then the constable said carefully, "Something like that."

Things slid into place for Norcross. Obviously Bighetty could not explain over the phone. "I'll be there later today. Can I buy you a coffee?" He lightened his tone and made the question sound casual as he stated a timeframe.

"Sounds good." Bighetty named a coffee shop off the highway, south of Duncan. "I'll meet you there."

Norcross ended the call and tucked his phone away in his right jacket pocket.

Beth was on administrative leave while she was under investigation. Bighetty probably wouldn't say what it was, not on the phone anyway. Of course it was this thing with Winslow Thrust, and Norcross knew this with the same certainty that he knew Beth Leith needed his help.

Chapter Four

Beth squeezed the trigger of the Smith & Wesson 9mm. The pistol barked seven times. She did not blink nor did her aim waver. Her delivery was smooth, yet crisp, making the seven plastic water bottles leap off the wooden rail as each round impacted the target object with a muted 'thunk'.

The sunny October morning was still, with no breath of a wind. The day promised more heat to come. Beth had already removed her brown work coat and flung it on the back table where her Ruger 270 rifle waited along with the pistol case for the 9mm. She had the range to herself. The shooting was peaceful despite the fact the weapons she used were shattering that quiet. Not that she could hear much while wearing sound suppressors over her ears.

Normally, Beth looked forward to autumn. Today she barely registered anything around her. Not the poplar trees splendid in glowing yellow-gold or the azure blue of the cloudless sky. She saw nothing beyond systematically loading the weapons, aiming, and hitting the targets. All with methodical movements.

This morning she'd received an email update from her union rep, and it had not left her in a good mood. Probably Miles Draper emailed her because he knew she would not be happy the investigation was moving at a snail's pace.

After two months literally nothing had changed except for the ramped-up smear campaign Winslow Thrust was waging against her in the BC media. Just this morning he questioned her work last year on the Paul Flete murder investigation. His quotes in the *Times Colonist* newspaper said she must have some kind of agenda against climate activists. Maybe all her case work was tainted by personal ideology? Did she side with the radical protestors two months ago instead of doing her job? Could she be trusted? Thrust said he was merely an innocent bystander when she singled him out and arrested him. He had nothing to do with the looting, it was guilt by association, and he was innocent.

Beth knew what the provincial politician was doing. He was hoping to taint public opinion against her so when his case went to court, potential jurors would side with him. It also looked like he was trying to get the story picked up by the national media to expand his profile. Without a doubt Thrust had an agenda of his own.

To prevent inadvertently saying something she would regret, Beth closed all her social media accounts. Once anything was out there on the Net, it was nearly impossible to remove it. While rebuking Thrust or stating her side of things was tempting, nothing would be accomplished by engaging in an argument. It all made her angry and frustrated. Especially tracking the story online, something she couldn't seem to stop herself from doing. This was her career at stake for heaven's sake, and she was not used to sitting on her hands. Hence the trip to the gun range to burn off some steam.

Beth ejected the empty mag and slid in a new one. Took aim on the next seven water bottles she'd taken out of the recycling bin. Beth concentrated on not gritting her teeth which would throw her aim off.

The visual of the water bottles leaping off the fencing felt much more satisfying than a paper target. When the last container smacked against the earthen berm behind the railing, she relaxed her two-handed grip on the pistol and lowered her right hand to her side. Now she allowed her shoulders to drop, more tension ebbed away.

When she was shooting, she could channel the anger. That was better than compartmentalizing it. The emotion became a tool to sharpen her focus. Her anger was not completely rational, Beth knew that, but it didn't matter. The negative emotion flowed through her and out the barrel of her pistol. At least an hour at the range target shooting took some of the edge off and improved her mood somewhat. Anyway, she figured it had to be better to be angry than depressed.

From long practice, she ejected the magazine and checked the pistol chamber to ensure it was clear. She forced herself to slow her actions and complete each task methodically. With a glance at the Monday morning sun, Beth realized it was time to get going. Her mother would have dinner— the mid-day meal in this part of the country— ready soon. It was time to pull herself together and go back home. Maybe there would be a message from her boss, Inspector Taggard. He was her main line of communication, along with the police union rep and lawyer. It was over two weeks since she'd spoken to him.

Beth began to pack up her gear. The rifle and pistol were carefully placed back into their respective cases, and then stowed in the mobile gun vault bolted to the floor inside her arctic-white SUV.

She returned the shooting range flag and sign back to its neutral state from live fire. Checked she'd collected all her brass in the bucket, and then climbed into her vehicle and pointed it back toward town.

Fifteen minutes later Beth crossed the railway tracks and her phone buzzed. She was back in cell tower range. That might be Taggard, but Beth's lips twisted into a line of resignation. More likely it was her mother with a reminder to pick up the package at her brother's business.

The SUV engine hardly laboured as it traveled over the tracks, and then rolled smoothly past the Co-op on the left, and a farm equipment supplier on the right. She signaled and pulled into the truck dealership also on the right. The sign still made her lift one eyebrow in disbelief. 'Leith Trucks', named for her second oldest brother, Derek, the dealership owner.

Once parked, she checked her phone and confirmed the message. It told her to remember to stop here for the carburetor kit for one of the grain trucks.

"Yes, Mom." She allowed a fondly ironic smile.

With harvest over, repairs had begun on the equipment to ready it for next spring. Of course, grain, canola, and peas still had to be hauled to the elevator in the neighbouring town during the winter to fulfill the contracts. This put the grain trucks at the top of the to-do list.

Running to town for her brother Dawson who did a lot of the repairs, as well as other odd jobs, kept her occupied. No doubt if she were here longer, hauling crops to the elevator for her oldest brother and father would fall to her as well. Unfortunately, the longer she waited for a judgment from the review panel, the more it appeared this would be the case. Even so, it was good to stay busy.

Beth knew Derek allowed their father to run a 'bill' or tab at his business. She suspected her parents were silent investors in her brother's venture, so it made sense.

She scanned the lot. The stretch of asphalt held several new vehicles and six used. Half-tons of various sizes and vintages outnumbered all else. In this part of the country, a truck was a tool, not a status symbol. She didn't see her brother's black 250, but he might park behind the building.

Going inside meant she'd have to interact with people. Beth breathed in deeply through her nose and released a long slow breath. She used to like people.

It was okay to allow herself one brief moment of self-pity, and then pushed the emotion away. Nothing would be accomplished by wallowing, and it wasn't like the last couple of months could be undone.

Beth climbed out, pushed the heavy door firmly closed, double tapped the key fob and then tried the door.

The locks were engaged, ensuring the SUV was secure, and the weapons locked up before she left the vehicle. Partly her actions were from her professional training, and partly from the discipline her parents instilled in her when it came to firearms.

Her own SUV reminded Beth of her work vehicle. Would she ever get back behind the wheel of an RCMP vehicle again? The stray thought made her pause for a second and blink. Things weren't that bad, were they?

She knew they were, and that realization came with a touch of fear. The fear triggered the anger, and her teeth came together. Defiantly, Beth stuffed the keys into her left coat pocket and tossed her dark braid over her shoulder. She regretted nothing.

Turning on her heel, Beth made for the glass doors. The faded canvas coat was worn, but more than acceptable. She wasn't out to impress anyone anyway.

As the glass door slowly closed behind her, Beth walked up to the reception desk. Her dark brown eyes scanned the large open area and displays as she went. This was her first visit to Derek's business.

It occurred to her that it didn't matter how you prettied them up, all garages smelled the same. The scent of grease, a bit of oil, and transmission fluid permeated the air, complimented by some kind of wax that was used on the showroom floor to give it a mirror polish. Then they drove cars over it. She shook her head.

An older man, roughly her father's age, was leaning on the customer service desk. He was speaking to the middle-aged woman behind the computer.

"I heard there was an inquiry. There might be charges laid." The man said as Beth came near and she frowned. It sounded to her like the two were talking about her situation, although as far as she knew no inquiry had been called yet. The realization made her hesitate for a fraction of a second, and that uncertainty annoyed her. "Don't be so sensitive," Beth muttered to herself and straightened her spine. She forced her features to form a stiff smile as she approached the two.

"What do you think the old man said?" the woman asked typing something on the keyboard.

"Who knows but I'd loved to be a fly on the wall for that conversation," the man said.

The woman shifted her spectacled eyes to Beth. "Can I help you?" She added a small smile as she pulled her green wool cardigan across her ample bosom and gave Beth a look of polite inquiry. The receptionist wore a 'Leith Trucks' ID pinned to the white blouse under her sweater. It read 'Millie'.

Beth realized she knew the woman. Small towns were like that. "Hi, I'm picking up a carburetor kit for Nick Leith." Beth took her hand out of her pocket and held her leather ID folder in her right hand.

"Oh? Uh, I thought Derek was taking the kit home for Nick." Millie's tone was uncertain.

Beth lifted one shoulder. "I've been directed to make a pickup." She leaned a forearm on the edge of the counter.

The older woman frowned and studied her for a second. "Bethany?"

"Yes, Mrs. Marshall, it's me."

"Oh, my word girl, it's been ages. You look so like your mother. Don't you think so, Burt?"

Burt turned moist blue eyes on Beth and looked at her with interest. He had to be in his late sixties, so not exactly a contemporary of her father. Nick Leith would be seventy-two this winter.

"Thanks." She shared her mother, Maria Leith's olive skin tone, dark brown eyes, and brunette hair.

"She does, doesn't she?" Burt smiled at Beth. "Your mother was quite the looker back in the day."

Beth returned the man's regard and slowly raised one eyebrow. "My mom is still beautiful." Maria was six years younger than her husband but in Beth's mind, looked at least ten years younger.

63

"Oh, yes, yes she is, sorry. I didn't mean to imply–"

"No worries." Beth flashed Burt a smile to let him off the hook. "I understand what you mean." She turned back to Mrs. Marshall. "If I could have Dad's order?" She tucked away her wallet. It appeared she wouldn't need ID after all.

"I know Derek has the kit. I think he left it in his office–" Mrs. Marshal gestured to the staircase bisecting the long wall in the centre of the huge showroom.

"Thanks." Quick long strides brought her to the stairs and up the steps, part way to her brother's office.

"I don't think he's in there, dear." The receptionist called after her when she got almost to the top.

Beth stopped and turned back to the older woman. She raised one dark eyebrow. "Do you know where he is?"

Mrs. Marshall rolled her bottom lip over her teeth and her eyes widened slightly. "He's gone to the municipality office. Derek got a call to go over. Nick is there."

Beth lifted her chin at the odd note in Mrs. Marshall's voice. "Has something happened?" She jogged down the stairs.

Millie Marshall shook her head and the artificially red curls bounced. "Oh, dear, I hope not."

"Thanks." Beth quickly exited the dealership. She could feel their eyes on her

64

back as she moved across the parking lot and their words hit home. Millie and Burt hadn't been talking about her. They were talking about her father.

She strode back to the white SUV. Got in and drove the three blocks to the Lone Spruce Municipal Office. Her father's battered 1977 powder-blue F100 truck was parked directly in front of the double doors. Derek's shiny black super-cab was parked right next to it, dwarfing the older model.

Beth heard angry voices before she even made it up the concrete steps of the seventy's era brick building.

Her father did not sound too happy about something. "I won't have strangers tramping around on my land or digging up the riverbank."

"Nick–"

As Beth entered, the clerk behind the tall counter was making placating gestures with her sun-spotted hands. Her dark eyes shifted to Beth and her expression smoothed out some.

"Dad, please, it isn't Reggie's fault." Derek stood as tall and broad as their father, but several pounds lighter.

"Do you know what will happen if those archaeologists find some artefact? It will become a full-fledged dig, and I'll never get my new granaries built. The old ones have had the biscuit after that last windstorm. I have nine hundred bushels of canola to move and dry before the whole crop rots." Nick flung up his hands but did lower his volume somewhat.

"I know, and I'm sorry, but it's provincial law. I have to follow the government policies. This is how these things go. There's nothing I can do to stop it now," Reggie said. "I am sorry, Nick."

"This is ridiculous. If anyone in my family came across any type of prehistoric finds, we would have reported them to the authorities and turned them over to the town museum. We've been renting that property from Morris Freeborn for years. No one has ever found anything."

"It's only ever been grazing pasture. How would you know?" Reggie asked.

"I've been all over that property, hell, so have my kids. There is nothing there to dig for. Honeyweld is lying. He wants to stick it to me anyway he can because he's an arse who likes to cause trouble merely because I bought the property."

Beth reached out to stem her father's words. "Dad," she said in a low tone. She knew there was no love lost between Rupert Honeyweld and Nick Leith, the whole municipality knew that.

Nick Leith turned to his daughter when she put her hand on his arm. His face was brick red and he was blinking rapidly, making her think about the condition of his heart.

She didn't insult him by telling him to calm down, but merely raised an eyebrow at him.

Nick took a long deep breath and let it out. He turned back to the clerk. "Sorry for yelling at you, Reggie." His tone was mildly contrite.

"No problem, Nick." Reggie gave the older man a sympathetic smile. "I understand your frustration. Unfortunately, Rupert filed paperwork with regard to his find. He's filed more papers with the Saskatchewan Archaeology Department than anyone else in our municipality. You know I have to follow their direction." She shook her blonde head. "I'm sorry, my hands are tied." Reggie lifted one thin shoulder in a 'what can you do?' manner.

Nick gave her a nod that he understood. Then he tapped the counter with his right index finger. "This is high-handed government overreach." He jerked his thumb, pointing over his shoulder. "Those people are already moving in, camping on our land. Asking for my permission was only for show."

"I'm sure they are nice people, just trying to do their jobs," Derek said. His own face held a florid flush from too little exercise and too much time behind a desk. His light brown hair was peppered with grey, but not to the extent that their father's was.

Nick gave his second son a dirty look. "You are not helping, Derek."

"It will be fine, Dad." Beth squeezed her father's forearm and wondered when it had gone from beefy to boney. She turned to the clerk. "How long do we have to allow them on our property? There has to be a timeline for how long they can stay," she asked Reggie. "A dig can't last forever."

"They have thirty days to uncover something worthwhile. Then, if they do, they have to file for additional permits to expand the site. Someone has to evaluate what they find. The chief archaeologist, I believe. If nothing further is found, it all goes back to normal. It all takes time. At least, that's how it was explained to me." Reggie gave Nick another shrug.

"Okay, then." Derek nodded. "We can still put up the bins in November, can't we, Dad?"

Nick made a rough noise low in his throat that neither agreed nor disagreed with his son.

"Come on, Mom will have dinner ready." Beth tipped her head toward the door.

Still frowning, and shoulders set, Nick Leith lead the way out.

Beth hung back and looked at the clerk. "Are you sending Dad a copy of the agreement with the terms and conditions included?"

"Absolutely." Reggie bobbed her head, no doubt relieved the elder Leith had left taking his thunderous mood with him. "You guys should drop by the museum. They're cleaning the things Rupert Honeyweld found so far, it's all so fascinating."

Beth glanced at her father's stiff posture as he retreated to his truck. "Not...today, thanks."

Beth strode after her family. "Dad," she called after him.

Nick hesitated with the driver side door open. He shifted angry eyes to his daughter as she reached him.

"Let me look over the paperwork and see what options we have. I'm sure there's something I can do." Why she promised this she had no idea, but hoped it was true to relieve her dad's fears.

"I doubt it." Nick shook his head. "I'll see you at home." He folded his big frame into the truck, started the engine, and then rolled out of the small parking lot.

Beth and Derek watched their father turn left on the highway.

"Well, that could have gone better." Derek ran a hand over the short light brown stubble on his head. "I'm glad you got here when you did." The hazel eyes he shared with their father lightened. "Dad was getting pretty intense there for a second."

"I saw that, and you weren't helping much."

"Hey, I do what I can. It's not my fault he doesn't listen to me."

Beth waved away her brother's words. "Did you give Dad his carburetor kit?"

Derek winced. "No, it's on the passenger seat of my truck. Come on, you can take it home with you." They crossed to his vehicle. "Reggie called me as soon as she saw Dad arrive." He opened the door and leaned in to extract a cardboard box.

"Probably a good thing you did." Beth eased her tone, cutting Derek some slack.

"Yeah, I know, even if I wasn't helping much." Derek mimicked her earlier tone as he handed his sister the kit. "Dad and Honeyweld haven't gotten along since their fight over who was actually president of the Lone Spruce Historical Society."

"The Christmas party argument didn't help either. Why can't they just let it go?"

"I agree." Derek waggled his head. "According to Mom, it has gotten worse since Rupert found that arrowhead."

"Honeyweld was trespassing on the new property. That didn't make things any easier."

"No, that's for sure. Reggie was telling us Honeyweld wants the whole length of the Assiniboine River scheduled protected."

"That's hundreds of miles of riverbank." She shifted the box to her other arm.

"Yeah, not really feasible, that's when Dad kind of lost it."

"Poor Dad, this must be infuriating." Beth compressed her lips. "The evidence still has to be verified by archaeologists."

"That's true, but the upshot is Dad can't put cattle on that land or expand the bin yard on those forty acres if the province wants to dig it all up."

They shared a look of trepidation.

Chapter Five

Norcross closed the document he'd been reading on his smartphone and tucked the device into the inside pocket of his jacket on the seat beside him. The charter plane landed smoothly on the grass runway with hardly a bump.

The view out the port-side window showed him the asphalt airstrip and expanses of emerald green grass surrounded by a chain link fence. The sun shone warmly on the vibrant green prairie surrounding the main runway and crosswind landing strip.

From his background research of the area, Norcross learned this year had been a particularly rainy one. The wet days alternate with warm humid ones, and now rolled into a warm and pleasant autumn. So much so, he'd removed his black jacket in the aircraft before they even departed Saskatchewan's provincial capital city, Regina.

Norcross gathered a battered briefcase and jacket. It was then he spotted the out of place SUV shining in the sun as they taxied past the mid-point of the airfield. It was hard to miss the large black vehicle parked off by itself away from the others in the lot.

As the 180 Cessna trundled over the apron and tie down area, a slim male figure stepped out from the driver's side. Norcross noted the male was dressed in a dark suit jacket, slacks, and a navy-blue dress shirt with coordinating tie. Slicked-back hair and heavy framed sunglasses completed his look. This, no doubt, would be his promised contact. The younger man stood even more out of place than the SUV. He probably had shiny patented leather shoes on too.

Not that it mattered. No one would care if some suit showed up looking like *Men in Black* or even if the vehicle had dark tinted windows, not here in the city of Yorkton. Anyone would assume he and Norcross were businessmen of some type. Still, a half-ton truck and attire similar to business casual would have been more appropriate and less memorable.

Once the plane came to a halt in the tie down area, the pilot killed the engine. The prop came to an abrupt stop and silence reigned.

"Thanks for flying with Tumbleweed Charters, Mr. Norcross." The forty-something brunette woman said over the Clark headset.

"My pleasure, Laney." Norcross removed his headset. "I have your card, I'll be in contact when I know the date for my return trip."

"Sounds good. One moment and I'll get your door." She tossed her dark ponytail over her shoulder and hung up her headgear on the left handle of the steering column, popped her door open, and climbed out.

Norcross hung up his own headset on the overhead hook he'd removed it from forty-five minutes ago, before they'd taken off.

By the time he unbuckled his harness, she had the door open and moved on to the luggage compartment for his bag.

The scent of baked earth, and crushed vegetation combined with airplane fuel, oil, and some other smells he could not identify, greeted him. October in central Saskatchewan, this was something new. He was interested in seeing this part of the country, but mostly he was interested in seeing Beth.

Black jacket and briefcase in hand, Norcross ignored the stiffness in his back as he emerged from the small plane. He looked over at the vehicle and then his contact and lifted his chin. The younger man took this as his cue and eagerly jogged over.

"Mr. Norcross?" The younger man asked through the chain-link fence as he removed his shades.

"Yes."

"I'm Mark Stone." The younger man wore an earnest expression and held a black portfolio.

"I'll meet you on the other side in a couple of minutes."

"Yes, sir."

The pilot placed Norcross' single black suitcase beside him.

"Thank you, Laney."

"Anytime, Mr. Norcross." She smiled at him.

With a nod, he picked up the case and turned to walk to the terminal building with Stone shadowing him along the fence.

Through the building and out the front doors, Norcross turned left and headed over to the waiting young man and the shiny black SUV.

"Nice to meet you, Stone. I'm guessing that's my ride?"

"Yes, sir. If you'll just sign for the truck, please."

"SUV, not a truck." Norcross said as he placed his case on the grass next to him and slipped his arms into the sleeves of his jacket to shrug it on. Leith had corrected him only last year on that score.

"Sir?" Stone blinked questioningly at him.

"Never mind." He held his hand out for the folio and Stone handed the document over. He gave his employer's standard department form a cursory glance. All was in order so he scrawled his signature at the bottom. He noted the rental agency for the oversized vehicle was local. "How are you getting back?" He handed the folio to Stone.

"I have my own wheels, sir." He pulled a slip of paper out of the back cover. "This is your reservation for Sleepy Hollow B & B in Lone Spruce, the town one hundred and four kilometres north of here."

"Thank you." He tucked the slip of paper away in his trouser pocket. He already knew this and had a digital copy on his phone. Still, he remembered his first taskings and wanted Stone to feel appreciated.

Stone's mouth twitched as he clutched the folder. "Do you...need any assistance while you're here? I can make myself available as backup, for whatever it is you're assigned to do." Stone was obviously eager to be engaged in field work, any field work.

Norcross shook his head. "Not at the moment. I'll let you know if the situation changes. I have your contact information."

"Oh, yes. Absolutely." Stone nodded, his feet shifted and dark grey dust drifted up and over his polished shoes. Yes, black patent leather.

"Anything else you're supposed to give me?"

Stone looked panicked for a moment. "Um, I don't think so."

"Keys?" Norcross prompted.

"Oh yeah, right." Stone handed over the key fob. "Sorry about that, it is push start though."

"Yes, I know. I'll be in touch when I've finished up north, if not before."

"Let me help you with your luggage, sir." Stone snatched up Norcross' case and jogged it over to the SUV.

Perforce, Norcross was made to follow. Well, Stone was nothing if not helpful, good initiative that, he'd remember it.

Stone opened the rear passenger door and placed the case on the spotless black floor mat. "Do you need directions or anything?"

"I'll be fine." Norcross gave the other man a steady look. "That will be all for now, Stone, thanks."

The younger man understood the dismissal. He nodded and strode around the hood of the huge vehicle.

Norcross closed the rear and opened the front passenger door to store his briefcase on the seat.

The rev of a four-stroke engine split the air and Stone departed down the airport road at mid-speed. A red helmet covered his head and face, and his tie trailed over his shoulder in the wind. Seconds later, Stone was on the two-lane highway, revved the motorcycle's engine again, and he headed south.

Stone's offer to partner up with him made him think of his last outing with Zara Dare, working with a partner seemed to be happening more frequently. Not actually a bad thing. He wondered if Mufisso had made any more progress with getting the last CINS Engineering executive out of his bribery scrape. There was always some wrinkle in these things. He should get an update from his young friend and see if there was anything he could do to assist. He did feel a touch guilty abandoning Mufisso with all the tedious paperwork while he and Zara put an end to the hijacking.

With Stone gone, the quiet settled over Norcross as he looked around. He knew the blacktop road which ran parallel to the airport fence was number nine, the highway he'd be taking north to reach Bethany Leith.

It had been many months since he'd assisted Sergeant Leith with solving the murder of Doctor Paul Flete.

She made a great partner. Their week together had been enjoyable. Discussing the evidence, brainstorming motives, and interviewing suspects, he'd thoroughly enjoyed it. That is, if one could enjoy a murder investigation. He knew it was the company and not the work which made it attractive. Many times during the ensuing months he thought about contacting Beth, but held back. What would he say? What could be his reason for contacting her?

Norcross thought he had made a real connection with the sergeant. Then it was all over so quick. Maybe there really wasn't anything there. Maybe he imagined it due to his need for some human connection. That thought made him frown.

Beth had gone home for Christmas, at least he assumed so. Shapiro had recalled him back to Ottawa and life returned to normal. Well, except for the fact he still had to figure out what to do with his mother's house. Not to mention Perkins, her cat. At least now he had the estate organized. He still had to make time to read his mother's letter. The infamous letter was in his briefcase on the passenger seat. It remained unopened for now, but he promised himself to deal with it when this issue with Beth was resolved.

Perkins remained at Mrs. Murphy's house for the moment. His mother's housekeeper was willing to keep the feline and play the caretaker for the Norcross family home for as long as he needed her to, she'd said when he'd drop by to check in with her and insisted she take the rise in payment he'd offered her. Perkins was not an easy cat to live with.

He was fortunate there. Even if he did pay her well, he knew he couldn't ask her to keep doing him this favour indefinitely. It wasn't fair to his mother's friend. Some final decision would need to be made about the property and soon. Perkins was a whole other matter.

Norcross shook his head at his dithering. He climbed into the vehicle and started the engine. The sun was dropping on the horizon. The ridiculous SUV rolled out of the small airport and Norcross pointed it due south. First he'd deal with his transportation, and then find Bethany Leith. There was some information about her suspension he was fairly sure she didn't know.

Chapter Six

Dusk was taking away the last traces of the sun. The moon had begun to rise and shone brightly down on Calvin Rokeby. He rode the four wheeled vehicle in the ditch, along the grid road at as fast a pace as his headlight and the moon would allow.

Five minutes later, Calvin made the turn into a copse of trees. It was much darker in amongst the poplars and spruce. He stood to gain a better view as the quad ate up the distance. At least there had not been any rain in the past two weeks so there was no risk of bogging down in the exposed stretches of clay rich earth. He turned left and took a side trail through an even denser cluster of trees. Calvin leaned forward to angle his ride up the ridge along a game trail just wide enough for his quad.

The knobby tires bit into the turf and from the exposed black dirt, he wasn't the only one to use old man Leith's property as a shortcut to get to the north side of the river. He thought he could smell the bonfire already.

Calvin carried a twelve of beer in one of his saddle compartments and looked forward to some fun on a Friday night after a long hot week shingling houses.

It wasn't usual for his crowd of friends to gather this late in the year by the river party spot. The long fall with lingering warm weather was the carrot. And so too was Mary McCarthy.

He had his eye set on Mary as the future Mrs. Calvin Rokeby. So far, their relationship was one of friends, but that was still a good foundation. She'd just turned twenty-two, plenty of time yet. With this being Mary's birthday, it was her wish for them and their friends to have a fire and a few wobbly pops down by the river. It was cooler in the evenings in this part of October, so Calvin did not hold out much hope of a moonlight swim. Even so, it would be enough to sit beside Mary and share a laugh.

Calvin looked forward to seeing her, he would put up with her teasing him about being late, again. He had a carefully selected birthday present in his other saddle compartment just for her and he was hoping the gift would be well received and move their relationship a tiny bit forward. A guy could hope.

As the ATV rounded a curve in the trail, he spotted an obstruction. Calvin frowned as he arrived at the other vehicle blocking the trail. The challenge required him to finesse his way around a bright green quad taking up the whole trail.

Odd place to leave your ride, but the machine might have broken down. There didn't seem to be anyone around.

Calvin didn't ponder any of this as he was forced to swing left to edge past and avoid the quad. He was almost past the other ATV, so Calvin sped up. Unfortunately, he failed to see the tree and had to turn abruptly left again to avoid the deadfall.

As soon as he made the turn, he knew he'd over compensated, his tires sank in the loose dirt, and the weight of the vehicle pulled him into a darkly shadowed coulee. The bottom dropped out of his stomach as the sharp vertical wall of earth crumbled from under his wheels. Calvin cursed as he gunned the quad to get out of the soft patch. No good, he felt more earth give way.

Leaning hard to the right, he tried to counter the effect and get back in control. This was no help either he realized as the back end of the quad doglegged and spun out behind him. He squeezed the lever to max out the accelerator in a last-ditch effort to climb up the bank. That was when the machine hit a massive rock and abruptly halted the ATV. Gravity pulled Calvin down and the machine decided to roll over.

He had no time to jump clear as the four-wheeler threw him to the ground and bowled over top of him. Anger and frustration at his situation allowed him to ignore the stabbing pain in his left leg as the machine's weight pressed him into the fallen leaves. The smell of damp earth and rotting wood filled his nose. Then abruptly the weight was gone. He saw the headlight swing violently as the machine tumbled a couple more feet down the steep slope.

He struggled to sit up. The moon showed him exactly where his quad had lurched to a stop on its side. The machine sputtered and stopped as oil drained away from the engine effectively starving it. There was the smell of burnt leaves and exhaust drifting up to him on the light breeze.

Calvin spat out some not very nice words as he struggled to gain his feet with the help of a nearby willow. He didn't think anything was broken, but he'd made a mess of his clothes and leather jacket. Mud and crushed vegetation clung to his knees and elbows. He reached inside his coat and checked his phone. No, the device was intact, one good thing then.

Looking downhill, he doubted the quad was damaged much. He could still make the party if he could get out of this hole. Calvin activated the flashlight function on his phone and gingerly made his way down to the quad. His feet slid on the loose dirt and gravel as he favoured his left leg. When he reached the bottom, he released a sigh as he looked at the quad.

He calculated how he'd right the beast and where he could attempt to drive out of the coulee.

After four attempts Calvin finally managed to get the quad back on its wheels using gravity, the steep side of the ditch, and a handy tree. He was deeper in the hole, but confident he could get out if the machine started.

Calvin was dirty and sweaty by the time he turned the key to see if he could get the all-terrain vehicle running again. Mercifully, the machine started, and he closed his eyes briefly in relief.

His respite was short lived. Calvin smelled spilt beer and realized he was standing in a wet spot, his feet squished. Calvin opened his eyes and expressed his further frustration. He should have listened to his older brother about taking cans of beer instead of glass bottles. Stopping to buy cans meant a further delay, so instead he took what they had at the apartment. Kyle was right, again. Whatever.

Calvin limped around the rear tires. It was then he realized his plans for the rest of the evening had completely come off the rails.

The headlight shone across the bottom of the hole and illuminated a pair of legs clad in dark canvas trousers.

"Oh, no." He shifted his light as he walked over to the pair of legs as quickly as he could. A dark certainty settled over him.

An older man was lying face down between a spruce tree and a poplar.

Calvin knelt and touched the man's shoulder. "Hello? Are you all right?"

There is none so still as the dead.

Chapter Seven

Five kilometres away, the same moon illuminated the Leith farm driveway along with the overhead yard light.

Beth parked the yellow Polaris quad in front of the machine shed and next to its fraternal twin, a red Polaris ATV. The sportsman 500 belonged to her dad. Really, both machines did, but the red one was his favourite.

It had been a good ride, though a long one checking fences. She'd skirted the area where some kids were having a bonfire by the river. She'd been young once too, and it amused her that the local kids still used the same location she and her friends had, back in the day. Well, and her brothers too, at some point.

"This is how you know you're getting old." Beth shook her head. She looked forward to a shower and washing away the mud and grime from her ride. And then some supper and possibly a couple of her mother's chocolate chip cookies. Not the most exciting evenings of her life, but better than most. Getting older wasn't all bad.

She opened the black storage bin on the back of the quad and removed her backpack as she debated grabbing something to eat first. There was no question she'd still have plenty of appetite left for supper.

The pair of dogs on the front porch stood and stretched. They meandered down the front steps of the veranda to greet her.

Beth had her backpack slung over one shoulder and was halfway to the house when the noise of an approaching vehicle diverted her attention. The long laneway was lined on either side with neatly trimmed caragana hedges. Headlights fanned the trees but gave no hint as to who approached.

Wayne and Shuster confirmed a stranger approached when the dogs took off barking across the yard. The German Shepard and Belgian Malinois charged over to the new arrival barking and jumping, destroying the calm as the truck halted.

Not one of the family then. Maybe a neighbour was dropping over? Beth changed direction to angle over to the new arrival. She also didn't recognize the Toyota Tundra truck. The tinted windows obscured the driver, and this alone made her slow her approach.

The driver's side door opened to reveal the silver haired, fit build of Adam Norcross.

As he glanced her way, Beth wasn't exactly sure how she felt about this new wrinkle in her life.

Typical of him, Norcross was dressed in black, but in practical jeans, and jacket, not a suit. He unfolded his long frame as he got out of the vehicle and his stout boots hit the ground. He was unperturbed by the dogs, but moved slowly.

Norcross' gaze never left hers. He looked taller than she remembered. As always, his bland expression played down his good looks. Even from this distance and the poor light, she could see he was deeply tanned. Why he chose to show up here, now, was unexplained. A negative thought made her wonder if he was here to escalate her situation.

Leith lifted her chin marginally as she watched Norcross take long slow strides toward her, meeting half-way. He was unhurried and appeared to scan everything around him. The yard light made his premature grey hair standout. He was trimmer than when she'd last seen him in December, thinner. No, not thinner, harder in some way.

From this distance his expression was not as clear as she would have liked. He stopped and dropped his gaze as he spoke to the canine advance party. The pair danced around him, and blocked his path, so he allowed the dogs to examine his scent.

Leith blinked but kept her first impulsive words behind her teeth. She'd given up trying to find out who Norcross actually worked for, too many roadblocks there. He was federal government and had access to areas of information most people did not. She had no good reason to think his arrival at her family's farm was anything but bad. Strangely, that wasn't the feeling he inspired if she were truthful and that made her frown.

His eyes settled on her, and the side of his mouth crooked up into a half smile and then it was gone. The dogs returned to her, and she gave each animal a pat. Then Norcross was there.

"Hello Beth."

"Norcross. What brings you out here?"

"I wanted to see you."

The porch screen door squawked as the spring protested. Beth glanced behind her. Nick and Maria Leith were walking across the veranda and then down the steps. Great.

The dogs abandoned her to greet their owners. Her parents arrived to stand beside their daughter.

"Hello." Beth's mother greeted the newcomer sharing a friendly smile. "Boys, sit." Maria ordered and the dogs complied.

She glanced at her daughter's expression and Beth knew her mother picked up the awkward tension right away.

Both dogs returned to run circles around Norcross.

"Calm down, Wayne." Her father reached for the dog's collar. "Shuster, sit." This time the Malinois complied, and it appeared to stick.

"Wayne." Norcross stared down at the excited animal. One long look at the dog and Wayne dropped his bottom onto the gravel, exactly like Shuster. Both animals stared up at Norcross riveted.

Vaguely Beth wondered how he'd done that. Maybe government agents were trained how to overcome guard dogs. Somehow this would not be surprising if it were true.

"Good evening, Mr. and Mrs. Leith." He nodded at her parents. "I'm Adam Norcross."

"Are you?" Maria offered to shake hands and elbowed Nick to follow suit.

"Norcross, why are you here?" Beth tried again. She had her suspicions as to why and her assumptions disappointed and annoyed her. Some of her feelings leaked into her words, making them sound sarcastic.

"Can't a man visit a friend?" His tone was innocent.

Her father merely raised his thick salt and pepper eyebrows as he studied the other man.

Beth compressed her lips as she gave him a hard look. Typical Norcross, he turned to her mother. "I'm an associate of your daughter's."

Maria continued to smile warmly up at the man. "Lovely to meet you, Beth doesn't bring her friends home much anymore."

Beth turned her head away as she rolled her eyes. By the crinkling around his eyes, she knew Norcross had caught her expression.

Finally, Nick Leith stepped up to the younger man and looked him in the eye as they shook hands. Both were of a height, but Norcross edged out her father by an inch.

"Welcome," the older man said. Beth could not decipher her father's look when he turned his eyes to her.

As the men stepped apart, another vehicle engine could be heard progressing up the driveway. The dogs were off again like a shot.

Norcross turned back to Beth. "Company?" he asked.

"Could be." Beth had learned to be more cautious with her words over the past weeks. Then the origin of the large SUV made Beth's good mood sink even lower.

Straightening her spine, she waited as the white RCMP SUV rolled up into the farmyard. This could not be good. She watched the vehicle park behind her own SUV.

"Are you expecting someone else, Bethy?" Nick asked.

Beth shook her head. "I wasn't even expecting Norcross." Now what? Involuntarily, her right hand gripped the strap of the backpack tightly as she walked over to the newcomer.

Not too fast, she wanted to see who emerged first. Only two other people knew where she was. It was possible Taggard or Bighetty could have passed on the information to someone else, but why they would and not let her know was disturbing. But then she hadn't turned her phone on in days.

"A bit late for an official visit isn't it?" Norcross was in step with her.

His action did not surprise Beth, and yet she was required to exercise some patience because of his action. She acknowledged how much on edge she was and it wasn't all due to Adam Norcross' presence. Thankfully her parents had hung back, no doubt sensing she wanted to deal whatever this was.

"Something's happened, something dire." Norcross nodded as they reached the vehicle.

"Do you know something I don't, Norcross?"

"Not yet, but I'm optimistic."

Before Beth could reply, the driver's side door opened and a tall, wiry figure in uniform, stepped out. The female cop turned toward Beth but paused to allow the dogs to sniff her closed fist to assure them she was not a threat.

"Can I help you?" The words jumped automatically out of Beth's mouth. She spotted the Inspector's rank as the other woman turned further toward her. Beth closed her teeth on a harsh expletive. This would not be good news.

"Yes, Sergeant Leith, you can help me. I'm Inspector Pelly from the Sturgis-Canora Detachment and we have a situation I need you to look into."

Beth came to a stop a short distance from the inspector. Thankfully Norcross stayed a step back.

At the senior cop's words, the muscles across her shoulders tightened. Both animals closed ranks beside her, one on either side. Shuster whined, a confused inquiry. Beth patted both dogs in turn to calm them. "Be good. Sit, boys." She then turned to look steadily back up at the inspector once the dogs complied. Pelly was studying her, so she schooled her expression.

"As a professional curtesy, your Inspector Taggard let me know you were home. I think he's a bit worried about you." Pelly was two inches shorter than Beth and her cropped dark hair was shot with silver. She wore no make-up to disguise a face lined by time and weather. The inspector's almond-shaped dark eyes looked tired. The dark circles made her skin look overly sallow. Of course, some of that could be due to the weird effect of the LED bulb the yard light produced.

Leith ignored the reference to Taggard. "Nice to meet you Inspector," she said woodenly. "I'd offer to shake hands, but I'm rather filthy." She merely gave the senior ranking officer a nod.

The inspector lifted her chin a notch at Beth's stilted greeting. "I'm not your enemy, Leith."

For her part, Beth slowly lifted one dark eyebrow. It was hard to tell these days who was her friend and who would willingly throw her under a bus. From Pelly's remark, the inspector no doubt also knew her recent history. Or at least the events prior to Beth's return home. It wasn't easy to maintain an apartment on Vancouver Island on half pay in this real estate market.

Beth was not on active duty, she owed Pelly nothing more than basic courtesy. Still, as her parents moved toward them she was reminded that wasn't how she was raised. She released a small sigh of resignation and relaxed her posture. There was nothing to be gained by being rude. "I didn't think you were, ma'am." Beth quickly introduced the other three people standing in the yard to the inspector.

She didn't explain Norcross, merely gave his name. Then she turned back to the senior cop. "What brings you out to my parent's farm at this time in the evening? What's going on?"

Pelly frowned at Leith's muddy attire then appeared to change gears. "We've had a call with regard to a fatality. I could use your help."

"I'm on administrative leave right now."

"I know, but you'll want to be dialed in on this anyway."

"Oh? Why is that?"

"The fatality is on your family's land."

"Where?" Beth snapped the word out.

Pelly gave her the land location. "I called Vic Freeborn first. He said the land transfer was in the works and those fifty acres are yours now."

Nick spoke up. "For all intents and purposes, the land belongs to us, yeah."

Interest and enthusiasm sparked in Beth for the first time in months. Even so she wanted to ask about the conflict of interest with her involvement considering the death happened on soon to be family land.

The inspector nodded at her father and turned back to look Beth in the eye. "We are stretched a bit thin at the moment, Sergeant. I could use an extra pair of hands and your experience."

Beth knew the problem the size of the districts in Saskatchewan represented for policing. It was the same in all the Prairie Provinces. The distances took law enforcement a significant amount of time to travel from one call to the next. Two calls could eat up a whole shift. Recruitment was down and every province had vacant positions. Still, she wanted to know why Pelly couldn't go herself.

Before Beth could ask any questions, Pelly supplied the information. "I have a hit and run north of here at a train crossing. Constable Buchanan is traveling here but he's at least an hour away."

Nick interjected. "Do you know who the fatality is? It wasn't one of the archaeologists camping by the river, is it?"

"Dad." Beth put a hand on his arm. She met his eyes and he narrowed his, but understood. He needed to let her handle it.

"So, is this a possible misadventure or something?" Leith rubbed her eyelid. This was all they needed. Since the land transfer wasn't one hundred percent complete yet, there was no insurance on the property at the moment. She hoped it wasn't any of the youths at the bonfire. "Do we have an idea of what happened?"

Pelly shook her head. "It's an older man. Possibly some kind of health issue, or something. Maybe a heart attack."

"The hit and run is higher priority."

"Yes, you see my problem."

"I do, of course." Beth nodded.

"Until the coroner can determine the cause, it's an unexplained death."

Beth nodded, there were protocols to follow.

"Has the coroner been called?" Norcross chose that moment to remind them of his presence.

The inspector turned her cool expression on him. "Mr. Norcross, if you would please stay—"

Beth held up one hand to forestall the senior officer's words. "Norcross has a higher security rating than you and I combined. He and I worked on a murder investigation together last December in BC."

"He's a civilian," Pelly accused with her tone.

"Not…entirely, Inspector. I'd like to offer my assistance as well." He reached into his inside coat pocket and extracted his identification.

It was readily apparent Pelly did not like his imperious offer. "I don't think–" The inspector began but stopped when Norcross handed over his ID.

Only Pelly could see the document she held, but Beth had read it last December. The man's credentials had raised the hairs on the back of her neck back then. She surmised Pelly was experiencing the same sensation. While innocuous at first glance, the seals and signatures smoothed Norcross' way. Beth had seen it firsthand.

What was it about Norcross' position that it could clear jurisdictional roadblocks? Was there something at an inspector's rank that revealed this special status Norcross held? The inspector did not say it, but Leith could tell by her flexing jawline, there was something there which allowed Norcross to impose his presence into this business. Abruptly Pelly handed Norcross the black leather folder.

Beth also wondered if Pelly knew just how complicated her incident report would become now that Norcross was involved. An unpleasant gift she'd experienced after last year's case too.

The Inspector's eyes narrowed briefly as she thought. Finally, Pelly glanced back up at Norcross. Again she gritted her teeth, and then took a breath. Apparently the inspector had something to say about Norcross, but suppressed it. Instead she replaced her first words with, "Thank you, I'll take all the assistance I can get."

"Glad to help," Norcross said without the tiniest note of hubris. Then his eyes shifted to meet Beth's and she swore she saw a twinkle of absurdity.

Beth lip's twitched as a quote popped into her thoughts. The nine most terrifying words ever spoken, 'I'm from the government, and I'm here to help.'

"Sergeant Leith? Are you going to handle this investigation?"

Beth knew what he was doing. Norcross was asking if she minded if he tagged along. Funny he was even asking after leveraging his government status with Pelly to get his foot in the door. "It looks that way."

Pelly's radio called for her to answer it, but she held her place until she saw Beth nod. Then stepped away to answer the summons.

Almost immediately she was back. "I need to get on the road. The coroner has been notified." Pelly clipped her radio mic back onto her tactical vest. "Glen Buchanan is on his way, he'll meet you out there if you would drop a pin in a map and text him the location. Same for the coroner. Calvin Rokeby is still out there, waiting beside the coulee where he found the victim." Pelly gave Beth a brisk nod. "Thank you."

"No problem at all." Beth said and gave her parents a shrug.

Pelly strode to her vehicle.

"You do what you have to do, baby girl."
Maria patted Beth's shoulder and accepted
the dusty back pack.

Beth nodded, but wished her mother
hadn't used the childhood endearment in
front of Norcross, not that she could do
anything about it now.

Instead she tipped her head at
Norcross. "Come on, the more the merrier."
It was impossible to keep the sarcasm out
of her voice as she led the way to her
vehicle. "We'll take my SUV." She dug for
keys in her jacket as she moved across the
yard.

Beth suppressed unidentified emotions
as she started the vehicle and Norcross
climbed in beside her. At some point there
would be a conversation about his motive
for travelling all this way to see her. Even if
she suspected she knew what that reason
was.

Chapter Eight

Beth's SUV headlights fanned the shape of a pair of ATVs parked on the dirt road.

On the road behind the first machine, some six feet away, stood a larger, black four-wheeler. This one squatted on the road with a male leaning up against the front fender facing them. He stopped scrolling on a mobile phone and lifted his head to watch their approach. Pelly said the reporting party was Calvin Rokeby and he was still on the scene. The young man didn't look too happy about any of it.

Rokeby straightened and tucked his phone in his back hip pocket with a solemn nod.

Beth halted her SUV and turned off the engine, but left the lights to shine down the rough dirt road.

On the drive over, Norcross told her coolee was not a term he associated with the prairies.

"The word isn't spelt the same," she assured him. "It has a completely different meaning."

"What does it mean, other than a derogatory term for a worker in Asia."

"A *coulee*," and she spelled it. "It's a kind of valley or steep ravine."

"Ah, so it comes from French Canadian, *coulée*, or *couler* 'to flow.'" He nodded in understanding. "Possibly cut by water."

Her lips twisted as she glanced at him. "You know, Norcross, knowledge is like underwear. Everyone has them on, but it isn't necessary to show them."

He chuckled, but this was an indicator for him to dial down the 'know it all' attitude. A fair point he decided.

Norcross exited the passenger side and stepped out onto the overgrown dirt road, which was little more than a game trail really.

The young blond man was in his twenties. Norcross could now see his jeans, T-shirt, and brown leather jacket were streaked with dirt.

Calvin Rokeby fidgeted by the second ATV, obviously his. The left side fender was scraped and battered. The marks looked recent. No doubt all results from this evening's events.

Grass and other detritus were stuck to Calvin's person, but it was the bleak look in the younger man's eyes that struck

Norcross. Was it possible Calvin had struck the victim and knocked him to the bottom of the ditch?

Norcross glanced her way as Sergeant Leith stepped from the vehicle, not Beth. Her professional persona was firmly back in place.

"Calvin Rokeby?" Leith led the way around the smaller quad, careful not to touch anything.

"What took you so long?" The young man was exasperated, but not too freaked out as he shifted his weight from left foot to right and back again. Was he nervous?

"I'm sorry Mr. Rokeby, I've just been told about this incident. I'd have been here earlier if I'd known." Leith walked over to the young man.

Somewhat mollified, Calvin Rokeby leaned once again on his quad. "Yeah, okay."

"I'm Sergeant Leith, you know my family owns this property?"

He nodded. "Everyone knows that. Isn't it a conflict of interest for you to investigate something like this on your own land?"

Norcross frowned, thinking the remark, well true, a bit odd.

"Not when the inspector for the detachment in this area tasked me with the job."

"Is that him?" Rokeby lifted his chin. "Is he the inspector?" Calvin Rokeby gestured to Norcross.

"No, that's my associate, Adam Norcross."

Norcross stopped just behind Leith's right shoulder. "Hello," he said, trying for a neutral, nonjudgmental tone.

"Oh, plain clothes." Calvin nodded. His tone said that explained everything.

Norcross was not surprised when Leith let that pass. It would take too much time to explain, and Rokeby didn't need to know anyway. "What happened here?" she asked instead.

Calvin took a deep breath and launched into a review of recent events. "My fault, I was going too fast and took the turn wide. My tires sank in the soft dirt, and I went over with the machine. When I was trying to right my ATV, that's when I saw the guy lying by some trees down there." He gestured to the dark pit-like depression to the left of their group.

Norcross shifted his gaze to look in that direction. All he could make out was the round opening approximately sixty metres across.

"Did you touch him? Or anything around him?" Leith asked.

Calvin nodded. "Yes, Sergeant," he said a bit stiffly. "I was a junior firefighter in high school. We all took first aid training, so

105

I thought I should check to see if maybe he was still alive." His tone held a touch of sarcasm.

Leith merely waited holding Rokeby's gaze.

"And he isn't, wasn't, whatever." Calvin shook his head and a fringe of dark blond hair fell on his forehead.

"I see. So he was down there when you got here."

"Yeah, I didn't hit him with my quad if that's what you're thinking."

The level of cynicism rang true to Norcross. In his mind, Rokeby was an innocent bystander. "Sergeant, I'm going down there to have a look." Norcross said and waited for Leith's acknowledgement. This time he promised himself he would work harder at not stepping on her toes.

Her lips twitched, but she gestured her agreement while still keeping her eyes on Mr. Rokeby. She knew what he was doing.

"Why were you even out here? And why do you reek of alcohol?"

"Well..." Calvin looked uncomfortable now.

Norcross did not wait to hear Rokeby's response. He strode to the edge of the coulee and clicked on the slim metal flashlight he'd dug out of his left jacket pocket. The small light was familiar in his hand and illuminated the narrow sides and a significant vertical drop.

He frowned at the ditch as he studied it. To him, the depression seemed artificial in nature. Even though several trees grew skyward out of the bottom and reached at least twenty-five, possibly thirty feet up past the lip. It was hard to see how runoff could carve out such a round hole. So coulee might not be the right term in this case.

Moving forward, he turned his feet sideways to control the speed with which he entered the ditch. Norcross navigated his way down the steep side of the hole. As he descended, he noted a significant amount of gravel and sand dislodged by his boots. He changed his clothing before leaving Yorkton after trading out the SUV for half-ton at the rental agency. There was no point in wearing a suit when jeans and boots would be more practical. He had no idea what he'd get up to in this location, but so far, it looked like his instincts had been right.

The grade levelled out as he reached the bottom of the depression. Glancing back up the way he'd come, Norcross judged the sides of the pit were a good fifteen feet high.

The area was inky black but his light found the target easily enough. Norcross could make out a human male shape lying face down, with the head turned away from him. Cautiously he moved forward. He swept the beam of his flashlight from left to right as he moved to ensure he didn't inadvertently disturb what in his mind was a crime scene. He had no evidence to back that up, but he knew he would find some.

Earlier, as he drove down the Leith family lane, before even speaking with Beth or Inspector Pelly, he had been struck with the 'something is coming' vibe.

It was no surprise to him that as soon as Inspector Pelly had arrived at the Leith farm, Norcross knew what was going to transpire. The situation had the same feel as last year and the murder on the Malahat in British Columbia.

This murder was going to complicate his assignment with Beth. Not that his 'task' from Shapiro would have been easy in any case.

Norcross found it was never a good policy to blindly follow orders. In his line of work, it was too easy to fall into taking directions for an outcome that could be deemed criminal in nature later on. In his book, the end *never* justified the means. And it certainly was not a good idea to taint oneself with questionable actions he or others might regret later. He knew what his boss wanted him to do. Or rather, those pulling Shapiro's strings from above, and that was enough for him.

He arrived at the body and squatted down, resting his forearms on his knees. He smelled blood. Shining his light on the dark mass on the back of the victim's head, he saw the wound suggested a suspicious death rather than unexplained. And yet didn't make that judgement completely conclusive.

Norcross leaned in closer to examine the contusion. To him it appeared to be shallow. Too shallow to cause death, however, looks could be deceiving, and concussion protocols existed for a reason. In this light he couldn't trust he could see the extent of the trauma anyway.

Moving the light to the man's face, he noted small cuts and bruising. Consistent with the man collapsing face first onto the ground. However, the victim's arms rested at his sides. Fanning the light to the hands, there were no obvious defensive marks or wounds.

Norcross frowned. The fingertips were discoloured. Was this bruising too? The colour was not the usual shade one found with a corpse and he found this curious. He'd let his back brain puzzle this out while he checked out the area.

Standing, Norcross took his time to look around the bottom of the ditch. There was no evidence the man just tripped and hit his head on something and rolled over. From what he could see, the floor of the hole was approximately thirty metres across and relatively flat. Several years' worth of fallen leaves carpeted the ground between the poplar trees and fallen tree branches. This was strange as there were at least twenty trees stretching up to the dark night sky. The moon's limited light wasn't much help. It merely cast shadows in the pit. Daylight or flood lights were needed to conduct a proper inspection of the site.

Exploring further he could find no blood, nor a weapon. Unless one included the shovel back up on the road leaning against what was probably this man's ATV.

Norcross could not touch the body until the coroner gave the go ahead. No doubt it would take some time for an individual to arrive from Saskatoon or Regina.

How long had he been dead? The lack of blood on the ground by the body was interesting. Something else caught his eye, the interesting amount of dirt coating the camo patterned trousers, and long-sleeved shirt the man wore.

What could he be doing here?

Norcross studied the wound on the back of the man's head again. It seemed too insignificant to be the cause, add to that the amount of debris stuck to the grey hair, the dried blood, and the laceration. Had the man fallen down at the edge of the hole and rolled in? Possibly, but that wasn't what his precognitive ability was telling him.

Turning to his right, he noted one area was clear of debris. The tree limbs, sticks, and other detritus were piled up to one side.

Could this man have been on a firewood expedition when things went awry? No, there was no chainsaw or axe to back up that theory.

Then he noticed something else. He walked over to take a closer look. Definitely not a firewood collecting venture, then. His flashlight showed him other things the sergeant would no doubt be interested in.

Norcross reached into his jacket pocket and extracted his phone. Flipping on the camera, he took photos of everything, including the body and the area surrounding it.

Satisfied he'd recorded enough photos to give Leith a good idea what they were dealing with, he followed his own footprints back to where he'd entered. He made his way back out of the pit and up onto the dirt road.

"Well?" Leith asked. "What's down there?"

"There is a deceased older man, mid-sixties or early seventies. Looks like he took a blow to the back of his head. The source of which is unknown."

"So an accident? He fell, or had a heart attack and collapsed?"

"Possibly." Norcross glanced over at Rokeby. He didn't want to say too much in front of the young man.

When he looked back at Leith, she gave a shallow nod of understanding.

111

"Have a look at these." He handed over his phone.

Leith gravely swiped through the first ones with the body.

"There's also a path worn in over there, on the far side of the hole," he said. "I'll go down over there and check it out."

She shook her head. "I'll go just so you don't trample on any evidence."

"No, that's not the best idea." He looked over at Calvin, who was scrolling on his phone again, then back at her. He dropped his voice. "Your status, for lack of a better word, is in limbo. Mine's not."

"And her dad has history with the dead guy." Calvin didn't look up as he commented. "Those two were always fighting."

Beth faced the younger man. "You know who it is? You can confirm the identity?"

Now Calvin did look up. "Well, yeah, it's old man Honeyweld. Didn't you know that?"

Chapter Nine

The headlights showed Leith's frown take on a more severe edge. "And how would I know that?" Her tone remained even, but Norcross wasn't fooled.

"You didn't know old man Honeyweld was squatting on your property?" Rokeby sounded sceptical. "Everyone knows he has it in for your dad. He wanted Nick out of the Historical Society. My mom said Honeyweld made Nick take a swing at him at the Christmas party so he could press charges too."

"Who's your mom?" Norcross asked. If Leith knew all this, then she was checking Calvin Rokeby's reactions to figure out if he was involved in Honeyweld's death beyond finding a body. Ask a question with question was a basic interrogation method.

"Betty Rokeby, she's the secretary for the society." Calvin shrugged his shoulders. "Why those guys are obsessed with who runs the thing is beyond me. Does it matter who's the president? It should be about finding something cool so people want to come to our part of the province to see it. Eastend has done great with the T-Rex Discovery Centre." He jerked his thumb over his shoulder. "Your dad is big into that stuff. Don't you guys have a bunch of people camped out on your land looking for stuff already?"

"Is there?" Norcross lifted his eyebrows as Leith.

"Sort of." Leith kept her eyes on Rokeby. "There's four people from Saskatchewan Archeology. They're camped on the north side of Conjuring Creek." She lifted her chin and addressed the young man. "Did you take any photos of this accident scene?"

"No, I'm not a freak." She'd have to trust him on that statement. There was no reason to ask for his mobile phone.

"Good, thank you. You can go now. You have my number if you think of anything else, or call the Detachment. I'll, that is, someone will be in touch."

The young man looked relieved. He did not waste any time stowing his phone and firing up his quad. Seconds later his red taillights disappeared around the next bend.

"Check the next couple of pictures," Norcross suggested. "The lighting isn't great, but still…"

Leith zoomed in on the profile of their victim. "Crap."

"Our victim is this Rupert Honeyweld?"

114

"Yep." She handed back his phone.

"And you have archaeologists looking for artefacts on this property?"

"Yeah, Honeyweld found an arrowhead over by the river a few weeks ago."

Norcross nodded. "You knew about Rupert Honeyweld trespassing on your family's land?"

"Yeah." She didn't sound happy.

He turned to look at the darkened pit. "How far is this 'accident' location from the campers?"

"A little over a kilometre, why?"

Norcross waggled his head back and forth. "I don't understand completely yet, but I think the archaeologists might be connected somehow to the death of your local historical society president."

"If that's the case, what's Honeyweld doing here? It's a bit of a hike from the base camp to this area. This area isn't part of the dig."

"I don't know, but there are some things down there you should see." Norcross gestured to the pit as he said this.

He looked over at the shovel leaning against the other quad. It looked remarkably clean at first glance. Norcross crossed the road to the green quad and squatted down. He ran his light over the blade of the shovel, and it was as clean as he anticipated. He clicked a different button on his metal flashlight and blocked the shovel from the SUV's headlights with his body. A different light intensity played over the metal.

"What are you doing?"

"Using a black light to see if there are any traces of blood on this shovel. There is an open wound on the back of our victim's head." He used a gas receipt from his pocket to cover the wooden handle. This paper barrier would ensure he wouldn't add fingerprints to the shovel as he turned it. Then he repeated the process with the light again.

"Where do you get a flashlight with functionality like that?"

"I know a guy."

"Sure." Leith snorted. "Find anything?" She asked from over his shoulder.

"No, it's clean, no blood or hair. I doubt this spade was used at all today by our victim. If it were, logically it would still be down in the ditch with the body. Still, we'll need forensics to confirm." He even went so far to look at the edges. Studying the spade gave him nothing.

He stood and switched his flashlight back to the standard setting. "If this tool was involved in Honeyweld's death, there's no obvious evidence of it now."

"So this death could be still be the result of an accident."

"Doubtful in my opinion. The wound is close to the crown of his head. It's hard to attribute a wound in that location to a fall. Although there is a slight possibility, I suppose."

Leith turned and pointed her flashlight at the hole and moved forward. "I've checked in with the Community Coroner. JD Zech will be here in half an hour or so." Leith walked over to the edge of the ditch and quickly descended. Norcross followed.

"Why is this pit even here?" Norcross asked when they arrived at the bottom.

She gave him a puzzled look. "What do you mean?"

"This depression isn't natural, it's almost perfectly circular."

Leith shook her head. "Not that it matters right now, but there are a few like this on the property. They've always been here." She turned away and her light quickly found the body. She moved forward, close to the body but not touching it.

Leith stepped to the far side so she could view his face. Her light hung on the man's features for a moment, and then she straightened.

Norcross noted her shoulders drop an inch. She'd held out a small hope the identity wasn't who Rokeby had said, but by her reaction, she knew who the man was immediately.

"Yep, it's Rupert Honeyweld." She rubbed her left eye lid like she had a headache. "I came across him by the river the day he found the arrowhead."

"Come look over here." He felt the need to distract her from her disappointment and led the way to the other interesting items.

"Why would he clean up the area?" She shone her light over the considerable stack of deadfall wood.

"That's not the least of it. You said this man found an arrowhead a few kilometres from here?"

"Yeah, he filed paperwork with the province. That's why Dr. Robert Orlinsky and his team of archaeologists descended on our property a few days ago. They are looking for more artefacts. They also hope to find some evidence of an indigenous settlement in this area from over ten thousand years ago."

"Our victim isn't part of the team of archaeologist?"

"No, Robert Orlinsky referred to Honeyweld as an antiquarian. An amateur, I guess."

"So what do you think he was doing over here then, do you think?" Norcross swung his light over to a neatly cleaned rectangular patch of ground. "I have my theory, but I'd like to hear yours." He estimated the dimensions were three feet wide by ten feet in length.

A tarp was spread out beside the excavation and held the discarded overburden soil. Smaller holes were dug at random intervals and a variety of levels ranging from a few inches to over one foot. Each held a white index card with a number and letter denoting something.

"He's got a fire laid at this end of the trench." She gestured to the dried wood stacked up over a few scraps of paper.

Norcross stepped forward. "I hadn't noticed that, interesting. Oh ah." He stopped two inches from a black plastic finds tray lined with newspaper.

The tray contained a smooth stone, five inches across, with an indentation running the circumference across the middle. This showed where lashings would have bound the stone to a handle, no doubt something wooden. "There are two flint arrowheads and a larger flint nondual in this tray."

"I'd say he was digging for artefacts." Leith looked down at the last item in the tray. She pointed, "What's that?"

Norcross ran his light over the object too. "That's a piece of obsidian."

"This all looks suspect. I'm not sure what Honeyweld was up to, but we will find out." A promise evident in Leith's tone, or was that a threat?

"Along with how he died." Norcross walked back to the pile of wood at the end of the trench.

"That too." She joined him at the stack of tree limbs. "What are you thinking?"

"To make the ground look like there has been a hearth over there, you need burn marks. The soil should look black, like it's been burned. I think that's what this pile of brush was for."

"How do you know this?" Beth's phone pinged.

"I spent some time as a student working for a British archaeological group. They taught me a lot." Operation Nightingale had been more than an education.

Leith removed the device from her sweatshirt pocket and glanced at the display. "Constable Buchanan is fifteen minutes out. I have to drop a pin in the map so he can find us."

Another text followed seconds later.

"That'll be JD, come on." Leith led the way up to the top of the hole.

"That was surprisingly quick." Norcross asked, striding up the now crumbling pit wall. His legs were longer, allowing him to reach the road mere moments before Leith did.

"No, he's the Lone Spruce Community Coroner." Leith was a touch breathless so maybe that was the reason for the pause.

Headlights from a truck bounced along the track behind the parked SUV. The vehicle slowed and then stopped all together. It was impossible for him to see the driver in the low light until the door opened, activating the interior light. A tall wiry man stepped out.

The new arrival was dressed in jeans, boots, and a sun-faded navy shirt. A popular brand of golfing gear was embroidered over the left pocket. From the state of the tattered shirt, Norcross doubted the wear and tear was from the golf course. The man leaned into the truck cab and extracted a Nikon camera and slung the strap from around his neck.

As he strolled forward, he snapped on his own flashlight, similar to the one Leith carried, and pointed the beam downward.

Light stubble roughened JD Zech's jawline. It matched the reddish-blonde hair above his ears. A faded black golf cap was perched on his head. It advertised the Lone Spruce Co-op.

"Hi JD, thanks for coming out."

Laugh lines crinkled. "It's not like I have a choice, Beth." He shifted blue eyes to look over at Norcross, but almost immediately returned his gaze to Leith. "Why are you investigating? Because this is your family's land?"

"Partly." She nodded.

"Where's the local RCMP?"

"Pelly said she needed the help. There was an incident up north on forty-nine highway. Glen Buchanan will be here shortly, I'll hand off to him."

JD nodded. "Pelly will be going to the hit and run by the train tracks, just south of Kelvington."

"Your next stop?" She asked.

"Nope, no one dead as far as I know."

Beth nodded her head in commiseration and then turned to Norcross. "This is my associate, Adam Norcross, he'll be observing."

The coroner opened his eyes wider, indicating this surprised him somewhat, but he shook hands with the other man all the same. "Nice to meet you, Adam. Just so you know I lead the investigation. Sometimes people get confused about that."

"Understood." Norcross released JD's right hand.

Technically, every coroner was in charge of each unexplained death investigation. All findings were brought to their attention.

"And Pelly's okay with this?" JD eyed Leith. He meant Norcross being present.

"She said she was."

"Fine, then. What've we've got?"

"This could be an accidental death." Leith let the suggestion part hang in the air, signalling she had some reservations.

"Usually that's the case, but not always. I'll need to confirm it one way or another. Where is the fatality?"

"Come this way." The sergeant led the way once again down the steep incline, but this time held back, waving Zech forward. It would be the coroner who proceeded first. She merely shone her light over the prone figure on the ground. "We can confirm it is Rupert Honeyweld."

JD made a sucking noise through his teeth as he glanced back at her, Beth frowned. Still, he said nothing about her family involvement. The coroner merely nodded and moved toward the still form for a cursory examination. Once that was done he then began taking photographs.

"Do you know the coroner well?" Norcross stepped up beside the sergeant.

"Yeah, this time it's my turn I guess. JD and I went to school together." That put him close in age to Leith, late thirties.

The sound of another vehicle approaching reached them.

JD continued his examination of the body unbothered by the new arrival. He lifted the victim's shirt and pressed his fingertips to the belly.

"That should be Buchanan." Leith made the climb once more, but instead returned with a couple of female EMS technicians. The EMTs carried a body basket and some supplies.

"Tessa, Kerry." JD acknowledged the women. "We meet again." He gestured for the blonde and brunette women to come over and spoke quietly to them for a moment. Then he returned to Leith and Norcross while the EMTs expertly, yet respectfully, inserted Rupert Honeyweld into a black body bag.

"Well?" Leith asked. "What do you make of it?"

Norcross waited for JD's response too. He also didn't think the blow to the back of the head was the cause of death, but then head wounds could be tricky and he wouldn't say anything until the forensic examination was done.

"I don't think his neck is broken. The head wound is puzzling. He could have fallen, but we will have to do an autopsy to confirm the extent of the head injury. Honeyweld died here, but it's inconclusive if misadventure was the cause. We'll have to send him up to Saskatoon for a full work-up."

"Why do you say that?" Leith tipped her head to look at the coroner to press the point.

"I think he collapsed. Possibly from a heart attack, or from some other medical reason. It's possible he did hit his head, but from the position of the wound, I think it's unlikely. I can say our victim was rolled onto his stomach after his collapse."

"Is that all you can tell us?" Leith wasn't giving up. Norcross noted her set jaw. She sensed JD knew something.

The coroner sighed, but then continued. "Rupert ticked off a lot of people in town and even more rural landowners. There's always the chance something more has gone on before he died. So, to cover all the bases, let's say it's a suspicious death until we know more."

"What did you see that makes you think he collapsed?" She, Norcross, and JD watched the body bag being placed into the carry basket.

"His lips and fingernails are discoloured," Norcross spoke up.

JD looked at Norcross and gave a small nod. "Yes." His tone was guarded.

"What do you think that means?" Leith's hands went to her hips as she turned to look at JD.

"I cannot comment, yet."

"How about the time of death?" Norcross interjected.

"I'd say our victim has been dead eight to twelve hours, by the fixed *livor mortis.*"

"So early morning?"

"I don't know yet." His tone was firm. She'd get nothing more out of him.

"Will the techs need any help retrieving Mr. Honeyweld out of this hole?" Norcross looked at JD. He wanted to let the medical people know he would help if they needed it, but did not want to push his way in.

Leith's phone rang. She stepped back to answer it.

"It would be easier if four of us take a corner, yeah. Thanks for offering." JD walked over to the loaded basket and grabbed a handle. Norcross followed and did the same.

Chapter Ten

The site was taped off before the coroner and EMTs took the body away. JD told them they would be taking the victim to Saskatoon. A pathologist, already alerted, would handle the scientific investigation into the death.

Beth watched JD get back into his truck, but her mind was elsewhere. Skin and nail discolouration was the usual indicator of poisoning. She hoped the pathologist could determine what Mr. Honeyweld might have encountered, if indeed, it turned out he was poisoned. She was trying to keep an open mind, but her gut was telling her Norcross was probably right. He wouldn't have mentioned it otherwise.

Fifteen minutes later, another RCMP vehicle arrived with a tow truck following him. The RCMP truck pulled in behind Leith's SUV and the male driving left the lights on. The moon had slid behind a bank of clouds and they could use all the lights they could get.

He got out and strolled over to Norcross and Leith. "Sergeant Leith? Glen Buchanan." The constable was Métis with close cropped black hair, dark eyes. He was a couple inches shorter than Norcross. The impeccable polish and crispness to his uniform belied his newly graduated status from the academy. Beth knew those habits relaxed slightly as one's career progressed.

"Nice to meet you, Constable." Beth shook his hand, then introduced Norcross and the men did the same.

"So, what did the coroner say? Is it a heart attack?"

"Undetermined at the moment."

"Do you have a working theory?" There was certainty in Buchanan's tone that of course she did. Part of the lower ranks' expectation of a sergeant.

"We only have guesses at the moment. I'd rather not voice any theories until we have more data to go on. All we know is Honeyweld was found face down, a wound on the upper back of the head. JD Zech, the community coroner, doesn't like the colour of his skin and nails."

Beeping emitted from the Lone Tree Towing truck as it backed up to within a couple of feet of the ATV. A short, wiry man in his forties jumped out of the commercial truck. He was dressed in jeans, boots, and a canvas jacket and red ball cap. Both cap and jacket advertised his towing company.

He squinted at Sergeant Leith and Norcross like he did not like what he saw. Even so, the driver strode over to them where they stood on the edge of the crime scene.

"Hi, I was called out by Constable Buchanan." He looked at each of them in turn. It was apparent he was trying to determine which of them was in authority as he used his right thumb to scratch his forehead. "Bruce Sangster."

"I'm Constable Buchanan, I put in the call but Sergeant Leith," he gestured to the lone female in the group, "is in charge."

"Hi, Bruce."

Bruce squinted at her, then his expression cleared. "Bethany Leith, I haven't seen you in years." Bruce had been ahead of Beth by two years at school. She remembered him as being car crazy back then and it was no surprise he'd taken over the family garage and gas station after graduation and a trip to college for a degree in business.

"It's been a while." She smiled in agreement. "You own the family business now?" Leith stepped toward the driver and gestured to his work truck.

"Yep, Dad's mostly retired. He still keeps a hand in while Mum runs the office. You're a sergeant in the RCMP, huh. I'd forgotten you joined up. How did you get dragged into this? Local cops short-handed?" Bruce glanced at Buchanan and

129

gave him a grin. Apparently Bruce found the situation amusing.

"Something like that." She walked over to the quad and Bruce followed. "Do you have a secure lot in Lone Spruce, Bruce?"

"We do." He settled his ball cap more firmly on his head to cover the receding hairline and told her the address. "We've kept impounded vehicles for a day or two for the RCMP before."

Leith nodded. "Ident will contact you tomorrow with regard to the quad."

"Sounds good." He handed her a card. "Thanks for the business, we are always glad to help." Beth figured this was Bruce's standard business tag line and when she glanced at his business card, she found it printed under their phone number.

"Let's go through the storage compartments on the quad before we spread a sheet of plastic over all of it." Leith told Buchanan. "Do you have gloves? We could use some evidence bags to catalogue the other items too. You'll also have to enter the contents into the chain of custody, and then file a report for Inspector Pelly's review."

"No problem." He all but sprinted to his truck to retrieve the items needed.

After a short delay to collect any evidence from the ATV, the machine was loaded onto the tow truck, with the three of them watching from the side of the road. Bruce gave them a wave and he drove off.

* * *

"How do you think the quad was involved in Honeyweld's death?" Constable Buchanan asked the sergeant as the dark swallowed the taillights of the tow truck.

"At the moment we don't know." They'd found a few items in the quad storage compartments; flashlight, empty plastic water bottles, used food storage containers, and the shovel, which had been leaning on the bumper of the ATV. Norcross wrapped up the shovel in plastic and handed it to the constable.

The sergeant put the other items into evidence bags along with the discarded cardboard shoe box found on the far side of the quad. All of the items found in the quad were stored in the back of Buchanan's truck for transport to the detachment. These would be entered into evidence and forensics would pick them up the next day.

In Norcross' opinion, none of the items were much help with building a picture of what happened just prior to Honeyweld's death.

"Possibly the ATV wasn't involved at all." Fists on hips, Leith turned to stare down into the pit. "There is other evidence to be collected." She took out her flashlight again. "We need to collect the items spread out on the ground down there."

"What did you find?" the constable asked as he passed Leith and Norcross a new set of gloves.

Norcross stripped off the old gloves and stuffed them in his back pocket. "Arrowheads, a stone mallet, flint, and some pottery shards." He pulled on a new gloves.

Leith looked at Norcross. "I think our squatter was excavating artefacts. I wonder what the team of archaeologists will have to say about that."

He gave her a steady look. "I'm not so sure he was."

Beth frowned at Norcross. "What do you mean? What else could he have been doing?" She tossed a touch of sarcasm into her tone.

"Anything is possible." Norcross wasn't sure she was paying attention to his tone.

"We can ask the archaeologists camping north of us what they think," she suggested, and then led the way back to the hole. "They are the experts." This was tossed over her shoulder.

Three flashlights bobbed in the darkness. Buchanan followed directly behind Leith, carrying more evidence bags, down the side of the pit with Norcross trailing. "There are archaeologists camped out on your family's land? I heard something about that." Buchanan paused to regain his footing.

"On the bank of the Assiniboine River, just to the north, yes. It's possible the finds here are related to their work up there." Beth crossed the ground and stood beside the rectangle that had been carefully cleared and dug out. She shone her flashlight beam over the exposed ground. The tip of an arrowhead caught in the light and reflected a spark back. A black plastic tray rested on the ground at the foot of the excavation, where they'd left it.

Leith picked up the tray and then looked down at the protruding arrowhead still partly in the ground. It too, had a white card identifying the find and its location.

"What's the plan?" Buchanan asked.

"We take these items into custody." She held up the tray. "We'll leave that one in place. It's something to show the archaeologists. Maybe they can shed some light on why Rupert Honeyweld was here, and why he felt compelled to dig up my family's land without authority or permission." She handed the tray to the constable and took photos of the contents with her phone. She also photographed the excavation and the insitu arrowhead. Photos were much easier to transport.

"I'll add these to the report too." Buchanan bagged, the finds one at a time.

"In this light it's hard to know if we've missed something." Norcross looked around him.

"True." Buchanan returned and Leith pointed down at the ground. "I'll meet you back here tomorrow morning first thing. Forensics will do a sweep of the area and we need to be here in case they find something helpful." They agreed upon a time. "I'll call Pelly and give report, but you should as well."

"I will. There's no death notification to do here. Judy Honeyweld passed away six weeks ago. Saskatoon Police Service are handling contacting Rupert Honeyweld's sister." This made sense to Norcross, Saskatoon was three hours away.

"A sister, is she our victim's only close relative?"

"As far as our office can determine, yeah. Once SPS talks to her, they'll find out if there is someone else to notify." He carried the lot back up to his truck. After that Buchanan drove off.

Quiet as well as full darkness crept back in.

"What do you want to do now?" Norcross asked as they returned to Beth's SUV.

"I want to check on our archaeologists."

"Yes, good plan."

* * *

Beth climbed into the driver's seat of her vehicle.

It occurred to her, Norcross was unusually quiet on this case. She debated

134

asking him what his motivations were for seeking her out but pushed that idea away for now and started the engine instead. At the moment, she had more pressing business.

Norcross got in his side. Instead of backing out like the tow truck and EMS vehicle, she drove past where the quad had been parked and down the track.

"So, what do you think?" She glanced sideways at him.

"It's too soon to say."

Beth twisted her lips. "Is there anything else you'd like to discuss?"

At her words, Norcross' face went completely unreadable. He shook his head. They drove for several minutes before Norcross spoke. It was the perfect time for him to bring up why he had tracked her to her parent's home. She waited for him to explain but instead he asked, "Is it common for farms to be archaeological dig sites?"

Beth's mouth turned down as she thought about it. "No, not at all. I've never heard of another farm having to deal with something like this. Although my dad has talked of nothing else for the past month. He goes from excitement to annoyance depending on the day." She glanced at Norcross and on impulse she did something out of character. She told him something personal. "My dad and Rupert Honeyweld do have a history of not getting along." She briefly explained the dropped assault charges. "I told you I caught the guy on this property, over by the river. He showed me an arrowhead he'd found. He's the reason the archaeologists are here with a dig team. Honeyweld filed a report with the province and once that was done, nothing can go ahead on the property until Archaeology Saskatchewan gets what they need."

"Do you know what the archaeologists need to find?" Norcross looked at her expectantly.

"Evidence, or a lack there of. Then they can declare the site a restricted area or allow my parents as the landowners to go on with their lives. At the moment, the team is still digging."

She didn't know why she let the words tumble out, but she continued anyway. "Yesterday, the group's site lead, Robert Orlinsky, asked for permission to extend their dig across the river to a parcel just over that ridge, also my family's land." She flicked a hand toward the headlights.

"Your father is none too happy about the situation I gather."

"You've got that right. Dad is a private person he isn't thrilled to have strangers tramping around on his property. Add to that, people digging up his riverbank and possibly causing erosion. However, the main issue is the delay this is forcing on him. His plans for this property can't go ahead until Orlinsky gives his 'okay'. And well, Dad's grumpy old guy factor is now multiplied by a factor of four." Her mind jumped to the previous evening, and she described it for Norcross.

"Dad said Robert Orlinsky asking permission was only for show. He was upset and said some things I think he'd like to forget about or take back."

"He was annoyed nothing can happen while the scientists are working at the site?"

She nodded. "Dad just needs to be a bit more patient. I told him it will be fine." Beth lifted one shoulder.

"What did your dad say?"

"Probably not." She looked over at Norcross and grimaced.

Norcross nodded. "Your father needs to wait for the final report on the dig. Much like when a building company finds remains or artefacts during construction."

"Exactly, but that's only part of it. Do you know what will happen if the team finds some evidence of a village or settlement of some kind? It's a full-fledged dig, and it could be months before we can get the new granaries set up on the west side. Let alone allow us to pasture the new livestock on the rest, if at all. The whole place might become scheduled land, protected."

Leith shook her head thinking her father had been right after all, it wasn't fine. He was angry, but not to the point he'd get physical. "My dad would love some artefacts to be uncovered, something they could add to the local museum, but not at the expense of his livelihood."

"It's good he can see both sides."

"The government will do what the government will do. At least this year's harvest is in the bin. We just have to wait them out."

She turned her attention to the road. Rupert Honeyweld was dead and some of the evidence pointed to something more than a suspicious death, but was it murder? She hoped not.

Maybe JD was wrong about the location of the head wound and the blue discolouration. Maybe it was merely a heart attack. Unfortunately, she knew this was never going to be the case. Three separate people, along with her father, said Honeyweld made many enemies in Lone Spruce. What could he have done that was severe enough for anyone to want to kill him?

She glanced at her passenger.

So far Norcross had not told her why he'd suddenly had a need to see her. She didn't buy the 'old friend' excuse he'd given Pelly for a second.

Beth narrowed her eyes as she stared through the dark at the track illuminated by her halogen headlights. They bumped and lurched over the uneven road. She could stand it no longer. "Why are you here?"

He glanced over at her, his gaze steady. "I think you know why, Winslow Thrust."

Involuntarily her jaw tightened, and shoulders went stiff at his calm even tone. "What about him?"

"Thrust is trouble and he wants to cause you more trouble."

"He's already done that. I'm on administrative leave. I'm sure you know all about it with your connections. Did someone send you here to twist my arm? Make me recant my report and say I was mistaken. That I got it wrong, and Minister Thrust had nothing to do with the charges I brought against him?"

"Yes." It was a simple answer but loaded with implications.

"How do you plan to do that?" Her hackles were rising. If he wanted a fight, she'd give him one. Hell, she'd tell him and the rest where to go. She was not going to back down.

"I don't."

Beth stepped on the brake, making the vehicle lurch before she put it in park. She and Norcross had arrived at the ridge which curved down to the riverside where the camp was located. She glared at Norcross.

His grey eyes were studying her.

"What are you saying?"

"Winslow Thrust is without a doubt, guilty of the charges you brought against him."

"That wouldn't stop his AG brother from trying to make it all go away."

"No, it wouldn't stop him, but this isn't a Hollywood movie. He's not going to hire henchmen to threaten you or make you disappear."

"I suspect that's what you are for. You are the government henchman."

A ghost of a smile appeared and then disappeared far too quickly. "I'm not in the habit of following orders blindly. I also don't work for Attorney General Thrust, nor do I subscribe to his methods. This country is run on the rule of law, and no one is above the law. Not even a federal minister's family members." He opened his door. "Shall we go check on your scientists?"

Beth narrowed her eyes at Norcross. "We are not done with this topic."

"I didn't think we were. I just want you to know I'm not here to pressure you into doing something against your principles. I hold similar ideals. I also have a problem with Attorney General Thrust. I need to figure out his agenda. He's up to more than trying to get his kid brother off theft and assault charges."

Chapter Eleven

Mollified in a small way, Beth got out and led the way past a hand full of vehicles to the area where a generator ran the portable lights and cast illumination on the four camper trailers. There, they found the archaeological team. Two men and two women, arranged around a central communal area with plastic folding tables dividing them up like workstations.

The tables were laid with everything from tools, finds trays, and the detritus of the evening meal scattered randomly. There were also several open bottles of wine and half-filled glasses.

In the distance, just barely heard over the sound of the generator, there was the faint sound of music and laughter from somewhere downriver. Beth wondered if Calvin Rokeby made it to his party.

"Hello!" called a flush faced man in his late sixties. "Beth, lovely to see you again my dear. Come in, come in. Who is your tall friend?"

"Adam Norcross, Dr. Robert Orlinsky, lead archaeologist. Adam is my associate."

"Associate? My, my." He winked at Beth like there was an inside joke. "We don't get many visitors. Come and have a lovely glass of shiraz."

"Thank you, but I'm fine." Norcross shook Robert's hand.

"None for me." Beth said as a seated middle-aged man held up a glass of wine. "Fine, fine, come and meet the rest of the crew." Robert led the way to a ring of folding chairs and tables. Robert was around middle height, and balding with a ring of grey speckled brown hair on the back of his head. The man was deeply tanned with an overabundance of laugh lines around his eyes. He moved well, so was reasonably fit. His blue plaid shirt and jeans were wrinkled and dirt encrusted.

Robert waved a hand at the first woman. "Hilda Barker, Finds Administrator, Mike Rockwall, First Nations liaison and a cracking digger, and Selma Dali, our photographer and vlogger. Gang, this is Beth Leith and her friend Adam Norcross."

There were general greetings, but no one got up from their seat. Each member of the group was dishevelled and looked quite exhausted.

"Nick Leith is your father?" Mike asked, reaching for his glass of wine. "Sure you don't want to have a drink?" Mike too was dressed in dirt-stained jeans, and a denim shirt over a white T-shirt which had seen better days. His curly dark brown hair appeared to have a life of its own as it spread out from his head and moved in the light breeze. His boots were kicked off and the wool socks were stuck in the tops. He wriggled his knobby bare toes in the grey and brown sand under the table.

"Maybe some other time." Beth knew her smile was stiff, but wanted to stay at a distance from these people. She wanted to remain impartial.

"What can we do for you?" Robert turned toward her, and it was clear this was not their first bottle of wine this evening. She had to concede it was well after six o'clock.

Before she could answer, Selma brought out two folding chairs and placed them close to the circle of scientists. Her short dark hair lifted gently in the light breeze, and she gave Beth and Norcross a shy smile. "Please have a seat at least, it's a lovely evening. A great time of year, almost no mosquitoes."

As she and Norcross took their seats, Hilda piped up. "Your dad dropped by this afternoon to give Robert the 'okay' to start test pits across the river." She gave them a thin smile as she dipped her small brush into a bucket of water by her chair and continued to gently scrub at a rock-like object on the table. The rock was bisected in the middle by a ground out indentation.

The grey and pink material looked like granite.

"Is that a hammer stone?" Norcross asked. He stepped around the folding chair.

Beth couldn't miss the intrigued note in his voice and apparently neither did Hilda.

The other woman beamed a smile at the younger man. "It's a grooved maul." By Beth's reckoning Hilda was at least sixty, but fit. She had long dark blonde hair streaked with a lighter shade, and pulled back from a striking face. And although she was significantly older than Norcross, the woman was attractive with her fresh scrubbed peaches and cream complexion and hazel eyes fringed with black lashes. These she fluttered at Norcross.

"How interesting," Norcross said. He accepted the nonverbal invitation and crossed over to Hilda and leaned over her shoulder for a closer look at the artefact.

"Yes, like hammer stones, grooved mauls were used for everything from pounding in stakes to tools for quarrying stone. Many of the larger mauls are grooved like this to facilitate hafting." She gave Norcross a coy look. "Do you know what hafting involves?"

"Attaching the stone onto a handle through the use of the grooves and strips made out of leather."

Hilda nodded, pleased Norcross understood. "True, or animal muscle as well

144

as a binding agent to help glue the constituent parts together." She stroked a hand over the rough stone as she spoke. "Smaller pecking stones are un-grooved, but can be identified by the impact scars. That is, areas where rock has broken off due to impact."

Beth could not figure out why she found the conversation between Norcross and Hilda odd, but she kept her expression neutral anyway. Archaeology had never been one of her interests.

"Would those smaller pecking stones be used in the chipping of stone tools, such as flint knapping? he asked her.

"In some cases."

"Bell-shaped grinding stones were used for pounding and grinding, like a pestle, weren't they?" He continued with another question and Beth rubbed her forehead to shield her expression.

"Exactly, pestle stones were very important. They were used for grinding everything from dried meat and chokecherries for pemmican, to earth paints for adornment."

Beth had serious news to impart to the team and wanted to get to it. She looked away from the pair and became aware Robert, Mike, and Selma were looking at her expectantly.

"Is there something we can help you with?" Selma added a smile. "Do you have any questions about this dig?"

Beth lifted her chin, she as glad of the opening. The awkwardness was new for her. It hadn't been that long since she worked a case. "I'm here in an official capacity."

The three looked puzzled and Hilda ignored her as she showed Norcross a view of another piece of some kind of rock.

She had no ID to show them but carried on anyway. "I'm a RCMP officer. I have to ask you where you all were today."

"You're a cop?" Mike sipped his drink. His black eyebrows were raised as he studied her over the top of his stemless wineglass.

"That's what I said."

"Why do you need to know?" Selma tipped her head to the side as she too, studied Beth.

"Please just answer Sergeant Leith's question." Norcross interjected this as he returned to sit beside her.

Robert waved with his hands in a 'whatever' gesture. "It's no problem to give you the information." He gave each of his team a meaningful look. "We need to keep lines of communication open, it's a two-way street."

Selma shrugged her round shoulders. Mike continued to study both Beth and

Norcross silently over the brim of his wine glass.

Their leader continued, "We were all working here today and have been for the past three. We've opened up a four foot by twenty-foot trench along the west side of the hill." He got up and walked over to a separate table and returned with a black plastic tray to show the visitors.

Beth noted the tray was similar to the one they'd found by the victim.

"Here are some of the items we've uncovered so far." The tray held many samples of stone in colours ranging from white to pink to grey, and black. There were also several shards of clay pottery.

"This is all from today?" She glanced up at the archaeologist.

"Yes, we sent the earlier finds to the University of Saskatchewan with my assistant, Rachel. She left yesterday morning." Robert took the tray back and returned it to the table.

"You were all here together, all day?" Beth asked, watching their reactions.

"Yes, either working in the trench or cleaning the finds." Selma nodded as she looked at her co-workers. "Oh, well, Hilda did make a grocery run."

"What time was this?" Beth looked at Hilda.

The older woman pursed her lips as she put down her scrub brush. "Late afternoon, we needed something to barbeque tonight for dinner for the boys and a vegan option for Selma and me."

"You went to the Co-op grocery store?"

"They have the nicest selection of eggplant." Hilda nodded.

"And good quality T-bones." Mike put in.

Beth could see the remains of steak and eggplant rind on a couple of plates, so she accepted this explanation. The information could always be checked out if need be.

"A lovely meal." Robert released a small belch. "Your coleslaw was amazing, Hilda."

The older woman flashed Robert a smile and then turned back to Beth. "What aren't you telling us?" Hilda placed her rock down on the newspaper in another tray in front of her.

"I'm afraid I have to inform you of a death on the property."

The shock and disbelief was pretty much what Beth expected. Still, she watched the four scientists for their reactions as Norcross added details of the situation. She could not detect anything out of step with the group.

"I'd like you to look at some photos of items from that site." Beth extracted her phone and set it to display the photos she'd taken of the finds from the crime scene.

"These items look like they are from a dig as well." The archaeologists all got to their feet and clustered around Beth to look at the pictures.

"That's a nice example of a flint knife." Apparently, Robert Orlinsky was an expert in this field.

"Robert, is that–" Mike was cut off by Robert.

"It certainly looks like it."

"What?" Beth looked at first Robert, then Mike.

"The arrowhead in the finds tray, it's a Clovis design," Robert told them.

"What does that mean?" She handed over her phone so Dr. Orlinsky could get a closer look.

"A significant find, indeed." Robert had his nose close to the screen. He adjusted the brightness of the display.

"A very important find for sure." Selma stared over Robert's shoulder. "When can we see these finds in person?"

"It might be a while. They're part of the investigation at the moment." Beth said.

Mike was frowning as he looked over Robert's other shoulder. "Bob, swipe to the trench photos again, please."

"Not my area." Hilda said after a cursory glance. She moved away and retook her seat at the cleaning table.

Robert complied and Mike leaned closer, still frowning darkly. "I don't know.

This could mean a village settlement but it's hard to say without seeing it in person. And with daylight." Mike glanced over at Beth. "Where were these photos taken? Geographically, I mean. On a hill? Or in a field?" He straightened to look directly at Leith.

"In a coulee." She glanced at Norcross. "Or maybe it's more of a pit."

Robert and Mike's eyebrows both lifted as she said this.

"That's…" Mike drew out the word. "Rather odd."

Robert nodded in agreement. "Not something we usually see."

"Odd how?" Norcross asked.

"Well, it's not a location anyone would want a village or shelter, for that matter. Poor drainage in harsh weather for one thing." Robert shrugged. "A hillside or a flat stretch of prairie close to a water source is usual." He handed back Beth's phone.

"Why are these artefacts part of the investigation?" Selma folded her arms over her stomach.

"All I can say is as soon as we determine if the items add value or not to the inquiry, our Inspector may release the finds to you for study."

"All artefacts belong to the province. Who should I contact so we may expedite the process?" Selma had her phone out to record the details.

The sergeant passed on Inspector Pelly's contact information. By the determined glint in Selma's eyes, she figured Pelly would be hearing from the scientist fairly soon.

* * *

Beth was silent as they drove down the dirt track. She made a left-hand turn to get them back on the grid road, in the direction of the farm.

When she made the turn for the driveway, once again they were met by the pair of dogs who now treated Norcross as one of their own. One ear rub each and the pair retreated to the front porch.

"What are you going to do now?" He asked once he'd walked around to the driver's side. They stood under the yard light and the moment felt awkward.

Before she could answer, her phone pinged with an incoming text. She quickly glanced at it. "It's Pelly. I have to give the inspector a verbal update."

He nodded. "I'll head to my accommodations then."

She frowned at him. "Where are you staying? Or are you driving back to the city?"

"No, I'm staying in town at the Sleepy Hollow B & B." Adam didn't want to leave. He wanted more time with her.

Merely giving Beth a heads up about Thrust and his manipulations to get his little brother out of trouble did not feel like he was doing enough. There wasn't much else he'd planned, no matter what anyone else wanted. He didn't feel like he could leave her just yet though. "I want you to be careful when it comes to Winslow Thrust. He has powerful contacts."

"I already got much the same advice from Inspector Taggard. People like the Honourable Geoffery Thrust think people like me are disposable." She gave a snort of derision. "Not my first rodeo."

"Still, be cautious, please. Thrust wields a lot of power, at least in his own mind."

She looked steadily at him for a moment. "Yeah, that's the same vibe I got off his little brother. Especially when he said, 'Do you know who I am?' when I was putting on the cuffs." Beth laughed dryly. Then she gave him a half smile as she cocked her hip. "Thanks for your help." She dialed Pelly's number.

That was it. She was giving him the brush off. "No problem."

Beth gave him a wave as she spoke to Pelly.

He was worried Beth did not fully comprehend how nasty dark politics could get.

Norcross did not buy her off-handed cocky attitude. With the right leverage, anyone could be bought, or pressured into doing things he or she found distasteful.

He'd seen it before and had to deal with the fallout.

Chapter Twelve

Norcross replayed his last conversation with Beth over in his mind as he drove back to town.

He knew without a doubt Thrust's goals meant more to the AG than those people he trampled upon. One of those goals appeared to be assisting his brother's climb up the political ladder by covering up any indiscretions. Chances were good the older brother had plans for the younger. Norcross was sure there was some self-serving agenda at the heart of it all. If he was going to figure it out, he needed more information to be sure.

He used his hands-free Bluetooth connection to send an email to Maisy Greenwich, his assistant. Making it possible to keep his attention on the road. He requested everything his assistant could lay her hands on about the Thrust family.

Next, Norcross had his phone dial Zara Dare's number.

"Is this you calling in your favour already?" Zara chuckled without saying hello.

"No, not yet, when I do call in that favour, it will be for something much larger than this small request."

"I should have known. What can I do for you?"

Briefly, Norcross brought his old associate up to speed with regard to the current case he was on. "I need you to dig into something for me."

"Isn't that what Maisy is for?"

"The information I need is above her pay grade, I'm afraid. This also requires an experienced light touch."

"You don't want Shapiro to know what you're after." It wasn't a question.

"Trust me, he won't want to even acknowledge I'm thinking along these lines. It would bring him a huge headache." More so than what was already on his shoulders.

"Plausible deniability, eh?"

"Something like that, yes."

"This 'favour' won't negatively affect me?"

"You scare people too much for that."

"True." There was no hubris in Zara's tone. "What can I do for you?"

"The BC Crown prosecutor has charges pending against Winslow Thrust. The arresting officer was Sergeant Bethany Leith. I want anything pertaining to any

155

counter suit and what the RCMP review board has achieved so far."

"That sounds straight forward."

"Here's where it takes a right turn. See if there is any connection to Rupert Honeyweld's death and Sergeant Leith. What does the chatter say? If there is a connection, and if so, how far up the chain of command is this case talked about."

"Which agencies or ministries do you want to concentrate on?"

"Just see what is in the general rumour mill. Theoretically, there should be very little, if anything at all. Our victim is a little guy and shouldn't be on anyone's radar outside Saskatchewan."

"And if this guy's death is on the minds of the powerbrokers?"

"It could be a setup or is this something else."

"You think it's something else?"

"I don't know yet. I do know this unexplained death wasn't an accident."

"Ah, yes, your superpowers at work?"

"More like basic investigation skills," Norcross said dryly.

"Something else you're good at. Is this your new hobby, solving murders in your off hours?"

"Not hardly."

Zara laughed at his response. "I'll see what I can dig up for you."

"Thanks, buddy."

Adam parked in the small lot next to the Sleepy Hollow Bed & Breakfast. The lot had the look of a recent addition. Possibly, a small house from the 1940's had been removed and the yard added to the grounds of the larger, older palatial property to form a parking area for guests.

A huge elm tree stretched well above the heritage building's third story. The branches disappeared into the darkness above the structure. A burl, some two feet across, had been removed from the front of the tree. With the rounded knotty growth gone, a hollow remained. He could see through the tree, although the hole was partially closed from tree growth. Tucked inside was a small gnome in the action of using an axe.

He wondered if this was where the 'hollow' in the B & B's name came from.

The tree had to be over a hundred years old. The elm must have been planted when the house foundation was dug.

In the street light glow, and the carriage lights on either side of the wide front door, the massive tree shone like a yellow flame. Adam took his bag out of the Tacoma and locked up. He followed the winding path and climbed the wide wooden steps.

Adam paused a moment to get a good look, he liked the three-story timber frame house. The exterior was painted white with black trim and shutters. The wide veranda reminded him of his mother's house in Maple Bay. Well, his house now. The floorboards were painted dark grey, and he admired the square Shaker-style finish of the wooden pillars, which were painted white too.

Before Adam could knock, Theodore Key, owner of the Sleepy Hollow Bed & Breakfast met him at the front door.

Teddy, as he was told to call the man, was in his middle fifties. Dark-haired with specks of white he had a lined face, he was slender with stooped shoulders, but had all the energy of someone much younger and an infections grin.

"Nice to meet you, Adam. We have your room all prepared. Please, come to the desk and sign in."

There was an honest-to-goodness book ledger which turned on a brass pedestal. For some reason, this pleased Norcross. It was like he'd stepped back in time over a hundred years as he plucked the fountain pen out of its holder to write his name into the tome.

The front desk, like the rest of the entrance was fashioned from red oak which also panelled the walls and was underfoot. Half-way up the walls, the wood stopped, and alabaster white plaster took over and continued on to the vaulted ceilings. The foyer was three stories high, and a crystal chandelier illuminated the front of the house. A pair of round-fronted glass curio cabinets flanked the walls on either side. Each cabinet appeared to be chock-a-block full of intriguing items. Adam wanted to stop and check them out, but he'd have to save that pleasure for later.

Teddy picked up the suitcase to take him to his accommodations. "We have you on the second floor." His host led Adam up the sweeping red oak staircase.

He paused for a moment to admire the wolf head carving on the newel post. Here, the walls changed to red wallpaper with a large dark gold pattern from the turn of the 1900's. "We were expecting you earlier in the day." There was a small admonishment in the owner's tone.

"Sorry about that, official business got in the way." They reached the second floor.

"That sounds interesting," Teddy said in a leading tone. He gestured the way down a high ceiling hallway. "Your visit wouldn't be about Rupert Honeyweld, would it?"

"I can't confirm or deny any information at this point." It was probable Rokeby had told people about finding Honeyweld's body earlier and no doubt news spread quickly.

At the end of the corridor, was a wide window complete with an inviting built-in seat covered with rich green embroidered pillows. The seat overlooked the back gardens. Adam caught a glimpse of red roses and the shapes of lilies in the glow of thousands of fairy lights strung among the trees and shrubs of the back yard and illuminated the large area divided by a stone walkway.

"I understand, but news travels quickly in this part of the country." Teddy stopped at an oak panel door. He held up an old-fashioned skeleton key with a flourish and glanced at Adam to ensure his guest was paying attention as he opened the room's door, obviously proud of the décor and the attention to detail.

As he should be. "You run a beautiful establishment."

Teddy smiled as he handed Adam the key now that the door was opened. "Thank you."

On impulse Norcross asked, "Did you know Rupert Honeyweld?"

"What does anyone know about their neighbours?" Teddy flipped on the bathroom light. "I've given you the only room that has an en suite. The rest of the rooms share bathrooms. You are my only customer at the moment, so you won out."

"Thank you." The four-poster bed looked large enough for him. Adam was sure he would be comfortable.

"I hope you will enjoy your stay with us."

"I'm sure I will. Mr. Honeyweld was your neighbour?" Now Norcross used a leading tone.

"Yes." Teddy placed the suitcase on the open rack fit for the purpose. "If you are going out, just drop the key in the lockbox. It's on the counter at the entrance." He hesitated. "What do you want to know about Rupert?"

Norcross knew he really shouldn't be saying anything at this point in the investigation, but local information might be a help and also might move things along more quickly. "He was found deceased, this afternoon. I am helping with the investigation into his death, and it doesn't look like an accident."

"Good lord." Teddy shook his head sadly. He looked and sounded believably shocked, just as the four archaeologists had after Beth imparted the same information.

"Did you know him well? Can you tell me about him?" Norcross gently prodded.

"Mm," Teddy said and dropped his hand. "Rupert lives or lived across the road and two doors down. He bought the Carson house about seven years ago, I believe."

"So Honeyweld hasn't been a resident of Lone Spruce very long?"

"No, it only felt that way." Teddy sighed. "He was always picking a fight with someone. Nothing was up to snuff for him. I

161

sincerely don't know why he would move to a little town if he didn't like small town life."

"In what context?" Adam put his briefcase down on the desk by the window.

"Well, in small communities you have to be tolerant. Everything doesn't happen all at once or sometimes as you would expect it to. Patience is the key for us all to get along. And we all need to be friendly to others."

"What do you mean?" Adam removed his jacket and hung it on the back of the desk chair.

Teddy flipped one hand. "For instance, when there is only one clerk running the check out at the grocery store. You just queue up and wait your turn no matter how long it takes. It's a good chance to visit with others. Our population has a great number of senior citizens, and they sometimes need a hand in the store. Helping or being patient while others give assistance is how we know we are all still human beings." The innkeeper gave Norcross an emphatic nod. "Rupert would rant about the speed of service. In the store, at the town office, how it took people forever to return a phone call. Trades people are busy. They will get back to you eventually, just not exactly on your timeline. If you aren't used to that, it can be frustrating."

"The good ones are always busy, even in the city, in my experience."

"Exactly. It's small potatoes stuff, but Rupert would carry on to anyone who'd listen and many who didn't want to. He wrote letters to the editor of the local paper complaining about the lack of professionalism in Lone Spruce." Teddy shook his head. "He turned a lot of people off with his fault finding and complaining attitude." Teddy paused, frowning. "How did he die?"

"We don't know yet."

"Right, and that's why you are doing the investigative thing? JD will be on this too, I'm sure."

"Yes, JD and I met earlier."

"Was Rupert actually found on Nick Leith's land? He was always dragging a shovel or metal detector to someone's property. He acted like he had carte blanche to investigate anyone's place because he was an 'antiquarian'." Teddy did air quotes.

"So Mr. Honeyweld snooping around the Leith's property wasn't unique?"

"No, it's just that Nick Leith doesn't take crap off anyone, least of all someone like Rupert Honeyweld." Teddy shrugged. "What time would you like breakfast?"

"How early do you usually serve it?"

"How is seven-thirty?"

"Perfect." Norcross was just about to ask where he could grab an evening meal when his cell phone rang.

"I'll leave you to it." Teddy closed the door behind him.

Norcross glanced at the display. Unknown, still it was a 306 area code.

"Hello." He knew who would be on the line.

"Norcross, once you're settled, drop by the house for supper. I've got some news from Pelly."

Chapter Thirteen

After Adam cleaned up and changed his shirt, he made a brief stop downtown. He purchased a bottle of wine from the independent liquor store open late on Friday evening. He chose a merlot on impulse but felt it was the correct choice. Adam never liked to show up empty handed.

As he drove back to the Leith farm, he reviewed some of the information he'd uncovered from his research on Beth's family.

Adam had found Nick Leith, father, farmer, and past president of the Lone Spruce Historical Society had gotten into trouble last year. This was in December, roughly near the end of the Flete murder investigation where he'd met Bethany Leith. The case was currently working its way through the courts system, with much coverage by the media. Norcross would never be called as a witness for either the Crown or the defense, and for that he was grateful.

He did remember the tense phone call Beth received during one suspect's interview. The call may have pertained to her father's legal troubles.

Yes, that felt right.

Nicolas Ruben Leith and Rupert Julian Honeyweld had both been charged with assault. Beth's father and Honeyweld had got into it at the yearend Christmas party No doubt alcohol had played a part in the dispute. The charges resulted in both parties paying a fine.

This wouldn't be the last time Nick Leith and Rupert Honeyweld clashed. At the annual general meeting of the LSHS the following January, Nick Leith called out Rupert Honeyweld and his practise of trespassing and digging holes on land he didn't own. "Permission for test pits must be obtained and only an ass-hat would not respect his neighbours."

According to the information, Rupert Honeyweld responded with, "*Leith, you are an ignorant hick.*" After that remark other LSHS members had jumped in to separate the two men. Another report was filed with the RCMP and both men given a warning not to come near each other in public again.

The final incident happened in a local cafe, Leith accused the other man of endangering his livestock by digging test pits and leaving the holes open, unfilled in. He'd lost valuable breeding stock to a broken leg from Honeyweld's negligence. At least that time both men went their separate ways before the cops showed up.

Nick Leith launched a civil suit for his losses. Currently, the lawsuit was ponderously working its way through the system.

Not that Adam could blame Beth's father for his anger. Honeyweld sounded like a right menace.

He slowed the truck to turn the corner. Once off the asphalt highway he took the grid road to the farm.

Other than the brief handshake he'd shared with Nick Leith, Adam was as yet undecided about the man. They had assessed each other, much as two unfamiliar males did at any introduction, but that was all there'd been to it. His precognitive talent had remained silent. Typically, he'd receive some inkling about a new acquaintance's character upon meeting someone for the first time.

The chance to share a meal with the family would give Adam an opportunity to assess Nick Leith. So, he'd better not be late for supper.

* * *

Adam wasn't sure what the mood would be at the Leith household as he slowly walked up the steps to the veranda. Both dogs flanked him.

Earlier, when he'd first met the dogs, he'd employed a method Zav Koering had shared with him when dealing with unfamiliar animals. The 'alpha stare' as Zav called it, worked remarkably well if one remembered to also adopt the alpha attitude which was required to go along with it.

As he approached, Beth pushed open the door. Light from the kitchen spilled out and felt welcoming. "Hi, come in."

Adam opened the screen door and the dogs lurched forward too. "Not you guys, you've been fed. Go check the property." She said the last as though it was a command and it must have been, since the pair of canines bounded down the steps and into the dark.

"Thanks for inviting me." Adam felt suddenly uncomfortable but covered it by offering her the plain brown bag which contained the wine.

"Thanks." Beth nodded as she took the offering and led him into a spacious eat-in kitchen.

The rich fragrance of roasted beef with garlic and vegetables filled his nose and he sighed with pleasure.

"Hello, Adam. So nice you could join us." Maria Leith came forward and placed a hand on his arm to steer him to a place at the table that was set for five.

Beth rolled her eyes at her mother and held up the bottle of red.

"Oh, nice one. I'll get some glasses for us." Maria bustled away and grabbed wine glasses out of one dark maple cupboard. "You pour, Beth, while I get the gravy ready for the table." She handed her daughter the glasses and turned left to lean on the door frame. "Nick, Dawson, supper," she called in to the rest of the house, and then continued onto the stove.

In short order, the elder Leith appeared in the doorway. Norcross automatically stood.

Nick Leith frowned at him but said nothing. A younger version of Nick came in behind his father. Dawson looked to be in his early forties. There was no wedding band on his left ring finger, but there was a faint outline where a ring had been.

"You know my dad, Nick. This is my oldest brother, Dawson." Beth placed a glass of red in front of Norcross.

Greetings were exchanged and a handshake between Adam and Dawson. Adam liked Beth's brother immediately. He gave off a clean, honest vibe with a healthy dose of integrity. There, his talent was still at work.

Nick took the head of the long wooden table. He dropped a napkin onto his lap and ignored Adam completely as food was delivered to the table.

Finally, Maria sat down on Nick's left, his daughter on his right next to Adam and Dawson took the place at the foot of the table.

Maria gave her son a waiting look and Dawson made the sign of the cross and all bent their heads as he said grace.

Then it was time to load their plates. Adam waited for questions to be asked but none seemed to be forthcoming. This surprised him somewhat, there was plenty of body language and shifting of eyes. Neither Nick nor Dawson drank any wine, they stuck with ice water.

Five minutes into the meal Maria finally looked at Adam and smiled. "So what brings you all the way out to Lone Tree, Adam? Don't say it's this investigation." Her tone told Adam she knew better.

Adam finished chewing the tidbit of beautifully cooked roast beef and swallowed. He glanced left at Beth, but she kept her head down. All right then.

"I've just got back into the country and found out Beth had left Vancouver Island. I called her old partner, Collin Bighetty and he told me she was here."

Beth briefly closed her eyes and then sat up straighter. "My family knows I'm on administrative leave, Norcross."

But not what was truly behind it, Adam guessed as he returned her look. "I had hoped to keep in better contact." He turned to look at Maria, "However, communications in that part of the world can be spotty at best."

"Where were you?" Dawson passed Adam the basket of rolls and he selected one before handing them on to Beth.

Adam took in Dawson's close cropped brown hair and his posture and made an educated guess. He added this deduction to his earlier impression and decided he could trust Dawson. "Libya."

"What were you doing there?" There was a guarded note to Dawson's tone as he added butter to his roll and carefully placed his knife on the side of his dinner plate.

"Assisting an associate with a difficult security matter." Adam figured it was best to be vague.

Beth studied him for a moment. "Libya," she guessed. "Afriqiyah airline flight 112, it's been on the news."

He nodded as he looked back at her. "Yes. They didn't want a repeat of 1985 in Malta."

Dawson narrowed his eyes in a frown. "1985 was bad?"

Adam shifted his gaze to Beth's brother. "Yes, it was terrible."

Nick was looking between the two younger men and appeared to read something he liked, Adam noticed.

The elder Leith lifted his chin in a manner Adam had seen Beth do a hundred times. "But why are you here?"

"It might not be our business, Nick." Maria tempted her husband with the beet pickle dish.

"I'm here to ask if Beth would consider accepting my proposal."

Everyone else froze as Beth's head snapped up to look at Adam, more than a bit horrified. "What proposal?" Her voice had a strained note.

"I need someone to live in my house." He looked at Maria and her shocked expression. "The property is outside of Duncan." He continued innocently. "I work and live in Ottawa, and I don't want to sell the house. It's been in my family for several generations. I thought who could be better than Beth to keep an eye on things? You'd be close to work, and it would be doing me a huge favour, so no rent."

"What about Perkins?"

"Who's Perkins?" Maria asked.

"My mother's cat," Adam said to Maria. "He's part of the deal I'm afraid." Adam accepted the butter dish from Maria with a thank you. He turned back to Beth. "He shouldn't be a problem, Perkins likes you. It's rare for that cat to like anyone." He broke off a chunk of roll and swiped it with butter. "I would have called ahead, but I didn't have Beth's mobile number." He raised his eyebrows at her, looking as innocent as he could.

Beth narrowed her eyes but did not contradict him. If he wanted her personal mobile number, she knew he could obtain it. Surely she realized he just wanted to see her and make sure she was all right.

"Long way to come to get a house sitter," Dawson murmured.

"What was that, Daw?" Beth lifted one eyebrow at her brother.

"Nothing. Please pass the pickles, Mom."

It was time to change the subject. "I understand from Beth your family just lately purchased the property across the road?" Adam asked Dawson.

"That's true, grandad ran cattle on it for years."

"If you don't mind me asking, why buy the land now?"

"We've always wanted those fifty acres, but Morris wouldn't sell." Dawson shrugged.

"*Becky* wouldn't sell," Maria put in. "She is Morris' wife. The land was hers and that parcel across the river too. When Morris married Becky, they used the north side mostly for cereal crops. The south side, our piece, floods in the spring every other year. Morris didn't have cattle."

"So not preferred for grains?" Adam asked.

"Not great for pulse crops either. No, that land is better for cattle." Nick wiped his mouth with a napkin.

"We reduced our cattle numbers for a few years, but it's time to ramp up again. The market is looking good." Dawson added rich brown gravy to his mashed potatoes. "The plan was to expand the bin yard across there too, and we'll still do that, but we have to wait." He met his father's eyes, and they shared a grimace. "On everything."

"Oh?" Adam asked, and then took a sip of the red he'd brought.

"I told you he showed me one when I caught him on the land." Beth stabbed her carrots.

"Probably quartz or quartzite." Nick breathed in through his nose but did not look up from his plate, his distain obvious.

Beth reached over and placed her hand on her dad's for a moment. "Honeyweld then filed paperwork with the province and demanded an archaeologist check the whole area for a settlement. He wants or wanted both sides of Conjuring Creek investigated."

"While the team of archaeologists is camped over there, we are at a standstill with our plans." Dawson's lips twisted. "We can visit the sites, but that's it."

"No access to the river at all," Maria said. "I'm glad I harvested the Saskatoon berries and hazel nuts before that bunch arrived. I hope they are gone before spring."

"In time for some fishing, I've gotten the odd pickerel out of the river around there." Beth laid her fork and knife down.

"You mean grandad did, and you watched." Dawson teased his sister.

"Jealous."

"Ha!"

"Kids." Maria's tone was reproachful. The land line in the next room rang and she excused herself.

"I doubt they'll stay after the first snow flies." Nick finished his meal and reached for the salad bowl to load his plate. Beth passed him the small glass salad dressing jug.

With interest Adam noted Nick sprinkled ground flax seeds and sunflower seeds on his salad then the homemade red onion vinaigrette dressing.

"Let's hope this is the limit of their stay." Dawson too had his salad at the end of the meal.

Nick snorted. "Honeyweld anticipated the attention his meddling would bring. He knew how it would bugger up our plans. He did it on purpose."

"The Saskatchewan Archaeological Society examined the artefacts he sent them. That's how it led to a full-fledged dig." Beth's tone was level with no hint of condescension as she glanced up at Adam filling him in.

Her father waved her words away. "These people are supposed to be scientists and work from evidence and facts, not from what some hack says. I can't believe they are giving that fraud any kind of credit to his claims."

"Don't speak ill of the dead, Bunny." Maria retook her seat.

Adam blinked at the endearment Mrs. Leith used for her rather tall and burly husband. He glanced at Beth. She was softly smiling as she helped herself to salad.

Nick merely grunted then continued his rant. "The earliest projectile points found in our province are Clovis and dated to roughly 12,000 to 11,000 BC. Only found in isolated areas, virtually untouched land and very remote. There has been no intact archaeological site dating back to that period and certainly not in this area of Saskatchewan. The only site I might believe has something of interest would be the seventeen acres across the river. There's no road access to the land, and it's unbroken prairie."

"This could be a first for us then," Dawson said. "Besides, that guy," he shook his head. "The lead archaeologist, Dr.?"

"Robert Orlinsky." Beth supplied.

"That's him." Nick forked some salad into his mouth and munched, eyes glinting.

Dawson nodded. "He said at the community meeting that he was keeping an open mind on what was found out there so far. He also said they needed to be sure of their findings before deciding anything conclusive, let alone announcing any conclusions."

"That doesn't matter. There is no Clovis settlement out there, there never was." Nick gestured with his fork.

This sounded like an old argument to Adam.

"I don't care what type of artefact Honeyweld said he found. He's a liar."

"What about the arrowhead he showed me?" Beth asked.

Nick compressed his lips and released a long slow breath, possibly to get a hold of his temper. "I saw the photo in the paper that trespassing ass-hat showed you, it was made from quartzite and was too small. You work with evidence all the time, Bethy, and facts. Neither of which support Honeyweld's claim he found a Clovis point."

Beth glanced at Norcross and their eyes met briefly before she turned back to her father. "You've kept tabs on what's being done on the property?" she said to change the subject.

"Of course I am. The team began by investigating with test pits and moved on to a couple trenches to identify what was actually going on. If the result looks worthwhile, then Orlinsky will bring in ground penetrating radar to gather geophysical data to back it up before expanding the dig, if need be."

"I see," Beth said to her father.

They all went quiet for a moment before Dawson picked up the conversation with a new topic. "I finished the fence repairs this afternoon. Tomorrow we can move the cows across to the old pasture." He glanced at Adam. "And nowhere near the archaeologists' camp."

"Or the incident scene." Beth raised one eyebrow at her brother.

"Or there either, the cattle will be up on the higher ground, where it overlooks next year's canola field."

"Are any of the heifers still open?" Nick asked his son.

"No, Walter took care of business."

Chapter Fourteen

It took little convincing for Adam to get Maria to agree he and Beth would take on the dishes and clean up after the table was cleared. "Nobody eats for free." He smiled at Beth's mother.

Maria willingly gave up the chore in favour of a walk with her husband. "We like to walk every evening."

"Do we?" Nick gave his wife an wide-eyed look.

"All right you do, but I come with you several times a week." Nick grunted agreement with this statement.

"Where is this walk taking us?" Maria gave her husband a fond smile while buttoning her red sweater. She pulled on a ball cap over her grey-shot dark hair and tugged her ponytail out the back.

"I need to check the trail cameras. I want to see if old Roughneck is back." Nick shrugged on a black windbreaker that had seen better days.

"Oh, that buck you missed last year? You think he'll come back? That's interesting." Her eyes sparkled with mischief as she winked at her daughter.

"I did not miss, that buck ducked. I'm not as good with a bow as I once was, that's why I switched back to my rifle."

"Of course, love. Have you seen anything good on the cameras this year?"

"Some good size does, and a small buck on the north camera." Nick held the door for his wife. "From the camera looking toward the main road, three combines. I have a couple on the new property, I'll show you where the new hopper bins are going to be installed too." Nick's enthusiasm was genuine.

"Oh boy, and it's not even date night."

"I could take you for a drive out to the dump if you'd rather." The sound of their voices died away as Beth's parents strolled down the steps.

Dawson had left earlier to go to the equipment shed. He'd said something about checking on the welds he'd done on the 9600, apparently the piece of equipment was a combine.

"Roughneck?" Adam shifted his eyes to meet Beth's as they walked back into the kitchen.

"Last year, when my dad still bow hunted, he took a shot at a five-by-five buck." Beth reached the counter and finished sealing a container of leftover gravy. "The buck moved at the last second and the arrow got him in the neck, but not fatally. Dawson and I helped Dad track him to the river. There was only the odd speck of blood along the way, and when we got to the water's edge it was clear old Roughneck had made it across Conjuring Creek by the cracks in the ice."

"What time of year was this?"

"Middle of November last year. Anyway, Dad called the Freeborns, and we checked out their side of the river too. Couldn't find any trace of him, he was in the wind."

"So still alive?"

"Yep, a couple of people told Dad they had a glimpse of Roughneck since then. Not too many have a white neck scar. Now the buck's a local celebrity." Beth crossed the kitchen to put the container in the fridge.

Adam began to unbutton his left shirtsleeve. The books tucked into a recessed shelf in the wall beside the kitchen table window caught his eye. All by the same author, Ivy Blackwood. He quickly turned his back and walked to the sink.

With the house quiet, Adam figured it was a time to speak with Beth privately. "I'll wash." He began rolling up his other shirtsleeve now that the food was put away.

"Why do you get to wash?" Beth lifted her chin at him as she handed him a serving bowl to rinse.

"I don't know which cupboard to put anything once it's dry."

"Good point." Beth allowed a small smile.

They worked companionably for several minutes, but once the counters were wiped off and the dishwasher loaded, the actual dish washing ensured they stood side by side for the task. It was time to bring up the reason he was there.

This simple chore was something Adam enjoyed immensely. He liked Beth's company more than he could say, or even admit to himself. Something best not to dwell on.

After a few items were dealt with he decided to start with small questions and work up to the big issues. "What does 'open' mean when referring to cattle?"

Beth dried a chef's chopping knife. "It means a heifer that isn't pregnant. If Walter, the bull, isn't successful with the female, we may sell her at auction."

"Ah."

"Walter is pretty reliable. Last year he sired twenty-three calves."

Adam let the silence settle on them for a few more moments as they worked in concert. Finally he asked, "What happened with Winslow Thrust."

She dropped another knife into its slot in the block with a solid 'thunk'. "What? Can't your office find out about something as insignificant as charges brought against a sitting BC Member of the Legislative

Assembly? Or a suspended RCMP Sergeant?" Bitterness was evident in her tone.

"I have the official report, but those documents don't always tell the full story. I want to hear what happened from you. I want your perspective."

"Is that really why you're here? To uncover something missed by the review process?"

"Partly." Adam nodded as he rinsed a pot and placed it on the drying rack. While not strictly true, if he did uncover something that should be included in the report, he would raise it with Shapiro. "You said you know who Winslow's brother is." It was not a question.

"Of course, Attorney General Geoffery Thrust." After a moment she added, "A very influential member of federal cabinet and number two in the power structure, even before the deputy prime minister."

Adam was impressed but knew he shouldn't be. He'd learned firsthand Beth was sharp and a good investigator. "Yes, that's true."

"So what's your involvement?" her manner was stiff.

"Apparently AG Thrust called my boss, and Shapiro contacted me. I'm to put pressure on you to make the charges go away." He gave her a look he hoped relayed the ridiculousness of that ask. "He

183

wants Winslow let off with a warning. At the most, the AG would agree to a public apology, possibly some community service work if pressed."

"Uh huh." Beth dried the pot, added the lid, and then put it in its drawer. "It's bad enough the AG would interfere with any legal case, let alone one at the provincial level. A law enforcement officer was assaulted."

"Yes, I heard. Who was the officer?"

Beth ignored his question. "You surprise me Norcross, I thought you had more integrity than this. Do you actually think you can strong-arm me into doing something unethical and just plain wrong?"

He turned slightly to his right and gave her a half smile. "No, I would never ask it of you. Actually, my boss wouldn't ask it of me either. We had a conversation regarding the situation. He never tasked me, not formally, with this assignment." His boss was careful about that, Walter Shapiro was always careful. "It was merely suggested. I'm telling you what has transpired and the reason I'm here. I have lines of communication you don't."

"You're not going to pressure me?" She sounded hesitant, afraid to believe him though she sounded like she really wanted to.

"Not at all. Besides, what leverage would I possibly use?"

184

"My father's involvement with a dead antiquarian?"

"I'm betting Nick Leith had nothing to do with Rupert Honeyweld's death and no doubt has an alibi for the time of death."

"We don't have a time of death yet from the coroner. I also haven't asked Dad what he was doing yesterday or early today." Beth shifted her gaze away from him. "I know early this morning he was supposed to be taking delivery of the hopper bins on the south side of the new property." She rolled her shoulders like the statement made her uncomfortable. "Because he can't use the new property, not without the okay from the province, Dad had them temporarily set up over there. I can show you the row of five shiny new bins set up there now."

He could tell he'd disturbed Beth even though it was her choice to bring up her father's relationship with the deceased. "That's not necessary, as I said; I doubt your father was involved in Rupert Honeyweld's death."

"Yes, but why would you say that?" She stared at him, even when accepting the rinsed gravy boat to dry. Her tone was suspicious, no doubt due to her trust in the system being broken.

Adam tipped his head at her. "Striking someone on the back of the head isn't your father's style. It doesn't fit his profile."

"What?" Beth looked confused for a moment. "How would you know–" He saw the exact moment she figured out how he knew anything about her father.

Beth's eyes widened as she stared at him and then narrowed and not in a good way. "Norcross," she said slowly, a warning ignited in her eyes. "Did you do background checks on my family?"

Uh oh. The only escape for him was to be honest. He placed the lid to the roaster carefully on the drying rack before meeting her eyes. "Yes. I could say it's force of habit, but I wanted to know who and what I would be dealing with before I got here." He tried to sound neutral, bland even.

"Why would you need to do a background check on my parents?" There was promised retribution in her tone. "Why would you need to know anything? These are good people."

"I don't know them." This sounded weak even to his own ears.

She glowered at him as her next thought occurred. "Did you do a background check on me when we worked together last year?"

"Yes, of course I did. And Collin, Taggard, the suspects, everyone."

"Again, why? Especially me?" She leaned a fist on her hip, the tea towel hung forgotten in her other hand. "And my coworkers." She added belatedly.

"It's my job to know everything I can, as soon as I can, about a given situation and all the people involved well before I engage so I know what I'm getting into." He knew he would have to explain more fully. Without honesty, there would be no trust. And without trust, she would never let him get close to her. "I don't like surprises."

Adam breathed in deeply and slowly released the air. It was never easy to explain what he could do. Finally he met her eyes and said, "I have a skill, talent really. I…I know things."

"We've established that already."

"No, you don't understand. I mean before they happen. I also know when someone is lying to me. And, I know when an investigation is traveling down the right road." He waited for Beth's snort of derision.

It didn't come.

She looked back at him steadily. "Go on."

He nodded in acknowledgment she wasn't scoffing at him. "The more information I have, the sooner my precognitive ability kicks in. I know things before there is concrete proof to back up the knowledge. That's the best I can explain it."

"I have questions."

"Of course. Ask me anything." Adam was a touch relieved.

187

"What could my parents and brothers possibly have to do with Winslow Thrust and his criminal behaviour?"

"Nothing probably, but still I found—"

She cut him off with an upheld hand. "Rupert Honeyweld's unexplained death didn't happen until you were on your way here. He's been dead less than twenty-four hours, I don't need JD to tell me that."

"You still think Honeyweld's death is merely unexplained? I'd call it suspicious."

"I don't know, do I? Answer my question, the previous question." Her irritation was rising.

"Are you sure you want to know?"

"Norcross, you are beginning to really tick me off. What did you find on my family?" she asked. Her tone told him he should not push her any further.

"I'm trying to, but if you don't like the data, you can't blame me."

Leith's steely glare said she'd more than blame him if he didn't spill the information.

"Your father has an assault charge pending against him from last December. I thought you might know about the charge. You got that call while we were investigating the Flete murder, I could see you were upset at the time. Then you went home as soon as Taggard could spare you."

"I came home for Christmas. What do you know about my dad, or any of this?"

"I know Rupert Honeyweld and your father had a physical altercation. If Honeyweld's death is anything other than accidental, you father will be on the suspect list." He shrugged. "The charges are not going to go anywhere now though."

"The charges were never going any further, the judge tossed the case. Two old guys who had too much to drink and got stupid, it was a mutual assault. Not much more to it than that." Leith breathed in deeply through her nose. "But now this could come back to haunt us. Their fight will make Dad a murder suspect." Her voice crept up in volume as she spoke.

"Well, yes." He was a tad confused why she was upset. "Even so, I know your father is innocent of any involvement in Honeyweld's death."

She ground her teeth, no doubt striving for calm. He'd seen his boss do this a time or two and recognized the action.

"What evidence do you have to back up that statement?" Beth asked.

Adam waved her question away. "Nick Leith may have bopped Rupert Honeyweld on the nose at a Christmas party last year, but he didn't kill the man. Why are you so upset?" He couldn't fathom why Beth was getting distressed.

She flung up her hands. "I know Dad wouldn't kill anyone, but can you prove that? Do you have proof we can show the Inspector my father would never kill a man he once assaulted?"

"No, not as yet. It's a–"

"Do not tell me you are hanging my father's fate on a feeling you have, a stupid hunch."

"My 'hunches' are very reliable." He sounded haughty even to himself.

"Good Lord, help me to understand..." she said covering her eyes with her left hand and shook her head. "Whatever. I don't have time for this right now I have to get Dad a lawyer."

Adam put a wet hand on her green T-shirted shoulder to hold her in place. "Your father will have the finest legal counsel we can find if and when he needs it. That's not important right now. You need to think this through." He gave her a long hard look.

"I don't–"

"Your fear for your father does you credit, but it is merely a distraction. Take a step back and expand your view of things. What is peculiar about this whole situation?" He waited, his hand grew warm, but he kept it in place even though her shirt darkened with the moisture from the dishwater.

Beth paused when he'd placed his hand on her shoulder. She blinked rapidly as she processed what she knew. It didn't take her long. Beth's lips flattened, and her chin came up. "Why would Pelly put me on this case, I'm on administrative leave? She knows about the assault charge against Dad. If I'm involved, I could cause all sorts of problems with the investigation. I could be accused of tainting evidence if Dad is under suspicion. He's in trouble and I've made it worse."

"Exactly, but to what end? Who would benefit?"

She shook her head. "I don't know. Winslow Thrust I suppose if I am discredited and accused of interfering with a murder investigation where one of my family members is a suspect."

He nodded and released her shoulder, satisfied she now knew the full implications of the situation. "Then they would have something on you." He did not like the look of fear in her eyes. "This is what I think has happened. Any data surrounding you and your family, entered into the system will be flagged for Thrust's attention. I suspect the AG found the same record of charges against your father and thought he could leverage it to his benefit, or rather his brother's. All he had to do was find a tool to use as a hammer."

"Honeyweld's death could well be accidental. Thrust couldn't know the guy would drop dead and implicate my dad.

Your theory is pretty thin. This could well be a–"

"Don't say it's a coincidence, there's no such thing." Adam frowned. "Thrust thought as far as my boss, but I wonder if Thrust factored in me."

"Could Thrust have been informed this quickly?" She twisted her lips thinking about it. "There's no way he could know about the reported incident yet."

Adam lifted dark eyebrows. "Why not? Everything is digital. Databases are seeded with key words to flag specific phrases and send notifications to the particular people who want to know."

Beth opened her mouth to deny his statement. She sighed instead and nodded. "Yes, I know how it works." Beth compressed her lips as she thought about it. "Even so to get Inspector Pelly to go along with this, it's disturbing."

"It is," Adam agreed. "Unfortunately, this is not the first time the PMO has used the RCMP for its own ends."

Beth gave a vague nod in agreement. "We've worn a lot of crap for them in the past. You think Thrust put pressure on the commissioner?"

"It is possible, and in turn, the commissioner put pressure on Pelly."

She shook her head. "Why, for what possible reason would the commissioner do that?"

"Career goals, past indiscretions, future considerations, I don't know yet. However, it all comes back to you. Thrust wants to hurt you or motivate you into doing what he wants. I doubt he cares about Pelly's career or yours."

"Have you been told directly, to get me to drop Winslow Thrust's charges?"

"As I said earlier, not officially. I'm afraid I'll hear from my boss again in the near term now with regard to Rupert Honeyweld's death." He sighed and put his hands back into the water to tackle the bottom half of the roaster. "So, tell me what transpired back in BC."

Beth sighed and nodded. "There are older reports on Winslow Thrust. He is a person of interest, although nothing had ever been proven previously. No charges either, only accusations. You can't prosecute someone on gossip."

"Only in the court of public opinion." Adam's mouth twisted after he said this.

She gave him an acknowledging nod and took the cleaned, wet roasting pan and proceeded to dry it. "There was video from a homeowner in his neighbourhood from last year. They claimed they caught him on camera, stealing delivered packages from the front steps. The perp had his face averted and it was impossible to prove it was Thrust. Later there was more, again the same neighbourhood and this time a partial look at the face."

"It was Winslow?"

"We think so, but he wasn't stealing anything, he was licking the camera from the security system. One of those doorbell jobs."

"How repulsive."

"I know, the woman who handed over the video was so creeped out she moved."

"No wonder. Could you charge him?"

"The Crown wouldn't take the case, they wanted undeniable proof who the perpetrator was, which we didn't have and even with it, there was no assault merely creepiness."

"So what happened next?" He pulled the plug on the sink and began rinsing the suds out.

"Two days after the doorbell thing, I was dispatched to have a chat with MLA Thrust. I informed him of the disturbance at his neighbour's home and we were looking into the report. If he had any intelligence at all, he'd realize we have the incident documented with a possible link to him, and that should have been enough to ensure he behaved himself from then on out. You know the drill."

"I do."

"While there was no reoccurrence of theft or lewd behaviour, he did up his game. Thrust attended a music festival in

Vancouver. It all started out very sedate, until a riot broke out because the headliner for the festival canceled his performance. All the audience got was the warmup act. Security turned them out onto the street and it got nasty after that.

"Thrust obtained a megaphone from somewhere and climbed up onto a car hood. He began inciting the crowd. It didn't take long to build up to a riot. Again, it was all captured on video." Leith kept her tone level, dispassionate. "The rioters trashed several cars, lit one on fire, all this outside the venue before they were dispersed. The legitimate concert audience members were long gone, and our boy slipped away before the arrests but was detained the next day."

"Charges were brought?"

Beth nodded. "The judge let all those responsible off with a warning. The victims were left to file civil suits if they wanted remuneration for their damaged property." She huffed a laugh. "ICBC, government auto insurance is suing the identified protesters, but it's a slow process."

"The next time was a different protest. This time with parents from several school districts uniting to demand more control over school curriculum. Again, it began fairly innocuously on the face of it, with a mixed crowd of parents, teachers and on lookers. The gathering was in front of the provincial legislature on a sunny Saturday morning which again unravelled into chaos. It took a couple of hours to sort through who was a troublemaker and who was merely there to protest."

"Why was Thrust at that particular event? Was he there as an MLA chosen to represent the government and to speak to the crowd?"

"No idea. His doesn't have a cabinet portfolio." Beth's expression was grave. "This last time, was almost a month later, there was an incident during another demonstration. You're right those things always attack bad actors with radical agendas, paid protestors, and criminals. They cover their faces with balaclavas or handkerchiefs and so did Thrust." She tipped the drying rack to drain into the sink. "Rocks were thrown through store windows. This happened on a side street away from the fires, one was a jewelry store and the other was a shoe shop. Our guy Thrust was videoed entering the businesses with other rioters following him. Armloads of runners among other things were taken. Our guy wasn't happy with just a few pair. He left and got a shopping cart from somewhere. I caught him leaving the premises pushing the cart loaded to the brim with stolen Nikes. There was also an engagement ring and other jewelry found on his person from the other store next door." She glanced up at Adam. "When I approached him, he began by throwing shoes at me and yelled obscenities. We got his face on video. I'm inclined to think he has some kind of mental difficulty, but now I'm not sure."

"It could be both. CCTV footage from the city and businesses, copies were taken?"

"Absolutely, and logged into evidence. Strangely enough, somewhere along the line, all videos pertaining to Winslow Thrust were lost or destroyed. Right along with the old doorbell video. It's even disappeared off YouTube." Her tone was bitter. "It smacks of an inside job, someone paid off to mess with the chain of evidence is my assumption, but no department is immune to incompetence. I couldn't prove it anyway."

"So it's your word against his." Not a question, still Beth nodded.

"If it were only the shoes and jewellery, I'm sure his legal council could get a judge to be lenient again. Heat of the moment and all that, but these new charges are more severe."

"Assaulting a police officer." Adam methodically folded the red dishcloth and hung it from the central tap spout.

"Yes, Thrust pulled a knife. When I was jumped from behind, he stabbed me."

Adam rounded on her. "Were you hurt?"

Beth blinked at the look in Adam's eyes but shook her head. "Nothing serious, my uniform suffered more. It's not like Winslow Thrust knew what to do with a knife." She shrugged offhandedly. "I had already pulled my Taser when Thrust pulled the knife. I fired on the person with their arms around my neck, and she went down. I was afraid she'd try for my service pistol. My VPD backup fired his Taser on Thrust and he went down too. Turns out the female who jumped me, she was Thrust's girlfriend."

"Then you arrested them?"

"Oh yes." She gave him a tight smile. Beth didn't say it, but it was there in her expression. She wasn't going to let Winslow Thrust get away with any of it.

"What is the exact charge against you?"

"I've been accused of harassing a civilian, stalking him actually. I suppose they believed I'd drop everything and behave like a frightened little bunny, dropping the charges in the face of overwhelming odds and threats against my career. The bosses just want it all to go away." She snorted.

"They don't know you very well, do they?"

She lifted her eyes to meet Adam's gaze. A slow smile slid across her face. "No, they don't."

His eye lingered on the long pink scar on her left arm.

Chapter Fifteen

"I still can't believe Inspector Taggard would lend himself to any of this. He's too by- the-book. How did you get my whereabouts?"

"I bought Collin a coffee. He's worried about you and when I offered my assistance, he gave me you parent's address." He looked directly back at her. "I can help."

"I believe you." She took in a deep breath. "Beside, you have already. You witnessed Pelly asking me to help in the investigation." Beth shook her head. "Why didn't this occur to me before to question my involvement?"

Adam gave her a soft smile. "You have extraordinary high ethics and you hold yourself to a high standard. Your first thought when it comes to a colleague's request is not a cynical one. You respond with 'how can I help?'"

Beth twisted her lips into a half smile. "Oh, I was cynical all right, but it didn't take much for her to convince me. I also want to be back on the job. The trouble is there's been a shift in the wind."

"What do you mean?"

"The parent school board protest. I was confused as to why we were ordered to be so heavy handed at the August protest. Even though he didn't say it, Taggard didn't like it ether. It didn't fit. A lot of us had questions. All those orders did was make a bad situation worse. Of course Thrust came out looking like a hero of the people."

"That's how his government spun it?"

"Yeah, after the last protest when we arrested Thrust's girlfriend, I was hoping she would give him up, but so far Collin tells me she is staying mute." Her eyes were hard. "Thrust's lawyer showed up to spring him on bail. Screaming about abuse of power and overreach, but we had them. Or so I thought. Anyway the same firm is representing his girlfriend, Carrie Belter."

Adam experienced a familiar sensation, this was important. "Which firm?"

She carefully hung up her towel on the oven handle to dry. "Biggerman, Case, and Abernathy. Paul Biggerman is her lawyer."

And there it was, like a puzzle piece falling into place. Adam turned his expression bland and folded his arms. He leaned a hip against the counter and waited for the rest.

She looked up at him. "One day the Crown prosecutor was going ahead with all charges against Thrust, and the next, all is forgiven. That's when I found out our video evidence was gone. She gave a sniff of derision.

"But I wouldn't dismiss the assault charge. A couple of days later two people from Thrust's political party met me in the parking lot at my condo building after my shift. Their job was to persuade me to drop the charges. Did I want to be responsible for Thrust's career being over? How could I live with myself?"

Norcross watched her carefully. "Did those two do anything?"

Beth shook her head. "They were only trying to rattle my cage. They made veiled threats about my career. It was like something from a formula cop movie from the 80's. After the threats, they made suggestions they could help me move up the ladder."

"That sounds familiar. Did you report this to Taggard or tell anyone else?"

"No, it was theatrics. I figured Thrust was grabbing at straws and if I didn't get him this time, there would be a next time."

"Did any of this make it to the media?"

"Not much. I think strings were pulled to suppress the story. How could anyone want to support a candidate guilty of assault and theft? Who would want to allow him to run?"

"You'd be surprised," Norcross said with a wry twist of his lips. "People have less than a three-minute attention span when it comes to politics. They will ignore a lot to get their chosen candidate on the ticket and Thrust has a following. Is that why you were suspended?"

Leith shook her head. "Not…officially."

"Oh?"

"I disobeyed a direct order, several of us did. The others received reprimands, I was selected to be the example I guess."

Again Adam waited Beth out. He knew talking about the events was miserable for her.

"The parent school board protests went on daily for weeks. I wasn't going to arrest peaceful protestors who were only exercising their Charter Rights. They weren't doing anything illegal." Her eyes hardened. "The government wanted the people to disburse, but the crowds were persistent. They demanded a meeting with the premier and he was too chicken to come out and talk to them. Nor would he send out a Minister to represent him. I was hoping for Winslow Thrust, but nope. The premier called our superiors. The government wanted us to charge the protestors with mischief."

"What happened?"

"Some of us heard rumours the province threatened to cancel the RCMP contract for BC. After that all orders were verbal. There was no record of what we

202

were told to do. Some members called in sick, took leave, some retired. The rest of us felt we had to be there to do what we could. We were understaffed and Victoria PD was also in the same boat."

"Cue the bad actors."

"Exactly. All dressed in black, faces covered, some carried bats." She shrugged. "You know how it goes. They used the real protestors as shields and it took us ages to sort through the mess. People were injured, bad guys and innocent alike. Charges were brought against members of both police forces. I won't let it go. I'm hoping for an inquiry. I want to know who the bad guys were."

"You shook the tree a bit too hard?"

"I guess. Anyway, my involvement was leaked to the press along with my connection with Thrust's earlier arrests. All charges were dropped. He's the hero. I'm the bent cop, with abuse charges. They put me on leave until this is all sorted out." She turned bleak eyes to Adam. "My parents know the basic story, but I see the shadow of doubt in their eyes and it eats at me."

"You're not giving in?"

"Never. I did my job. Winslow Thrust must be held accountable." Her lips twisted. "I will hang on until I'm vindicated. If what you are saying is true, then someone further up the chain is taking orders from some influencer outside our organization and the result is trickling down to people on the Force like me. You think Geoffery Thrust is behind the high-level manipulation?"

"Possibly, but I don't know yet. He only asked Shapiro to get the charges removed. Whoever is responsible, is trying to manipulate provincial policy from a federal level, and that cannot be allowed to happen. Provincial laws are not there to be manipulated by anyone."

"He's the one pulling the strings with his brother's case. I'm betting his hand is in all of this. Still, the school board protest, I don't know, it seems contradictory. Why push around innocent parents?" She frowned. "To what end? What's his goal?"

Adam shook his head. "I don't know yet."

"I think we have to pull at the threads we have, but first we have to find out what happened to Rupert Honeyweld."

* * *

The next morning, as early as he arranged it, Norcross went down for breakfast. Staying in a traditional B & B had benefits the alternative did not, like an actual hot breakfast.

He paused in the foyer to look into the cherry wood cabinets. There was a selection of items from the previous owners and the original family who owned the house. Family photographs, an invoice for garage building materials from Beaver Lumber, a hardware store, from the year 1906. There was a crystal doorknob, square forged nails, and a ring of antique keys too.

"Good morning."

Norcross turned to smile at a forty-something woman dressed in navy blue trousers and white blouse with a white apron worn over top. "Good morning."

"I'm Tilly, Teddy's wife."

"Nice to meet you."

"I see you're looking at the house history. Are you interested in history?"

"Always. Especially with the archaeological dig on the Leith's property."

Tilly snorted. "Not to mention an uncanny death nearby. Come with me in here then." Tilly crooked a finger at him and led the way into what was a common room for guests to gather.

The room reminded Norcross of a parlour or receiving room for visitors. The furniture was ornate, like from the turn of the 1900s.

"Have a look at this." Tilly gestured to a curio table in the middle of the room. This tiger oak table's heavy curved legs sat on a brown and green Persian carpet surrounded by two brown leather wingback chairs and a settee upholstered in deep green velvet.

Norcross walked over and looked down. Judging by the heavy hard-used glass lid and the fitted brass hinges to allow the glass to be lifted, the table was also an antique.

Through the spotless glass he could examine the treasures inside resting on red velvet. There were three flint arrowheads. These caught his eye and his interest. The grey stone was almost perfect, like the owner had lost the objects before he could use them to bring down game.

Oddly, a gilded snuff box lay next to it. The box's indigo lacquer was brilliant against the red velvet all the objects rested upon.

"These things all belonged to Ebenezer Wick. He built this house for his wife in 1890. His family owned a large track of land outside of town, big farm, but his wife didn't like being out of town. Possibly, she didn't like her in-laws who still lived there. Anyway, from the time he was a young boy, Ebenezer collected the things he found on the land. He continued to farm, but also started up a mercantile store. He bought this table to display his treasures." She looked fondly down at the table. "He and his wife never had any children, so he willed most of his collection to the University of Saskatchewan."

Norcross leaned down to inspect the contents. "But he kept some items?"

"Oh, he did give some to the local museum, but these artefacts we found in an old trunk in the basement when we bought the house."

"I saw a grooved stone maul yesterday. Did he ever find one of those?"

"Oh yeah, people would find those all the time. My dad used to get them on our farm. It's not so common anymore."

"And why is that?" He straightened to look at Tilly.

"Well, finding arrowheads, mallets, and axe heads were easy to spot back in the day when farmers walked the fields and rock picked by hand. Today it's all automated." She gave a shrug. "The tractor pulls a rock picker along behind it and then at intervals, the machine has to be dumped. If you don't check out the rock piles, it's easy to miss interesting things."

"I suppose it is." He nodded and then tipped his head. "I'm guessing Rupert was one of those who did check the rock piles."

"Oh, yeah, but only because he heard Nick talk about it at one of our meetings. Judy told me Rupert was forever getting chased off someone's property. He made life difficult for her. She was always apologizing for him." Tilly shook her head. "I'm betting you'd like some coffee."

"I would, yes. Thanks for showing me these items."

Teddy's wife led him into the breakfast room and after she took his order for the type of eggs he wanted, came back with the coffee pot to chat.

Norcross would never miss a chance to interview a local when he had the opportunity. This was how he usually got inside information. In this instance, he could gauge how Honeyweld's neighbours regarded him.

"Had you heard about Rupert Honeyweld from Teddy?" Norcross asked as he lifted his cup for a sip of the steaming brew she served him. The coffee was excellent.

"Oh my, yes." Her expression went somber. "Not much stays secret in a little town like this." Tilly pursed her lips as she rested one hand on an ample hip. The rising sun shone through the window behind her, making her auburn hair glow almost as much as curiosity did in her dark eyes. "I hear you and Beth Leith are on the case. Is that true?"

Since he was the only guest at the moment, Norcross had her undivided attention. He gave her a smile, there was no polite way to deter her question. "We are doing what we can."

A bell in the kitchen rang and Tilly turned her head, making her curls swing across her shoulders. "I'll be right back."

She returned with a tray this time and served him a glass bowl of fresh fruit medley and a smaller bowl of yogurt on the side. "Tuck into that while you wait for your cooked course." Tilly smiled at him making the crow's feet lines around her eyes crinkle.

"Thank you, this looks delicious." Norcross drew the white cloth napkin across his lap and picked up his spoon. "And thank you for putting the yogurt on the side."

"We've started doing that since people began asking for non-lactate dairy. Lots of allergies out there."

"Very true." Before taking in a spoonful, he asked, "Did you know Mr. Honeyweld well?"

"A bit. I knew Judy, his wife better. We were in the Ladies Auxiliary together." She lifted her eyebrows at him like he should know what that meant. "She passed away, a few weeks ago from cancer." She gave him a small nod, like he'd understand.

"I'm sorry, it's a terrible disease."

"It is, and poor Judy soldiered on through it all. I drove her to her chemotherapy treatments several times." Her lips compressed into a straight line. "She never complained. That husband of hers, what a piece of work." It was clear Tilly didn't think much of Rupert Honeyweld. "I know I shouldn't speak ill of the dead, but honestly, he's not much of a loss. Judy looked after that man completely, she did everything. Even as sick as she was from the chemo, she'd cook him meals and made-up food so he wouldn't have to do for himself when she went into hospital. He couldn't be trusted to take her to her appointments. She couldn't contact him half the time." Tilly shook her head sadly.

"Oh?" Norcross inquired munching on a grape.

"Yes, and there was Judy, she would defend that man until the cows came home. Who knows why? She found out Rupert had a record when they tried to go to Arizona to visit his sister and maybe patch things up, Judy said."

Norcross paused, spoon almost to his mouth. He blinked, this was news. "Criminal record?"

"Yep, anyway, U.S. customs wouldn't let Rupert cross the border, not with what he had in his history." She shook her head. "I think Rupert lied to Judy their whole married life. She was some shocked I can tell you. I don't think she actually knew who she was married to."

"This is interesting." Since only this morning he'd requested a full background on the dead antiquarian from his office. Norcross determined Tilly might be of significant help. He'd sent a request to Maisy in his office for the details. Her report would take time, but he usually used her information to confirm his hunches anyway.

"Yeah." Tilly folded her arms across her middle, her expression pleased she could share the scuttlebutt. "Old Rupert has a rap sheet from his earlier years. Bit of a car thief and a scrapper I hear. Of course, being a fighter when you're a young man isn't surprising, but it is when you come from an upper crust background like his. Judy used to talk about how her in-laws had it all. Apparently, when Rupert was a teenager, he got into all sorts of trouble, but nothing criminal, or so she thought."

"Did Judy talk about the details of Rupert's record?"

"No, but she did say in his twenties his parents cut him off. Judy would say Rupert thought he was going to come into big money when his parents died, but it never happened. She said he resented his parents and the sister who got everything. As far as I know Judy never even met any of his family."

The bell in the kitchen rang again.

"I'll just get your next course." She picked up the dishes and left him with his coffee.

Seconds later, Tilly briskly returned with a large plate of eggs, bacon, fried tomatoes, and dark brown beans in maple syrup. She placed the laden plate in front of him with a side of whole wheat toast. It was

211

a far cry from his usual morning porridge and smelt amazing.

Norcross gestured to his plate. "That's interesting, the baked brown beans for breakfast."

"Well yes, you have to have fibre to combat the bacon. Balance is so important."

"Do you know anything about Rupert's sister?" Norcross picked up his fork and knife. "

Tilly shook her head. "His parents are dead. I'm not exactly sure where his sister lives, Saskatoon I think. The 'who-who' area along the river somewhere. Rupert's family had a big house in Regina too, and another in Yuma, Arizona. That's why Judy and Rupert tried to go down there last winter. With their parents gone, I think he was trying to reconcile with the last of his family, but it was a short trip."

Adam's phone pinged and she left him.

* * *

Much like the giant elm in the yard at his lodgings, the farm laneway trees had lost their glorious gold and yellow leaves to the chilly breeze. Overnight the canopies were gone and the leaves swirled behind the truck tailgate as it rumbled down the lane.

When Norcross arrived at the Leith farmyard proper, he was again met by

Wayne and Shuster. He got out and after a quick scratch and rub, walked toward the house with his new friends. Beth met him halfway.

"The coroner called?" Norcross was not completely on board with Beth's plan to continue to investigate Rupert Honeyweld's death. There were things in motion he couldn't yet define. This was the first time in a long time he felt a foreboding concern for someone else.

"No, I called JD and he shared the preliminary information."

"What about Constable Buchanan and Inspector Pelly?"

Leith shook her head. "Pelly sent Buchanan off to find the driver from the hit and run from last night." At his reaction she lifted one hand. "Two injured pedestrians, fortunately no fatality. The driver had a vanity plate so not terribly difficult to figure out whom to arrest. It's just a matter of finding the relative who has taken him in. Pelly asked me to continue on the investigation." She met his eyes fully for the first time that morning. "I need to see this through. You can decline to participate if you'd like. I will understand."

He studied her for a moment and realized Beth would not let this go. If there was something else bad coming down the pike, she'd meet it head on. "Not likely."

Norcross shook his head. "You need backup too."

This response won him one of Beth's rare smiles. Then she waved away her reaction. "Thank you. Back to our victim, there was a serious blow to the head, just as we figured. However, the pathologist isn't confirming that's want killed him." She tipped her head toward her white vehicle. "Let's use mine." She dug into the pocket of her down filled jacket for her keys.

"Okay." He knew she needed to drive, sitting in the passenger and navigating wouldn't work for her. Not when she needed to problem solve.

"I got JD to send me the preliminary report from Dr. Knighly. In it he says while there was a blow to the head, which probably didn't help, Knighly doesn't think it was enough to kill Rupert Honeyweld."

"What about the blue colour of the deceased's skin?"

"Yeah, the pathologist thinks it's something, he's going to run a full tox screen, but it will take a while."

"It will be well worth it if Knighly can narrow the field of possible contaminants."

"There's the chance the two things in combination caused our victim's death." Beth opened the driver's door. "I hope the results will be definitive enough to help us solve this murder."

"So no longer an unexplained death?"

"Pelly is still calling it suspicious, I call it murder."

Chapter Sixteen

Norcross buckled his seatbelt as Leith started the vehicle. "Where are we going first?"

"To the scene of Honeyweld's death. I want to have a look at it in daylight. Forensic Identification Services will be here shortly too. We need to look for field scatter and probably things we missed last night when we trampled all over the area."

"Is Ident there now? They won't be happy with us."

Leith grimaced in agreement. "No, they won't, but it can't be helped. They should be there shortly after we are."

Leaving the farm behind, Leith drove the dirt road across the property to the location they'd investigated the previous evening. While they drove, Norcross brought Leith up to speed with regard to the conversation he'd had with Tilly Key.

"Criminal record, huh? That's interesting."

"It is. I contacted my office to get the full data. I wasn't sure you had access to local resources." He left unsaid the risk she was taking delving into the investigation instead of staying at arm's length. Still, if he were in her situation, he doubted he could sit on his hands either. He wasn't good at that, hence jumping in to help Beth now.

"Pelly told me to utilize the local office resources and tools, but I don't want to test it. I'd rather use their information to confirm what we think we know." She slowed so the SUV springs could absorb the rough terrain. "I'll have to go in for briefings, and you should come too."

"Are any scheduled?"

"First one is at six o'clock. We'll head to the Canora Detachment for that one. Pelly will meet us there. I would have thought Sturgis was a better idea, it being the halfway point between our crime scene and the full team at her office in Canora, but apparently not."

They arrived at the place they parked the previous evening. The scene looked different in the light only some of the trees had dropped their leaves.

Leith checked her phone as she closed her door. "Ident is two minutes out. We'll wait for them to set up." She crossed the dirt road to stand beside Norcross.

The wind blew tendrils of her dark hair around her head like a halo. She kept her eyes on the ditch where their victim had been found.

"You're right, this hole in the ground is weird now that I really look at it." She leaned forward to see down into the depression, resting her hands on her knees. "Funny, I never thought about it before now."

"Certainly not natural, the shape is too rounded."

"There are two more just like this one half a kilometre to the northwest."

Norcross looked at her with interest as she straightened. "Yes, you mentioned that last night. The same shape, I'm guessing."

"Yep. They all look roughly the same, a hole with trees growing out of it, about twenty to thirty feet wide."

"Do the archaeologists know about these depressions?"

"I don't know, it's possible Dad mentioned the pits to the archaeologist. I'll have to ask him. Maybe they used this route to get to the main grid road. I'm sure Dr. Orlinsky must have seen at least this hole. It's also possible Honeyweld told the team. He was the one who wanted them here in the first place."

"From their reactions, I don't think they knew Honeyweld was on the property let alone digging here. I doubt our victim shared his finds with them. I have a feeling he was going to pick his moment," Norcross said.

"Robert and his team were certainly interested in the photos I took. No one said if they were directly working with Honeyweld."

"Probably because no one was working with him. I got the vibe the team was surprised when we mentioned it." Norcross shared a sage look with Leith. "Then again, people lie."

"That they do." It was then the panel van rolled up and parked behind the SUV. Two people got out, one male, one female and introductions were done. The stick-thin female, Ginny Waterelk had her straight long dark hair tied back. She identified herself as being in charge. She and her co-worker, Vince Grey, bullet shaped and bald, suited up.

"You've already seen the evidence collected from last night?" Leith leaned a hip against her vehicle when the techs reappeared.

"Yes, first thing this morning. We stopped at the Detachment in Canora on our way out from Regina. Those artefacts look to be museum quality. We'll run tests on them for blood, DNA, and fibres." Ginny nodded to Vince and the two forensic techs climbed down the bank of the ditch.

In short order, the scene was processed. At first, nothing new was discovered on the excavated ground. Then Vince poked his head out of a dense corpse of poplars. "Ginny, come look at this." He was on the far side of the hole, close to the centre, and obscured from their sight.

Norcross and Leith watched with interest from the road as Ginny walked over to where Vince was, carrying her camera. She stopped and stared at something shielded by the copse of trees. Slowly she turned and looked up the hill at them. "You might want to see this."

Cautiously following the path the forensic team had marked out, Leith and Norcross entered the depression.

They crossed the bottom and arrived to see seven rocks stabbed into the black soil, to form a circle. The stones were each over three feet tall.

"Standing stones?" Leith sounded incredulous.

"This is…unbelievable." Ginny continued to take photographs. Whether for her own interest or the investigation wasn't exactly clear, but Norcross didn't think it mattered much.

Yellow leaf litter was scattered thickly in and around the slate grey stones. This, along with the booties on their shoes muffled their footsteps.

"Wow." Norcross blinked at the sight. "I wonder if the stones are larger than we think. They probably go quite deep into the soil." He gestured to the one on his right.

Vince dropped to his knees. "The earth is loose around all of them. This one looks to go down at least two feet deeper."

"This, combined with the trench over there," Leith jerked her thumb over her shoulder. "It looks like Honeyweld has been working out here for at least a couple of months."

"What?" Vince was taking notes. He paused to look up at Leith. "You're saying this is all new?"

Leith nodded. "Like I told Norcross yesterday, these coulees have been here forever, since I was a kid and my parents, too. I've never seen this collection of stones before and I've been all over this property. This circle is a fake and so too, I'm willing to bet, is the trench over there."

"You think Honeyweld built this?" Norcross waved his hand at the circle.

"Don't you?"

"Possibly. It's harder to say with the flint arrowheads."

"Well, we just happen to have some experts close at hand to ask. Come on."

Ginny paused in her picture taking. "We'll need a scientific expert, not just someone who knows local history. Who are you going to talk to?"

"Archaeologists from the University of Saskatchewan, they're just up the road digging up another stretch of property." Leith tossed the words over her shoulder as

221

she climbed the ditch wall. "I'll see if we can get one of them to come back with us and give us their opinion."

* * *

Leith halted the SUV on the ridge outside the archaeologist camp.

"What happened here?" Norcross climbed out of the passenger side.

She joined him. "This looks like a fight broke out or something."

"Mm, I'd go with the or something." Norcross moved forward.

The ultra-organized row of trailers now had an abandoned look with their doors hanging open. Claw marks marred the sides of two trailers along with smears of mud. The windows were open with curtains flapping in the breeze on a third. Items from a central table were lying on the ground and the table was on its side.

A loaf of bread lay torn open, and the slices scattered. The metal coffee pot lid had come off, and the contents spilled onto the turf. The smell of burnt bacon was in the air.

Folding chairs were strewn about. The gas barbeque was lying on its side. The hose was still attached to the propane tank, and Norcross could smell mercaptan, the chemical which gives the odourless gas the 'rotten egg' stench as a warning. He strode through the camp wreckage to the

222

barbeque and turned the tank gate valve off and righted the barbeque.

"Hello, Robert?" Leith strode north around the trailers looking for the missing team lead archaeologist. "Is there anyone here?"

Norcross took the opposite direction. It wasn't long before he found their missing scientist. "Beth." He projected his voice behind him and then knelt down to assess the crumpled male human he'd found by the rear tire of the fourth trailer.

"Doctor Orlinsky?" Norcross placed a hand on the man's shoulder. There was no bleeding, nor could he see any obvious injuries. The man was dishevelled, his clothing smeared with mud and grass stains. His hair had leaf particles dusting it and the skin on one side of his face looked scraped and red and his glasses askew.

Leith jogged up. "Is he okay?"

Abruptly Robert sat up. "I think I passed out." He turned wide eyes to them.

"Did you hit your head? Do you need an ambulance?"

"I might have." He felt his bald pate and looked at his hands. "No blood."

"Look at me, please." Norcross looked into the older man's eyes, gauging his pupils. "You don't appear to have a concussion. Any headache? Do you feel nauseous?"

"No, actually I feel fine." He adjusted the set of his glasses.

"But you were knocked out." Norcross took the man's pulse and found it was with in normal parameters.

"Well, maybe not." Robert Orlinsky looked sheepish. "I think I just fainted."

"What happened?" Leith examined his head for injuries herself but shook her head at Norcross when she found nothing.

"There was a bear," Robert swallowed as he looked at her. "A huge black bear. I must have surprised the creature when I came back to camp from my trench."

"Is there anyone else we need to look for?" Norcross asked.

Robert gave Norcross a glassy-eyed look. "No, the others have gone. I was here alone. I needed to check some things. These finds aren't adding up." He blinked rapidly, coming back to himself. "I was on a bear!"

"What?" Leith frowned.

"It... the bear, he was rooting in Hilda's trailer. I yelled at it. The bear backed out of the trailer and turned on me. He ran at me. Of course, I don't really know if it was a male. It could have been a female, I don't know."

"You didn't use your pepper spray." Norcross could see the metal cylinder still strapped on Robert's belt in its black webbing holster.

"No, I forgot in the heat of the moment that I had any on me. I yelled and swung my walking stick at it, but he just kept coming. I turned, I was going to run away, but the bear knocked me down and it fell too. I could feel his breath on my neck. No way was I going to be a bear treat, so I jumped on top of it and smacked it with my walking stick."

"That's when the bear got to its feet," Leith guessed.

"Yes, how did you know?" Robert turned a quizzical look on her and rubbed his hands together. "I guess I just hung on, by reflex." He worked his fingers and them choked out, "I was on the back of a black bear!"

"Yes, Robert, yes. We know."

"I can't believe I was on a bear!" Robert's voice was rising in volume and range.

"Okay, Robert, you need to calm down now," Leith said in a soothing voice as she patted his shoulder.

"But I was on the back of a black bear!"

"Yes, as I said—"

"I think I need to change my underwear." Robert bit his lip.

"Okay, then." Leith immediately stood and stepped back. So too did Norcross.

* * *

Fifteen minutes later the three were gathered around one of the camp tables.

225

"We have some questions for you, Robert, but first, what's bothering you about the finds?" Leith handed him a cup of tea. While the archaeologist recovered his composure, and made a trip to his untouched trailer, she and Norcross righted the camp as much as possible and then set about making hot, sweet tea for the doctor.

Robert took a healthy slurp and swallowed, closing his eyes in appreciation. "I should find a shot of whisky to put in here." Then shook his head. "No, that's probably not a good idea."

"Probably not." Norcross picked up his own ceramic mug and took a sip of his plain black tea.

"Anyway, you have questions?" Robert spooned two more sugar lumps into his brew and stirred.

"How much did Rupert Honeyweld tell you about this property?" Leith sat across from the archaeologist and blew on the surface of the tea to cool it.

"We had the geological surveys and of course the land location maps from the province. Rupert gave us his version of a map too. He wanted to meet with us and explain his vision. I didn't want that. I spoke to the team and we decided, as a group, not to allow prejudice to enter into our findings. While I know Rupert Honeyweld only wanted to be helpful, he could be a bit…much."

Leith tipped her head. "You knew him well before coming out here for this dig?"

"Only from his emails. His many, many emails." Robert settled back into his camp chair and extended his legs. "Rupert has been an enthusiastic antiquarian for some time. A supporter, if you will, of our work." He sipped his tea. "I think Hilda met him before though."

"How well did Hilda Barker say she knew Rupert Honeyweld?"

"She didn't mention it directly, but she did have an opinion on him and his work. She wasn't much in favour of this dig, but once I showed her the quartzite arrowhead he sent us, well, she was all for coming out." He took a long drink from his tea. "Of course the mallet find put her up on cloud nine. She'd mislaid a similar one a while back." The doctor looked down at his boots for a moment and sighed. "So was there anything else you needed?" He sounded tired, but then Norcross acknowledged it wasn't everyday one rode a black bear.

"Have you ever heard of any standing stones in this province or anywhere on the prairies?" Norcross asked.

Robert lifted his chin to stare at Norcross. "Standing stones? Like a medicine wheel?"

"Please describe a medicine wheel for us." Leith rested her elbows on the table.

227

He nodded to her. "Ah, well, it's a large grouping of stones arranged in a circular pattern, roughly 5000 years old. They can include a larger central rock pile or cairn with radiating lines of stones like spokes. They are usually ten metres or more across. We don't yet know the reason for the medicine wheels. Possibly they are markers or burial monuments. Some suggest astronomical alignment markers, but astrology isn't my field, so I won't comment on that aspect." Robert gave Leith a quick smile. "We are in the central eastern part of the province, so it's not out of the range or out of the question for a medicine wheel to exist in this location. It would be a good find for this area and I am very certain this is the first one to be discovered in this part of the province. That is, if it is indeed a medicine wheel."

"Correct me if I'm wrong Doctor Orlinsky, but those constructions consist of a single layer of roundish stones? As you said, laid out in a wheel and spoke pattern? The one we've found is half a kilometre away from this location. It is also significantly different than how you've described a medicine wheel." Norcross moved the doctor's mug away from the edge of the table so that Robert's elbow wouldn't knock it to the ground.

Intrigued, the archaeologist sat forward in his chair. "Different how?"

"Larger stones for one thing, fewer in number, and resembling more of a European-like standing stone site. Something you'd see in Avebury, in Britain."

"A henge." Robert breathed out the words reverently.

"Yes, do you happen to know anything about henges or standing stones? These ones are in the depression south of here." Norcross picked up his mug.

"I'll need to see them." The doctor's tone was excited. "By depression, do you mean a ditch?"

"Yes, however it's more of a round hole in the ground than a ditch or a coulee." Leith put her cup down on the table. "I've lived here half of my life and I've never seen these stones before."

"May I see the circle?" Orlinsky popped to his feet. "Can we go there now?"

"That's why we came to find you. We need an expert analysis on what's been found. In my opinion, the stones don't fit, they've been planted." Leith lifted one hand. "But, I'm not an expert."

Norcross found the circle interesting, however he too doubted the stone circle was legitimate. He drained his cup and placed it back on the table.

Leith's words had deflated Robert's excitement somewhat. "Mm, well that fits in with my theory as well." Robert up ended his cup and finished his tea. "Come with me." He put down the mug and gestured for them to follow.

* * *

Robert led them some hundred metres out of camp, and over to the riverbank.

Norcross had not said anything to Beth about the fact he got no reading at all from looking at the stone circle. If the henge were found to be real, it would be an important site and something he should get a feeling about. However to him, finding a stone circle here was an impossible long shot. "There is no record of standing stone circles ever being found in Canada. That is, unless you count the stone configuration at the bottom of Lake Huron, from the last ice age." Then again, science was only what they knew for a fact this week. New discoveries were happening all the time. He looked at Dr. Orlinksy for confirmation.

"True, or those stones at the bottom of Lake Michigan, again same time period." The archaeologist added with an accepting gesture. Robert came to an abrupt halt, startling a pair of mallard ducks from their swim. The male and female flew off, scolding the humans.

"I think mallard ducks always sound sarcastic." Doctor Orlinsky then waved his words away and gestured to the riverbank. "Come down here if you would. Walk on the boards, please, so we don't contaminate the site."

Leith went first, followed by Norcross. They placed their feet where the field archaeologist had stepped on the wooden planks. They were mere inches from the edge of the water.

"Now, it's been a very dry few years which is fortunate for us. The level of water typically should be higher and would cover most of this side of the bank when the weather cycle turns back to normal and wet."

Tall grass was hacked short, and the grey sand and black earth exposed. The clear water flowed quickly past them and the exposed riverbank. With the bank blocking the cool breeze, the sun made the air feel much warmer.

"Because of the dry state of this area, the stratification was easy to uncover." The archaeologist gestured. "Selma and I dug the overburden away to look at the layers of earth and create the timeline. Look here." He pointed to direct their view to a side cut in the soil.

"What are those numbers on the white cards? Dates?" Norcross leaned forward to inspect.

"Good eye, yes indeed they are dates." Robert removed a pair of wireframe glasses from a case he pulled from his vest pocket. "What I want you to see is this span of time we have mapped using the stratification. This is the location Rupert found the Prairie

Side-Notched projectile point." Robert pointed at a card. "Those arrowheads date from 1,200 to 550 years before present. Any artefacts found in this layer are part of the final Late Pre-contact Period."

Leith shrugged. "Okay."

"Now, given there could be some overlap as new technology is accepted, you would expect the abundance of flint arrowheads to dwindle as we go forward in time to the Contact Period." He looked back at them to ensure he had their attention.

"I would suppose so," Norcross allowed.

The archaeologist raised his hand at the 1600-1700 mark. "The matchlock musket came to Canada in 1583 with Sir Humphery Gilbert, but it wasn't until around 1608 when Champlain's gunsmith, and inventor, Marin le Bourgeoys, figured out the flintlock mechanism. We know about half-way through this period the flintlock and muskets were traded for fur pelts. This continued into the 1670's, when trading came to Hudson Bay. That said, it wasn't until later the plains people were impacted by European goods to a larger extent. People from this region would travel north to trade or traders would come to their villages. It wasn't until 1753 when the first trading post was established around Prince Albert. So, flint, chert, quartz, and quartzite remained the available hunting point materials for some time."

"Yes." Leith wished the doctor would get to the point, there was a crime to solve. Some of her frustration leaked into her tone. "How does that help us with our victim?"

"This information helps because it makes us ask questions. Why are we finding larger amounts of flint and stone tools to nap them, all the way through these layers?" He lifted his hand up to 1900. "It's just not logical nor is it realistic. Indigenous peoples were well versed in metal tools long before this. And while iron and steel rust away in the soil, we still find knives, rifle barrels, and household implements." His expression was not excited, but rather bleak and sad.

"What is your professional opinion, Dr. Orlinsky?" Leith watched the old man steadily.

Norcross knew what Orlinsky was about to say, but it was important for the scientist to voice his opinion.

"These artefacts we are uncovering." There was palatable anguish in his tone. "I have many, many questions about the validity of these finds."

Chapter Seventeen

"Just to be clear, what do you find fake? Not the flint arrowheads?" Leith asked, no doubt looking for clarity. "How do you fake stone?"

"The arrowheads themselves are not fakes, no. However, I'm beginning to get the sense some of this isn't right. From what you are telling me about the artefacts you've found at the crime scene, we are all in agreement."

"Do you have the artefacts here?" Norcross asked.

"Oh, my, yes or well, we did. You saw some of them last evening." Robert nodded, shifting his weight to his heels and rocking on his feet. "That's why the rest of the team aren't here right now." He removed his glasses and gestured north of the camp. "Mike found a Clovis projectile point this morning in his trench about seventy metres north of here." Orlinsky screwed up his face like he was in pain. "Along with several tusk and bone implements that point to Atlantic manufacture."

"You mean like from the Maritimes? How is that possible?" Norcross frowned.

Robert tipped his head in acknowledgement. "Nova Scotia to be specific." The archaeologist lifted his rounded shoulders. "It shouldn't be possible. It doesn't make sense to any of us."

Robert's tone dropped into what was probably his university class lecturing voice. "This might get a bit technical, but please bear with me."

The doctor smiled when his audience nodded. "The earliest projectile point type found in Saskatchewan was certainly Clovis, dating approximately 12,000 to 11,000 years Before Present." He ran his right index finger along the time noted dirt line. Some of the brown and grey dirt trickled down the wall, some stuck to his fingers. "The distinguishing feature on Clovis points is the presence of a flute or flake scar that extends from the concave base of the point up into the body, making them rather distinct."

"And identifiable to the lay person," Leith said.

"Yes, exactly right. The flute can appear on one or both sides. These types of spear points are found at isolated sites throughout southern Canada and into the United States. However, no intact archaeological

235

village sites dating to the Clovis period have been discovered in Saskatchewan."

"So finding a Clovis period site would be quite the achievement for an archaeologist?" Leith asked.

Robert Orlinsky waggled his head back and forth. "Clovis finds are not as unique as they used to be. In the past few years there actually has been more interest in finding pre-Clovis artefacts."

"Why is that?" Norcross asked.

"Because it seems the previously accepted notion that the Paleoindian culture, Clovis, were the first people, is proving to be not the whole story. Some in my field are not accepting this as fact anymore. They are pushing back the date for when North America was inhabited. Instead of merely 13,000 years ago, for the Clovis, some theorize–" Robert held up a cautionary hand. "And not without evidence, mind you, that another culture inhabited this part of the world as much as up to 100,000 years ago, this time period has been classified as Pre-Clovis."

"Still using the ice-free McKenzie corridor?" Norcross nodded.

"No in fact, but the Pacific Costal Migration Model, underpinned by evidence found at Meadowcroft Rockshelter and Cactus Hill."

"And Monte Verde?" Norcross suggested.

"Exactly, nice to see you have a handle on some of the archaeology, Adam." The doctor smiled, pleased.

Leith gave him the look she used on him when he was being a bit too smart. He winked at her and she rolled her eyes.

"Anyway," the older man continued. "These people were more than hunter gatherers. They also fished with nets and over generations migrated north from South America."

"Okay, I get that." Leith gave Norcross a narrowed eyed look before turning back to the doctor. "Let's bring this conversation back to the subject at hand. Which discovery would bring more status and attention to an archaeologist or anyone for that matter?"

"Certainly finding a pre-Clovis site would be more controversial, and many times rarer." Robert gestured to the trench several metres away. "While it's true the test pit or trench dig is led by one person, when an artefact is observed, the field *team* catalogues all aspects of the provenance data. I'm referring to information such as specific spatial data explaining precisely how, where, and in what context the pieces were found. These data are documented and then the objects in question are cleaned and secured in protective containers by other team members."

Leith and Norcross nodded as they listened closely.

"After that, the artefacts are transported to our laboratory/office facilities where experts analyze the artefacts. It's vitally important our finds are verified and our initial identification, are accurate and all pertinent records are captured. For us that's the University of Saskatchewan, Saskatoon campus. The Clovis spear point is too important to continue work without confirming our identification and securing the artefact properly." He scratched at a red welt on his cheek with dirty fingers, leaving a dark smudge.

"You're saying it's more the team really who receives the credit than merely one person?" Norcross asked.

Doctor Orlinsky gave a small shrug. "Well it's certainly true the archaeologist who actually lifts the artefact out of the ground gets a larger share of the credit, the team, as a whole, are also recognized. Case in point; Mike wanted to be one hundred percent certain our identification of his find was accurate with a second opinion and no doubt a third, just to be sure. In his excitement, he didn't want to wait for Rachel to get back so he took it upon himself to courier the spear point and the other items we found yesterday back to the university." He put his eyeglasses back in their case. "He'll want to show the spear point off too, the Clovis find could well make his career." His tone sounded doubtful to Norcross.

Leith squinted against the glare of the sun reflecting off the water. "You don't sound very excited by Mike's find."

"Oh, I am, but only as far as it being, what I believe to be, a lost artefact." Robert gave them a sad smile. "Ours is a small world, Beth. There are roughly 13,000 Clovis projectile points in all of North America."

"That sounds like a lot," Leith said.

"I suppose it does, many show up for sale on eBay and that is a shame." Robert shrugged. Then he smiled and spread his hands. "Or I could be vastly wrong. Maybe it's a new find. We do have access to all the records so we will know one way or another shortly. The artefact will be analyzed and if it looks like it's one that was previously identified, whether lost or stolen, we will know."

"What does a Clovis artefact go for online?" Norcross asked curiously.

Robert pursed his lips as he thought. "They can go anywhere from eight hundred to a thousand dollars, depending on the quality of the weapon point and of course the authenticity from the organization who issued the certification. Of course, black market sales are usually for more money, but then the artefact must be perfect or so rare an imperfect one would be acceptable to a collector."

"Did you mention your doubts to your team before they left?"

"Oh, yes. Only Mike and Selma drove up to the University. I don't think Mike paid me much attention. He's got stars in his eyes. Hilda understood the implications. She didn't accompany the others. She will be back at camp shortly after she gets a prescription filled for her allergy medication." Robert rubbed dirt off his fingertips on his trouser seam.

Norcross and Leith shared a look.

* * *

Beth did not mention anything about the attention such a find would have gained Rupert Honeyweld. Was fame his motivation for faking the archaeology? It seemed possible their victim had been after acclaim and possibly profit. By Norcross' expression, she knew he understood this too.

One thing was certain; this new information did not exclude the archeologists from their suspect list.

"Before we move on, I have to ask about this exposed stratification." Beth felt a need to know, at least on her dad's behalf.

"Yes, of course." Sunlight caught the lenses of Robert's glasses.

"What do you do with this exposed riverbank when your dig is completed?" She gestured to the cut away earth.

"We cover it back up. The same as with all the trenches and test pits we've dug. We will make it look like we were never here."

She nodded. "My dad is concerned with erosion."

"As well he should be." Robert sounded pleased.

"Can you come and have a look at the stone circle, please, and the trench we found?" Beth turned to lead the way back to the camp.

"Yes, I suppose I had better. Can I bring some gear?"

"Of course."

Twenty minutes later Norcross and the archaeologist stood on the rim of the ditch by the dirt road.

"The Forensics team is finished here for the moment." Beth had just spoken to Vince before she crossed the dirt road to join them. "They're moving on to Rupert Honeyweld's house to see what evidence can be found there. I've asked them to let me know if they find anything resembling the artefacts already recovered here or at your site, Doctor Orlinsky."

"We're going there next?" Norcross asked.

"Yeah, Buchanan is already in town at the Honeyweld residence."

"He found the driver?" Norcross referred to the hit and run perpetrator with the vanity plate.

"Yeah, they found him at a relative's home in Yorkton, hiding under the back porch."

Beth was torn between following the forensics team and staying with Orlinsky and Norcross. Still, she'd help talk the archaeologist into accompanying them back to—for lack of a better term—the crime scene. The preliminary pathology report didn't state it was a murder, not without more proof, but Norcross wasn't the only person who experienced gut-rolling hunches. Especially when backed up by the blue condition they both noted in Honeyweld's skin. The question was, where had the contamination, as the pathologist called it, come from?

"Is the circle this way?" Doctor Orlinsky eagerly followed the path down into the depression. He paused and did a fast scan of the area before he continued behind the copse of trees with Norcross and Leith following.

They caught up to the doctor and found the older man staring at the nine stones. Grey, lichen covered rocks formed a circle. "Incredible." He shook his head. "I wish I

could believe this configuration was real."
Then Robert sighed and moved between
the standing stones. "This arrangement
looks familiar." He leaned down to get a
close-up inspection of one. He sniffed and
straightened, frowning as he looked around
him.

The circle was roughly three meters
across with a third of a meter between each
stone. The fallen leaves littered the ground
in and around the circle. Beth had to admit
the scene felt permanent even though she
could not for a second believe the site was
real.

"I'd have to check with my records, but
this arrangement is extremely similar to the
Bronze Age stone circle known as the Nine
Ladies." Orlinsky stood hands on hips,
turning in a circle himself to see the whole
extent of the site.

Norcross pulled out his phone and
began typing.

"Where is that circle found?" Beth
moved to stand next to the archaeologist,
viewing the configuration from the inside.

Robert pointed the camera he'd brought
with him at the shapes and began photo
documentation. "The Nine Ladies are an
ancient megalithic structure located in a
woodland of Stanton Moor's National Park,
in Britain." He glanced over at her in
between shots. "It's a lovely part of the
country."

"Beth." Norcross offered her his phone to look at an image.

She stepped over to him. "Hm. Except for the grassy area, the size, shape, and the stone colour look very similar."

"May I see?" Robert lifted his head and looked at Norcross.

He turned his phone for the doctor to view.

"Oh yes, that's the Nine Ladies." He went back to photographing the circle.

"Where would someone get stones like this?" Beth watched Robert. "Local quarries?"

"I'm sure there are places that would cut the stones for you. There are ways to age the stone to make it look old too. Burying them in leaf mold is one way," Robert said helpfully.

The archaeologist gestured at the walls surrounding them. "This ditch is definitely man-made, certainly not a natural feature." Robert walked in a circle, his face turned up, taking in the steep sides.

Norcross accepted his device back from Beth. "I think the pit is manmade too, although not by hand. I suspect before trees began growing here, this hole was more than likely a gravel pit."

"Why would there be gravel pits here?" Leith tipped her head to the left as she spoke, looking at him. "It's kind of small."

"The sign by your family farm driveway. It says your family has owned that property since they settled here in 1908, correct?"

"Yeah, that was when the farm was established. My great-grandfather received a plot of land from the government when they immigrated. They actually arrived in 1907."

"Not an easy thing." The archaeologist used his thumbnail to scratch away some of the moss off one stone.

Leith rested her hands where her webbed belt would be if she were on duty. It was a habit that made her feel awkward, so she dropped her hands to her sides. "Leave everything you knew behind in the old country–"

"Scotland." Norcross said.

"What?" Leith looked him.

"Your family hails from Scotland originally, outside of Edinburgh actually."

"My dad's side, yeah. Why do you know that fact?"

"Just something I picked up somewhere. Like your surname, Leith, which means 'dripping water.' Probably something to do with the River Leith I suppose."

The archaeologist straightened and waved a hand at Norcross to hush him. "What was their story?" he asked, and looked at Beth.

Chapter Eighteen

Dr. Orlinsky's intent gaze encouraged Beth to tell the story. "Okay...well, great-grandad Ian was the third son, and if family stories are to be believed, a bit of a black sheep. He married Elspeth, and six years later with two children, took ship to Canada and landed in Nova Scotia. They made their way west by train to Winnipeg and in the spring, my great-grandparents drove a wagon over six hundred kilometres to find their new home. A bit of a hike back then."

"Oh my, yes without a doubt." Robert compressed his lips and looked at Norcross. "What has the farm sign got to do with these ditches?"

For his answer, Norcross asked another question. He addressed Beth. "How long has there been a grid road running by your family's farm?"

She shook her head. "I don't know. It's always been there during my lifetime."

"We could ask your father about the road and these ditches."

"I doubt there was much of a road back in 1908 when my great-grandparents received their land grant."

"Likely there was no road at all, it would have been built after the township was organized or later still with the establishment of the municipality," Orlinsky said this conversationally as he crossed the clearing to the excavated trench.

Norcross kept an eye on the archaeologist. "It makes sense they'd get the gravel for the road construction locally. Possibly the owners of this land earned some money for the first gravel pit, so they allowed two more to be dug." Norcross joined Robert at the trench. "Although they aren't very large, so how much material could they have excavated?"

"Maybe," Leith allowed and followed. "So what does that tell us? There's no way any of these artefacts are legitimate, since the pits were dug mechanically?"

"The time frame was possibly post-World War II." Norcross added as he looked at Beth.

"Actually, the work started in 1956, it took ten years and cost upwards of ten million dollars, but was vital for the economy of the province. We had to move grain to the elevators for rail shipment. My father worked on the project in the southern part of the province." Robert took a hand full of trench photographs then he turned to Norcross.

"If your hypothesis is correct, and I see no reason to dispute it, this means these earthworks are artificial, that is, dug for commercial purposes. Definitely not dug by Paleo-Indian people for a village or for a burial site." Robert let his camera hang from his neck as he came back to join them at the stone circle. "Or ritualistic even."

The archaeologist chuckled and Beth lifted one eyebrow at him. "Sorry, inside joke. Whenever people in my field can't figure some bit of archaeology out some of us say it has a 'ritualistic' purpose."

"I see." Her lips twisted at the implication. "Making it even more unlikely there should be any artefacts in this hole, and yet there are. I think we can confirm what was going on."

"Yes, I daresay we can, and it makes me sad." Robert shook his head. He rubbed his face with a tired hand. "I think you are correct. From the look of the trenches by our camp I'd say the land has been seeded with artefacts. Rupert Honeyweld was working backward to make it look like the finds have been here for centuries. At least to the untutored eye." He paused and rolled his bottom lip over his teeth as if reluctant to voice his next thought.

"What are you thinking, Robert?" Beth kept her tone even.

"I'm thinking these finds would be mind-blowing if they were legitimate. Our team was taken in by them, at least briefly. Rupert's motivation being, we would forget everything in our excitement. That we would ignore the fact the items are in the incorrect timeline ranges according to our investigation." He gave Beth a nod. "And also wrong for our geographical timeline as well. The abundance of artefacts is quite unusual, and the quality of the finds is amazing. That alone, begs one to question the validity of the finds."

"Actually, I'm willing to bet after some more thorough investigation, we'll find that all the artefacts are stolen." Norcross said as he slid his hands into the front pockets of his coat. The air was turning cooler and the wind was now up.

"Wait, you think the finds are all stolen property?" The older man frowned at Norcross. "You don't think he could have purchased them from eBay?"

"When the math is computed, I doubt it."

Beth nodded. "All right, if these things are stolen property, there has to be reports on them."

"No doubt a database somewhere. I'll send off a query to my office." Norcross worked his phone. "I'll have someone get us a list so we can begin verifying items."

"That will help." Leith stepped away and dug out her phone. "We'll need Forensics to come back and collect these things too."

Robert looked about to protest when Leith said this, but then shook his head and didn't comment.

"Doctor Orlinsky, what are the odds that some of these items, being so small and of low value–" Norcross halted when Robert held up one dirt smudged hand.

"Not all of them."

"True, however, it's possible some of the artefacts could have been taken from small museums or collections without being reported. Possibly no one knows they are even missing." He waited for the older man to comment.

The archaeologist gave a head waggle. "For some items, yes, I'd say you are probably correct, but others, like the Clovis artefact, I'd say that theft would certainly be noticed. This is going to break Mike's heart if that is the case." The doctor lifted his chin. "At least the spear point is safe and back in responsible hands. So that at least, is something." He put the lens cap back on his camera. "I'm wondering if Rupert Honeyweld was a collector, buying these types of artefacts online could not have been cheap."

"I suppose it's possible he was an unwitting customer of black-market antiquities," Norcross said.

Beth folded her arms over her front. "Then there is the third option, he was a thief. Why else would someone want him dead? So far, we don't have much else to go on."

The men both nodded at her words.

Robert rubbed his red welt, removing some of the grime. "I wonder which is true."

"Does it matter?" Beth looked over at the trench. "Either way he was murdered."

"No, I guess it doesn't." Orlinsky sighed and walked back over to the trench. "The size of the spoil heap isn't very big. I wonder how deep Rupert planted the finds, and where else he seeded artefacts." He squatted down by the trench like he could figure out the answer to his question himself.

"Hard to know exactly." She stood behind him.

"I'll call the university. We need to get the ground-penetrating radar team out here. I requested them earlier but was denied the funding. Well, Dean Pittman, you'll just have to suck it up." Robert's smile held an edge as he stood and dug out his mobile phone.

Leith walked back to Norcross. "We need to see what Forensics found at the Honeywelds' property. Stealing arrowheads and trying to pass them off as his own discoveries is not ethical, but is it's hardly a reason to murder someone. The thief part though, that feels right."

"It fits with his past, from what his neighbours told me. He has a criminal record from his youth at the very least."

"You're thinking there might be proof of some bigger crime?"

Norcross gave a small shrug. "I don't know, maybe. Or at least a clue as to someone who had an axe to grind beyond disgruntled landowners."

Her eyes narrowed. "You mean besides my dad." Sarcasm was heavy in her tone.

"Yes, other than your father."

"I'm annoyed anyone would try and implicate Dad by killing Honeyweld on our property."

The three retraced their steps back up to the dirt road and Leith's SUV.

Orlinsky was still on his phone arguing with his dean. They left him to it.

"Can you think of anyone with a grudge against your father worth killing Honeyweld over?" Norcross came to stand beside her. They both leaned on the SUV fender.

"The problem is lots of people know about the feud between Rupert Honeyweld and my dad. If someone local is responsible for cracking Honeyweld on the head, that says to me a lack of planning, an impulsive action."

"Versus the blue colour of his skin." Norcross reminded her.

"I had a heart attack victim turn purple on me once. The man was over eighty and driving his car with three passengers."

"This sounds like an old joke," Norcross said carefully.

"I guess it does, but in this case it was true. The only difference, this gentleman collapsed at the wheel. The Cadillac coasted up over the centre meridian and came to rest on the traffic light post. I was right behind him and ran up to give CPR. When I opened his door, his lips, ears, and hands were already purple. I got him out and called for an ambulance. Me and another passerby took turns performing CPR." Her tone was distant, detached. Norcross placed a hand on her back. She leaned into him. "The ambulance came, but it was too late."

"Lack of oxygen turns them purple. That's cardiac arrest, a problem with the electrical malfunction in the heart which prevents it from pumping blood to the brain and other organs. The heart just stops and unless you have access to a defibrillator, there wasn't much more you could have done."

"Yeah, I know. Still, I remember his wife and relatives just sat in the car. They were silent, in shock, I guess."

"No doubt."

She turned her head as a vehicle drove up the dirt road toward them. An RCMP truck rolled to a stop, again behind Leith's SUV, and parked. Constable Buchanan got out.

Beth straightened her posture, Norcross dropped his hand.

"Sergeant Leith." Buchanan strode up to her. She might not currently look the part, but some ranks showed even when the member was out of uniform.

"Constable, you have something for us?"

"Yep, I heard back from Saskatoon Police Service."

"And?" Leith prompted.

"Yeah, I spoke to the cop assigned to handle the death notification for Rupert Honeyweld's next of kin."

"Was the notification done?"

"No, no one was home and when Constable Hepworth went to where the victim's sister worked, he was told she's away for a few weeks."

"What? Like on a conference or something?"

"No, on an archaeological dig. Guess where." Buchanan lifted black eyebrows at her.

Leith sucked air in between her teeth. "What's the name of Honeyweld's sister?"

"Hilda Barker."

Chapter Nineteen

"Mrs. Hilda Barker is Rupert Honeyweld's sister. Isn't it strange she didn't mention this fact yesterday?" Leith breathed in deeply as she rubbed her left eyelid. "She never even gave us any indication she was related to our victim."

"It's possible the two are estranged. There was bad blood between Honeyweld and his family."

She shook her head. "That doesn't erase the family connection. We've got to talk to her again, like right now." Leith strode over to the archaeologist and put a hand on Robert's shoulder.

Immediately, he lowered his phone to look at Leith.

"Where is Hilda Barker?"

"She went into town." Robert's eyes widened at Leith's dead serious expression and tone.

"Lone Spruce?"

"Yes, the pharmacy, she should be back by now. Is Hilda in trouble?"

"Maybe. Come with us, then. We need to speak with her." Leith then turned back to Buchanan. "We've got a second forensics team coming out here to do a wider sweep. I told their lead you'd be coordinating the site. Establish a grid pattern to cover all the areas between here and the camp."

"More evidence to support the alleged murder?" Buchanan nodded.

"In a way, yeah. We are looking for stolen property. Honeyweld may have buried more antiquities." She quickly brought Buchanan up to speed with what they'd found and the related timeline.

"Will do." Buchanan gave her a nod. "When do you expect the second team?"

She glanced at her watch. "Not for a while. You should come with us to the archaeologist camp. We're going to question the victim's sister."

Leith looked at the archaeologist. "Doctor Orlinsky," she said formally. "When can we expect your ground radar people?"

"They should be here by early afternoon. I've sent them the topographical and geographical drawings along with my sketched maps so the team can hit the ground running."

"Good, give Constable Buchanan the contact names of this team so he can inform Ident when they get here. He'll coordinate. I'm willing to bet our guys can suss out likely locations for further buried evidence faster with the teams working together."

"I wouldn't guarantee it, but we can give it a go. We should be able to see ground disturbances at the least." Robert hesitated over his next words.

Leith tipped her head. "You have a question?"

"I do. The province is legally supposed to gets custody of the artefacts. Any idea of the timeline for that after they are no longer evidence?"

"We can sort that out later. Let's go."

* * *

Norcross suspected the determined glint in Leith's eye said the trip back to the camp would be a bit faster. He and the archaeologist piled in the SUV with Beth behind the wheel.

Buchanan followed in his own truck.

When the four of them arrived, they found a small white Ford Ranger truck was parked beside Robert Orlinsky's forest green Jeep.

There was no one about. "Hilda is probably in her trailer." Leith got out of the SUV and the others followed suit.

"I'll go get her, shall I?" Robert's tone had turned a touch timid in the face of Leith's uncompromising mood.

Norcross couldn't blame him. He knew by the dark red spots on her cheeks Beth despised being lied to. But then, who didn't?

"I'm sure Hilda has a good explanation as to why she did not mention that Rupert was her brother." Robert sidled away on an angle toward the closest trailer.

As Buchanan's vehicle door slammed shut, the trailer door opened and Hilda Barker came stomping out. "Robert!" She made her way down the metal steps and forward to her team leader. "What the hell happened in my trailer?"

"Um, we had a bear break-in."

"What?" Hilda blinked at him.

"A bear came into the camp and he got into a couple of the trailers. Yours was one of them. Sorry."

"This is unacceptable." Hilda tossed her hands up in the air. "The mess—"

"Never mind that right now Hilda, the police need to speak with you. And I think I need to speak with Constable Buchanan." Robert beat a hasty retreat.

"Mrs. Barker, if you would join us over here, please?" Norcross led the way to the cluster of chairs and the table which still had three tea mugs sitting on it. He held a chair out for her. "Please have a seat."

Hilda walked stiffly over to them and sat in the same chair Robert vacated approximately an hour earlier. "I have a lot to do. The finds have to be processed and I can't do that until I clean up the wreck my trailer is in." Her hands balled into fists against her thighs.

"This shouldn't take too long." Norcross collected the mugs and moved them to the side of the table. This gave Leith some elbow room as she sat opposite the archaeologist.

The older woman released a dramatic sigh. "Fine. What do you need from me?"

Carefully, Leith set her phone to record and stood the device propped against a tea mug. Then she looked up at Hilda and fired off the first question. "Saskatoon Police Service tried to serve you with the death notification. Why didn't you tell us you were related to the deceased?"

Without hesitation Hilda fired right back. "I didn't think it was important. I haven't spoken to Rupert in years. I can't be in two places at once. Not that this ridiculous dig site should be the priority." She gave them a flat smile. "How far I've fallen." Her tone was dramatic.

Robert drifted over to listen to the conversation when Buchanan's phone rang. He took a seat well away from Hilda.

"Your brother was found dead, a mere two kilometres from your camp and you don't think it's important to tell the authorities?" Leith had her occurrence book open and began taking notes.

"Rupert has been dead to me for some time. Now it's simply official." Hilda shrugged. "It doesn't take much effort to discover Barker is my married name. I'm divorced, have been for a decade. I didn't bother with the name change, my married name put some distance between me and Rupert, at least in the archaeological world."

"You sound a bit cold toward your brother." Norcross put a folding chair down behind Hilda's. She had to glance awkwardly over her right shoulder to see him. "You must have known we'd find out about your link to our victim eventually."

"I didn't care one way or the other. You know nothing about my relationship with my dead brother, you don't know what he put everyone in my family through, put *me* through. Cold?" she scoffed. "Hardly." Hilda folded her arms over her stomach and turned her glare back at the cop.

"Then help us to understand your side of things." Leith relaxed her tone, no doubt to draw the female archaeologist out.

Hilda snorted. "Rupert always was a greedy, self-centred narcissist. He's a thief, has been since he was a pre-teen. He took things, for no other reason than he thought he should have them. If my brother wanted something, in his mind, he should take it. If our parents wouldn't give whatever it was he asked for, he stole it. Simple as that." Hilda lifted one shoulder. "He was supposed to have this exceptionally high IQ, genius level. Bah!"

"This sounds like an established pattern of behaviour." Leith turned the page in her notebook and wrote something.

"Oh yes, it started small, candy from the shop in our neighbourhood, then toys, models, things he thought our parents should buy for him. When the shop owners called to complain about him, he got worse."

"Was his shoplifting ever reported?" Leith watched Hilda closely.

"To the police? A couple of times. It's a misdemeanour and most places would drop the charges after the cops picked him up. Rupert would egg their stores at night or break windows. Of course no one had any cameras back then and they couldn't prove it was Rupert." Hilda leaned forward looking at the sergeant. "But I knew."

"What happened after that?"

"By the time Rupert was fourteen he'd moved on from shoplifting. He stole our mother's car and wrecked it. He got out of the hospital and a week later, stole the next-door neighbour's truck. That time he was charged and things escalated from there."

"How can a fourteen-year-old steal a locked vehicle?"

Hilda snorted again. "Rupert had an aptitude for things like that. He gleaned information from various sources, including a few other juvenile delinquents who stole cars for joy riding. The vehicle thefts became a challenge for the bunch of them. Rupert told me they wanted to see how many they could make off with in a day. It was an underage crime wave in our town, thanks to that bunch." She shifted her gaze away from the cop.

"Our parents tried everything they could think of to get through to Rupert, to make him see what road he was headed down. It didn't matter because to Rupert, he never thought anything he'd done was wrong. Whenever he got caught and was asked why he did what he did, Rupert would look puzzled as to why anyone couldn't figure out his reasoning." Hilda scowled. She wasn't looking at Leith, but instead was focused on some memory in the past. Then abruptly the older woman raised her chin and looked back at the sergeant. "Do you know why he wanted the truck?"

Leith didn't answer. It wasn't that type of question.

"He needed something large to haul part of a T-Rex skeleton. Our father was a palaeontologist and worked with large dinosaur fossils in the southern region of the province. He was part of the team who found Scotty."

"Scotty?" Norcross raised an eyebrow at Leith.

"The world's largest T-Rex." Robert supplied. "It's at the Royal Saskatchewan Museum. This is the same museum where several Clovis age weapon points went missing now that I think of it."

"Do be quiet, Robert." Hilda was enjoying her confession, she wanted the attention. No, Norcross realized, she craved it.

"As I was saying, for Dad it was a passion, almost a religion. Rupert and his cohorts took the encased T-Rex skull from the worksite our father ran. Dad wasn't just a sponsor of the dig. He was in charge. Rupert damaged our father's career and his standing in the archaeological community, but more than that, Dad was professionally and personally embarrassed. How could he look anyone on his team in the eye after his own son stole their chief artefact and tried to sell it? It made him look culpable."

Buchanan joined the four of them. He took out his phone and placed the device beside Leith's with record running as well. It was good to have a copy of the confession.

"That's when the authorities discovered my brother had stolen other historical artefacts from the museum our mother worked for and tried to sell them too. She was devastated. No one would believe our parents were innocent. It was all Rupert. He was the one responsible for the crimes. Who, at fourteen, ran a criminal enterprise of that scale?" Hilda shook her head. "Our parents had money, they didn't need to steal. Rupert wanted to prove he was smarter than everyone else, and he wanted attention. So when our father told the police it was Rupert and allowed them to question him, he got that attention. Eventually he confessed and explained how he'd done everything to show how much smarter he was than our parents and the cops. Then he was convicted and spent six months in juvenile detention only because he wasn't able to actually sell anything. All the artefacts were found in an abandoned house."

"His time incarcerated didn't help, I take it?" Leith tapped her pen against her thigh.

"Not from his punishment, no, but he did change. There was an accident that made us believe Rupert had transformed his ways."

"What accident?"

"The other three hoodlums Rupert ran with, they stole a vehicle and ran a red light turning onto the highway. They were T-boned, killed instantly." Hilda's mouth turned down. "Rupert got much quieter after that. No more screaming phone calls from detention. When he came home, he seemed changed. He went to school, did his homework, and any chores our parents gave him without complaining. For all appearances, he made it look like he was reformed. The bad boy was gone."

"But you didn't believe him."

"Of course not, people don't change; they merely grow clever at hiding the things they don't want you to see." Hilda snorted. "Rupert excelled at hiding things. He did it with my parents for a while, at university, and I believe that's how he convinced a gentle soul like Judy to become entangled with him. In the early days, if she ever saw the real Rupert she'd have run like a scared rabbit. I tried to tell her before the wedding, but she wouldn't listen. Then it was too late, she was under his control. I was so sad when I read her obituary in the paper. I always hoped Judy would escape Rupert before it was too late. At least Mom and Dad wised up before they died."

"How did your parents wise up?" Norcross asked.

Hilda's mouth quirked into a faint smirk. "They changed their wills. The museum got a hefty endowment, what would have been two-thirds of Rupert's share."

Leith flipped back a page in her notebook. "It's possible Judy Honeyweld did know something of your brother's crimes." She glanced over at Norcross.

"Yes, a woman I spoke with knew your sister-in-law fairly well. She stated that Judy fought with your brother about some of it.

Certainly about the things he'd done since moving to Lone Spruce."

"That's not all he did. A year ago, my brother came to visit me in Saskatoon at the University where I work. I was processing artefacts from a dig we'd run that summer. Several antiquities were lying on a specimen table, where I was cleaning and cataloguing the items. Rupert deliberately picked a fight with me over money he thought he was owed from our parents' estate. He'd gotten his share already but used the argument as a pretext to upset me. When my back was turned, he stole several artefacts."

"A stone mallet was among the items." Norcross interjected.

Hilda glanced over her shoulder at him. "Yes, it was." She gave him a slow smile. "But I got it back." Then the smiled faded. "But not before I was reprimanded by my boss." She aimed a dirty look at Dr. Orlinsky. "And the faculty I work for."

The senior archaeologist pursed his lips and ducked his head but said nothing.

"It was humiliating. I was demoted for losing the artefacts. The resulting paperwork was ridiculous."

Norcross lifted his eyebrows. "You didn't tell the museum you suspected your brother stole the items? You didn't report the theft to the police?"

266

"How could I, without becoming a bigger joke? I decided to deal with Rupert myself and return the things he'd stolen. I wasn't going to let him do to me what he did to our parents."

Leith's lips twisted at Hilda's reply. "You said earlier you hadn't seen your brother in years. Now you say you saw him last year."

Hilda folded her arms over her chest. "I forgot." This through clenched teeth.

"How did you get the stone mallet back?" Leith kept her eyes on Hilda.

"I was out for an early morning run when I saw Rupert drive his quad thing down a dirt road by that ditch. I followed him. My plan was to demand the artefacts he'd stolen be given back to me. But things got out of hand." Now her eyes slid sideways, she no longer looked at Leith.

"What do you mean?" the sergeant pressed.

"He put in standing stones, and dozens of other pre-contact artefacts in the ground in that ditch. The idiot." She shook her head in disgust. "I always suspected he cheated his way through school. If he'd done any studying, he'd have done a better job of faking the site."

"You didn't like the standing stone idea? Based on the Nine Ladies?" Norcross asked.

"Oh, you figured out the circle he copied. Good for you." Hilda tossed the words over her shoulder.

"We've figured out more than that." Leith gestured for Hilda to continue. "What happened when you confronted your brother?"

"I demanded Rupert return the stolen artefacts. Rupert had them with him. He was going to place them in that trench he'd dug." She covered her face with her hands, making her next words muffled. "I'm sorry I did it. Even if Rupert did have it coming, for years."

"What was that?" Leith needed to make her say it. "What did Rupert have coming to him?"

Hilda dropped her hands and looked up. "His comeuppance, I suppose." Hilda said dully. "Punishment, for making our lives a living hell when he was at home. For breaking our parents' spirits and sending them to an early grave. Still full of grief for the man he'd turned into and for killing all the joy in their lives and mine. I lost my temper, it all boiled over."

"Why now?" Leith asked.

Hilda shook her head, dropping her chin. "He would not give the artefacts back. In fact, he laughed at me. Told me I would never measure up to our father, or our mother. I'd never be good enough." She was deflated, drained. "I lost my temper."

"What did you do?"

"He turned his back on me and I hit him."

"What did you use as a weapon? You didn't use the shovel and then clean it?" Leith asked.

"No, there was no shovel down in the ditch. I didn't mean to hurt him." Hilda's tone held faint regret. "It...just happened."

Norcross shifted in his chair. "You didn't use? Not the mallet, surely?"

Hilda turned on Norcross in horror. "Of course not! That mallet is a valuable artefact. I would never–" She got herself under control. "No. I merely used a large rock."

"What did you do with the rock after you hit your brother?"

Hilda looked down at her clenched fists. "I tossed it into the river after I got back to camp."

Chapter Twenty

Hilda Barker's confession and subsequent arrest sent Doctor Orlinsky in a tizzy.

"This cannot be happening." The archaeologist stared at Buchanan as he snapped handcuffs on Hilda Barker's wrists while reciting her a litany of rights.

"I assure you, it is." Hilda gave Robert a sunny smile. "I really don't have anything left to lose. I felt it was better to right some of the wrongs where my brother was concerned."

"Oh Hilda, don't say that. It's not true in any case. You took those missing artefacts too much to heart. This was a terrible price to extract. Nothing is worth killing someone over."

"Says the man with an intact career, and tenure." Hilda sniffed. "You'll have to find someone else to scrub the dirt from your finds. Make sure you get someone reliable, Robert."

Buchanan placed a firm hand on Hilda's arm. "Time to go."

"And don't forget to have someone sift through the spoils heap." Hilda called to Robert as she followed the constable's persistent insistence.

Inspector Pelly's SUV rolled up at that moment.

"I'll have to brief her on Hilda's confession." Beth said to Norcross and walked over to the Inspector.

Norcross folded his arms over his chest and focused his attention on Hilda as he watched the constable tuck the female archaeologist into the back of his truck. She was settled behind the mesh holding area and Buchanan buckled a seatbelt around the woman.

Thinking about Hilda's testimony made Norcross frown. She certainly had told them the truth, she'd assaulted her brother, and while she said she didn't mean to kill him, some part of this did not feel right. Was she lying? No, it was not merely her words, something did not fit. This case was not yet resolved. There was still something more to be discovered. He was convinced of it.

Pelly's mobile phone rang and she extracted the device. After a brief conversation, she spoke quickly to Buchanan who had waited for her. He then got into his truck and drove away with their chief suspect.

271

The inspector and the sergeant walked back over to the table where Norcross was still sitting. "The community coroner is coming out." She addressed this to both Leith and Norcross.

Dr. Orlinsky was rubbing his hands together, as though he needed something to do.

Leith put a hand on the archaeologist's shoulder. "Robert, would it be possible to get copies of your photographs?"

He blinked at her and then glanced down at the camera still hanging around his neck. "Oh, yes, of course. Can I email them to you?"

"Certainly, that would be quickest."

Leith extracted a business card from her phone case and handed it to Robert. Then she gently turned the archaeologist toward his trailer. "Maybe get yourself another cup of tea. This morning has been full of shocks."

"Yes, yes. That it has, I think more tea is called for. Or maybe something a touch stronger." Robert muttered to himself as he trotted off to his accommodations.

Leith turned her attention back to Inspector Pelly, who was speaking. "After the coroner's report, I have to get to the victim's house. Forensics has found some interesting things."

JD Zech arrived twenty minutes later just as Robert placed a full teapot on the outdoor table with clean cups and fresh milk. "At least Hilda brought out some supplies before she was arrested." From his back pocket, Robert pulled a micky of rye whisky and put a splash in his mug before capping the bottle. He looked up at the other four visitors. "Sorry, would you like a drop?"

Pelly, JD, and Leith declined, as did Norcross. Robert slipped the bottle into his back pocket again and added tea to the mug. No sugar followed this time.

Leith gave the older man an exasperated look as her phone pinged with an incoming text. She glanced at it and tapped an acknowledgement. She then put the device away.

"So, can we get to it?" JD took a seat and pulled a full tea mug over to him.

"Yes, you said something about nitrate?" Pelly dropped into a chair next to JD but refused Robert's offer of tea.

"I did. First, has anyone given a statement regarding Rupert Honeyweld's behaviour? That is, prior to when he was found in the ditch?"

"Not yet, but we are actively asking for the public to tell us anything they can about our victim and his actions before his death. Is there anything specific you're looking for?" Pelly pushed a mug of tea Leith's way.

"Yeah, I want to know if anyone noticed if he was disoriented, confused and if anyone noticed the appearance of blue in his skin, specifically, his lips." JD turned to look at Leith and Norcross in turn. "As you noticed when the body was discovered. Of course once we saw his tongue, which was almost black, the pathologist knew what we were looking for right away."

"Which was?" Leith took a sip of the brew in her cup.

"Ammonium nitrate." JD opened his hands in a 'ta da' movement.

The other four just looked at the coroner for a moment.

"Sorry, what are you saying?" Pelly asked.

"Our victim ingested ammonium nitrate, in large quantities too." JD reached into his coat and extracted a collection of papers folded vertically down the middle. He flattened the papers on the table and flipped to the second page. "See, the results of the tests are here." His finger underlined the quantities.

"Is that our cause of death in conjunction with a head injury?" Leith asked.

"The pathologist told us the blow to the back of the head was not enough to kill our victim." He flipped to a new section of the report. "The skin was broken, some dirt and sand was found in the wound, but bleeding was fairly minimal and there was no concussion."

"So Hilda didn't murder Rupert. This is wonderful." Robert lifted his tea mug as if in a toast and drank. "I'll be getting my finds expert back."

The others ignored Robert as they continued to question the coroner.

"Why and how did the ammonium nitrate cause Honeyweld to appear blue?"

"I don't know the why, I'll leave that up to you. But nitrogen is vital to all living things." JD was warming to his subject. "Nitrates are abundant in soil, animal waste, plants, and in spinach, cauliflower, collard greens, and beets. However, nitrates also come in the form of medications used to treat heart disease and hypertension and as creams used to treat burns. Volatile nitrites, otherwise known by the slang term 'poppers' are known to be abused for recreational purposes." He turned to the last page of the report. "Other commercial sources of nitrates include fertilizers."

"And explosives." Norcross said mildly. Both Pelly and Leith cast him a frown.

"Overexposure can lead to serious, negative health effects," JD continued. "Nitrates are converted into nitrites by bacteria in our saliva, stomach, and intestines, and it is primarily the nitrites that cause toxicity."

"Thank you, JD, could we cut to the chase?" Leith asked.

"I was merely giving the background so you would understand nitrites oxidize the iron component of red blood cells rendering them unable to carry oxygen. The resulting condition is called methemoglobinemia, and the lack of oxygen is the reason behind the characteristic pale to blue-gray color of the skin."

JD gave them a nod, assuming everyone was following his explanation. "The severity of methemoglobinemia is directly proportional to the percentage of red blood cells affected. The higher the percentage, the more serious the symptoms, and the bluer the patient appears."

"Honeyweld was practically Smurf blue," Pelly commented.

"We can't find any evidence he was prescribed any medication which contained a like substance. Nitrate medications are prescribed for people who have high blood pressure or heart disease in some cases. Their function is to dilate blood vessels," JD continued. "Poisoning can result from swallowing, inhaling, or even skin contact. People have been poisoned after drinking nitrate-contaminated rural well water."

"How likely is that to be true here?" Pelly asked and looked at Leith.

"Not very. There's no well on this property at all. Farmers get their wells tested at least twice a year around here as a precaution to spot any type of contamination. We're all informed about proper cleaning techniques for equipment." Leith lifted one shoulder. "With the price of fertilizer, a lot of farmers are using manure on their fields. We certainly are and I know the Freeborns do too. So Honeyweld wouldn't get methemoglobinemia from any of our properties. Although it's possible he drank water from someone else's well I suppose."

"Town water must be tested regularly as well. Have there have been no reports of anyone else suffering from this type of poisoning?" Norcross looked between Pelly and JD.

"No other reports," JD said.

"I'll call the town office to verify." Pelly gestured for JD to go on.

"Rokeby told us Honeyweld ranged far and wide in his trips to find archaeology," Norcross pointed out.

The inspector nodded. "As we are canvasing the public for information, I'll make sure this is included in the questioning. We are asking for anyone who has had a run in with our victim. The office is setting up interviews. We can ask about the fertilizers at the same time. I suspect our victim would need repeated exposure to the poison to build it up to toxic levels." Pelly looked back at JD.

"Yes, that is true."

Pelly pushed her chair in under the table. "So we need evidence our victim ingested this stuff more than once. Anything else?"

"No, that's about it in a nutshell." He offered Pelly the report. "An electronic copy has been sent to you as well."

"Then I won't take your hard copy. I'm going to check in at the office. Hopefully people are coming forward with information about our victim and his whereabouts prior to his death so we can build a timeline." Pelly stood. "We'll get Hilda Barker processed. I have to speak to the Crown attorney on how they would like to proceed." She didn't say what she was thinking, although her expression made it plain.

"This is still a suspicious death, not murder," Norcross said.

"That is the current status, yes." Pelly's words were firm. She gave Leith a nod and strode away to her vehicle.

"I should go too. I have paperwork to file." JD made to fold the report.

"Can I have that for now?" Leith held out her hand. "I'd like to read it over."

"Sure, shred it when you're done, or give it to the inspector." He handed over the sheaf of papers. "Let me know if you have any other questions."

"Will do." Leith got to her feet as well.

JD gulped down the rest of his tea and left.

"Thanks for the tea, Robert." Leith emptied her cup.

"Beth, if I may ask..."

"How can I help?" She placed her empty mug on the table.

Robert stepped forward. "This sounds like Hilda is innocent. She didn't kill Rupert. Shouldn't you let her go?"

The sergeant turned to the older man. "That's a very good question. I would suggest you contact a criminal lawyer for Hilda so that she can get advice when she is charged."

"But, she–"

Leith held up one hand to forestall Robert's next statement. "While it looks like our victim died from something other than assault, the fact remains Hilda did confess to attacking her brother. The investigation is continuing." She held the older man's gaze to ensure he understood. Robert finally nodded. "That said, even if Hilda was charged with her brother's death, the Crown will probably allow her bail. She has no prior criminal history, and I doubt she's a flight risk. For now, she's been remanded into custody until these issues can be sorted out. To speed things along, get her some representation."

"Yes, yes. Good advice, thank you. I'll make some calls." Robert began collecting the teapot and mugs.

Leith looked at Norcross. "Come on, you've been invited for lunch."

"Thank you."

She leafed through the information as they walked slowly to her parked SUV. "So our cause of death isn't the crack on the head after all."

"I questioned the assumption the injury was severe enough to kill him earlier. However, it's not my place to step on anyone's toes. I did second-guess myself again though when Hilda confessed, I must admit."

"Hang onto that thought. Something isn't right here." Leith handed him the report, then dug out her keys.

"Good, I'm glad I'm not the only one to think so."

Two minutes later they were back on the road.

"This is now officially a suspicious death. No matter what the pathologist found. Nobody accidently develops methemoglobinemia." Leith took a different dirt road upon leaving the camp. It appeared to be a more direct route to the grid road.

"Suspicious being one notch higher in the critical scale than unexplained?"

"I'd say so." The SUV accelerated smoothly as she sped up.

"Am I truly invited to luncheon with your family?"

She glanced at Norcross and his wistful tone. "Yeah, it's just leftovers."

"Still, I haven't thought to bring anything for your mother as a thank you. It means a great deal not to have to dine on takeout days in a row."

"I know. So does Mom, hence the invite. Don't worry about it."

"Hm, well, thank you." He paused and his lips twisted. "What aren't you telling me?"

"We might have some surveillance video of our crime scene. That's the other reason we are going home." Leith swung the large vehicle to the right as they took a sharp turn and a new laneway. "Back entrance to the farm," she explained, taking the dirt track by the tree row faster than Norcross strictly felt was necessary.

They arrived back in the parking area a few minutes later. Wayne and Shuster gave her a cursory hello, and then went to greet their new fascination.

"Nice to see you again too." Norcross gave each of the large dogs a scratch behind the ears.

"Bethy, Adam," Nick Leith called to them. He strode away from a two-story metal building as the massive door rolled

281

closed. He wore oil and grease stained blue coveralls and a snap back hat advertising his son's truck dealership. "Are you taking time to eat with us?"

"Yeah, we want to see your video too, Dad."

Nick grunted and gave a nod. He was pleased about their arrival. "Come on then. Get cleaned up and we'll eat." Nick kept to his brisk pace and his dogs abandoned Norcross to walk on either side of their master. "Your mother made her stroganoff."

When the kitchen door was opened, the fragrance of garlic, beef gravy, and fresh baked bread greeted them.

Nick turned left and shrugged out of his coveralls to hang in the porch. Beth and Adam went to wash their hands.

"Just in time to set the table," Maria said.

* * *

After lunch, Maria shooed all three of them off to Nick's office. "You two can wash the supper dishes." She winked at Adam.

By turns, Adam pleased to be invited to another wonderful home cooked meal, but apprehensive of Beth's reaction to her mother's obvious match making. Not that he had any problem with Mrs. Leith pairing him up with her daughter.

He did slide his gaze over to Beth to gauge her reaction and found her merely giving her mother a bland look. Adam could not make much out of Beth's response one way or another. Sometimes he found her thought completely transparent and at other times, like now, he had no idea what she was thinking, which intrigued him to no end.

"Come on," Nick urged them to follow him. "I have to get back to working on the 835, I need the spike cultivator ready to go when Dawson gets back from the elevator."

"835?" he asked Beth as he trailed behind.

"Tractor."

"Ah."

They entered the cluttered office to find Nick behind his desk inserting a SD card into the slot of a laptop. "I thought you should see this." He tipped a second screen their way and clicked his mouse.

They each took a wooden office chair and watched a short clip of Rupert Honeyweld. The man drove his yellow ATV past the camera and out of frame. The time stamp read 7:29 a.m. "That's all this one has on your case." Nick used the software to eject the SD card and swapped it out for another.

"We have our victim arriving at the site," Beth said.

"This card has more important video." Nick clicked open the file folder. Several files were displayed. He clicked on the first one.

Another angle of the dirt road was displayed, this one closer to the fork which led to the camp by the river. The figure of Robert Orlinsky walking down the track while using a walking stick popped into view.

"That time stamp says 6:40 a.m., Orlinsky was there before Honeyweld around 6:43 a.m." Adam lifted an eyebrow at Beth. "He didn't mention this to us. I wonder why."

"Probably because he didn't think it mattered. Oh, here we go." Beth leaned forward as Hilda Barker walked briskly into the frame. The older woman abruptly turned right and descended into the ditch. "This clip started at 7:10 a.m. She got there part way into this one."

"She was lying in wait for her brother."

"Yeah. This says she wasn't just trying to talk him out of his fraud and lost her temper."

"Premeditated, attempted murder." Norcross glanced at Beth, and she nodded.

The next clip was timestamped for 7:30 a.m. Three frames later it showed only the front fender of the quad and then a shovel leaned up against it.

The next ten second video at 7:40 a.m. showed Hilda leaving the ditch. She tossed the cardboard box in front of the quad and tucked her rolled up blue sweatshirt under her arm.

"Forensics should find Hilda's prints on that box. I'll give them a call." Beth turned and accepted the SD cards from her father. "Thanks, Dad, I'll have to give your cards over to Pelly."

"I figured you have to. That's not a problem." Nick nodded.

"May I ask a question regarding your new property?" Adam got to his feet.

Nick made a shrugging gesture. "Sure"

"Those ditches, or coulees by the east dirt road, were they at some point gravel pits for road building?"

Nick leaned back in his chair and laced his fingers over his stomach. "Some pits were dug in the fifties looking for gravel. I think only one actually yielded some, but not enough for the road. I remember my dad saying old man Freeborn was ticked off he missed out on the contract."

"You know where we found Rupert Honeyweld?" Beth said to her father as she stood too.

"Yep, in the deepest pit, across from that second game camera. Now that I think about it. I wonder how he missed getting recorded on my cameras before now." Nick's bushy eyebrows came together. "Where did you run into him that time, Bethy?"

"Further on, down by the river. He didn't have a quad with him, he was walking."

"He probably crossed over from Sheila Atwater's place. They've got a massive beaver dam upriver from us."

"Has she called you again looking to have the damn broken up?"

"Oh yeah, but she'll have to get off her wallet and pay somebody to get rid of it. Dawson told her we can't take the excavator up there, it's too swampy. Bank beavers don't bother me much anyhow."

Chapter Twenty-One

After Leith made her phone calls, she and Norcross headed into Lone Spruce and the Honeywelds' house.

"Buchanan should be here somewhere, I'll hand the SD cards off to him."

They parked across the street from the house in question, a seventies style bungalow. The Honeyweld residence was a one and a half story building with sun-faded tan vinyl siding. The trim was a darker brown. Patchy weathered paint hung from the window frames, door frames, and fence. The front lawn and flower beds were weed-choked and overgrown. Who knew how long it had been since the lawn was cut. The house had an abandoned feel even with the forensic team beavering away with both garage doors open.

Leith led the way across the street to a truck parked on the driveway. Plastic boxes filled with items were being packed in the back. This was where they found Constable Buchanan.

"Those the SD cards?" he asked.

"Yeah, I don't have any evidence bags." She offered him the cards enclosed in a plastic sandwich bag.

"It'll do." He flashed a smile at her as he took the bag.

"Finding much?" Norcross asked.

"Heh, way too much it turns out. Come have a look." Buchanan waved to toward the garage.

The pair donned foot coverings and followed the constable. "I have to say this, please don't touch anything."

"Of course not." Leith pulled black disposable gloves from her back jean pocket and offered Norcross a set. "Not without these."

"Yeah, right," Buchanan said with an awkward shrug. He went first into one of the garage bays.

Inside the building, a smattering of tools lined the boards attached to the walls, but the hooks were mostly empty. A small potbelly wood stove was situated in one corner. The rest of the area was occupied with empty discarded boxes from a provincial courier company. Some were broken down for recycling, but most were haphazardly piled in a heap. Next to this, a neat and orderly stack of plastic tote bins.

Buchanan gestured at the shipping boxes. "We've found literally dozens of shipments of fossils, arrowheads, stones with petroglyphs, and tons more." He pointed at the stack of plastic totes. "There's pottery, coins, bones, and artwork. In house, here in the garage, it's mind boggling."

The plastic containers reached the rafters of the garage. "Good grief," Leith said, following Buchanan's gesture.

"This isn't everything. Come through here."

Leith held up one hand. "Wait, you're taking the courier boxes as evidence, aren't you?"

"We have ten courier containers classified and processed as evidence already. Marty said they will take the rest and store them until the trial. We're tracing the shipments. There's only the destination address on them." Buchanan pointed at a customer account number on one box. "We're pretty sure these all originated from the same sender account number."

"Good to know." She nodded at him to proceed.

Buchanan directed them to a man-door at the back of the garage. Across the gravel pathway was another building which took up almost the entire backyard. This building looked new, twelve by sixteen feet and the metal siding was painted a flat white. "The neighbours thought it was a workshop."

"It's not, obviously." Norcross looked in through the back doors. The view through the open doors was of the back lane, where a truck could discretely make deliveries.

The three entered the structure. Artefacts were displayed in cases, and upon tables under muted lighting. The floor and surfaces were immaculate. "This looks like a museum."

"That's exactly what I thought," the constable said. "We had to order another truck."

"This is going to take a while to inventory." Leith shook her head at the sight. "There's thousands of items here."

"And from hearing Hilda Barker tell it, some, or all of this might be stolen." Buchanan stopped to study one index card beside a black stone spear point. "That means each item will have to have a search done on it to find the right owners."

Leith's lips twitched into a half smile. "It might be easier to send out a communication to registered museums and request they contact the RCMP with a list of stolen items, with photos, from their facilities."

"Yeah, you're right." Buchanan blushed briefly and cleared his throat.

Norcross found one display case particularly interesting and stared down at the contents. Had he ever been that young?

Buchanan changed the subject. "Have you sent your copy of the confession to Pelly?"

"Yep, right before lunch."

He nodded. "SPS is going to take forensics through Hilda Barker's residence in Saskatoon."

Norcross lifted his head from studying a display of locket sized painted portraits. "You may want to ask them to look for information on a second, possibly a third home. The parents had a place in Regina, and one in Arizona. Hilda would have inherited those properties."

"The brother wouldn't have stored stolen goods there." Buchanan looked at Leith. "Would he?"

Leith studied Norcross for a moment. "It's worth checking out. Who's to say Hilda Barker is all that honest? It's not like her confession was completely aboveboard. Any artefacts found in Hilda's house by Saskatoon Police Service might not be stolen but will need to be verified just in case."

"True." Buchanan extracted his phone.

Norcross moved to stand over a curio table made of maple. There was a hodgepodge of items under the flawless glass.

"This is an eclectic collection." Leith looked over his shoulder.

"Why am I not surprised?" Norcross straightened and looked at her.

"What do you mean? Why do you say that?"

He spread his hands indicating the table. "Do you know what these are? All these displayed items."

Leith looked around the room. "What are you getting at?"

"These are trophies." He tapped the glass top with his latex covered finger. "Each is a grouping of items Honeyweld acquired, probably from the same museum, location, or possibly from a collector and no doubt all stolen."

She nodded. "That's why snuff boxes are included with pottery shards. He took these things from the same place?"

"I think so. We'll have to investigate to know for sure."

"Constable? Sergeant?" A female tech in white disposable coveralls stepped into the outbuilding.

"What's up?" Leith turned toward the tech.

"My boss has found something he wants you to see."

Leith glanced at Buchanan, he waved at them to go on.

Norcross trailed behind Leith as they followed the forensic technician into the house.

They entered through the front door, also wide open. Protective matting spidered its way through the house and prevented the team from damaging any evidence. It made Norcross wonder why they all

292

bothered with foot coverings, but not his circus.

The living area was messy and cluttered with used dishes, newspapers, books and articles of male clothing scattered about. It was as if no one was in charge of tidying up. The disorder made the 1970's décor with its avocado green carpet and furniture appear even more abandoned. A dirty path from someone not removing their shoes was worn into the carpet. The path led from the master bedroom to the bathroom, then from the living room into the kitchen. There was also a good coating of dust on all surfaces. Well, fingerprints would be easy to acquire.

They walked through the living room and down the hallway, still the same carpet, brought them to a back bedroom. There was no dirt trail here. Pink carpet and walls contrasted with the white bedroom furniture and desk, all with gold pin striping. Silk flowers were full of dust and placed in several vases on multiple surfaces. Scarfs, jewelry trees, and other female articles filled in the available spaces between.

A tall reed thin male, also in coveralls, turned to greet them.

"Sam Malcolm." He introduced himself. "I'm in charge of this motley crew." He flashed them a bright smile as the sunlight reflected off his heavy framed glasses. A wisp of blond hair escaped his coverall hood. "Where's Buchanan?"

"Sergeant Beth Leith." She then introduced herself and Norcross. "Constable Buchanan will be joining us shortly."

"Okay." Sam did not comment on Norcross' presence, merely gave him a nod. Then he gestured to the room at large. "From what we can figure out, this was Judy Honeyweld's bedroom, separate from her husband's."

The bed was draped with pink cauzy material. The duvet and sheet were rumpled and pushed to one side. "The woman passed away several weeks ago. I don't believe our Judy lived her last days at home."

"No," Norcross said. "According to a friend of hers, Tilly Key, Judy died in hospital."

"Cancer, right? Do you happen to know what type?" Sam picked up a clipboard to make a note.

"I'm afraid I don't know."

Sam sniffed and walked over to the desk. The other two followed. "I thought you'd be interested in this." His gloved hand opened a pink covered book. The first page read 'this diary is owned by Judith R. Honeyweld, nee: Riskly.'

"We found this journal wedged between the box spring and mattress." Sam turned to the first entry. "I've only skimmed it, but early on Judy's entries are innocuous. About the plants she's started for spring, Ladies Auxiliary meeting notes, other community initiatives she was involved in. Family stuff, information her brother Malek shared with her about his family on their monthly video calls from Australia. Things like that." He turned to look each of them in the eye briefly to make sure he had their attention. "Then later," he said as he turned the pages to almost halfway through the book. "You can see where her illness is affecting her. The entries are fewer, and she is less careful, probably due to the chemo treatments." He showed them the scrawled writing on the pages. "Then things take an odd turn. Read this." He handed the book to Leith.

She frowned and read out loud; "*I can't believe he's doing it again. The garage and shed are stuffed full of this old crap. Why does he have to keep buying these things? No wonder we never have any money. Stupid garbage!*" Leith looked up. "I assume she means all the historical artefacts filling the house, garage, and shed."

"Exactly, but turn the page." Sam shifted from foot to foot. He seemed eager for Leith to find something.

She looked down. "*This has to stop.*" Her chin came up an inch as she read out loud. "*I need treatment, I want to try*

295

something else. This doctor doesn't know everything. Why won't Rupert help me? He calls it all quackery, but I'll die if we don't try something else." Leith tipped the book. "This is from May of this year." She flipped the pages forward. "By this, Judy is becoming increasingly upset."

"Until July." Sam points to a paragraph.

"*I am resigned to my fate.*" Leith frowned. "Now it's filled with canning information, pickles, tomato sauce, beans, and meals she's put by in the freezer."

"Is that the last personal entry?"

"It is. The rest of the journal is blank after the canning information."

"Then we found this in the wastepaper basket in the office next door." He waved a hand at a younger man. "Jason, where is the evidence bag with the papers you found?"

Jason dug into a plastic tote and came up with the requested item. He walked it over to his boss.

"Thanks." The pages were displayed back-to-back inside the evidence bag to easily display the printed words. "Have a look at these."

"These looked to have been printed from the internet." Leith took the plastic wrapped papers. "Sodium nitrate is commonly used as a preservative in curing meats and ammonium nitrate is found in instant cold packets." Leith glanced up at

296

Norcross. "It goes on, 'Symptoms of nitrate poisoning can vary depending on the amount and duration of the exposure. Those with very mild methemoglobinemia might not have any symptoms at all, or might appear a little pale and feel tired. Moderate-to-severe poisoning is associated with cyanosis, a blueness of the skin, confusion, loss of consciousness, seizures, abnormal heart rhythms, and death.'"

"Mm, yes." Sam rubbed his stubble-covered chin. "An old toxicology adage pops into my mind, by the 16th century physician Paracelsus." Sam looked up toward the ceiling as he recited. "The dose makes the poison." He looked back at Leith. "This truly applies to nitrates. No living thing can live and grow without them, but too much can be deadly. I'll be passing this off to our pathologist, Dr. Knighly."

Norcross took the pages from Leith and scanned them. "That's all there is. Still, we have a new suspect for Honeyweld's murder," he said, handing the pages back to Jason.

"Yeah, his wife, Judy." Leith frowned. "But how? All we have is an print out."

"I think we may want to look at Judy's preserves." Sam lifted his eyebrows at them.

Constable Buchanan walked into the bedroom. "Pelly is on her way. What's going on in here?"

297

"I'll leave that up to you, shall I? I have a pantry to investigate." Sam grimaced a smile. He picked up the journal and slid the book into an evidence bag. "We have a few other things to process too."

"Thanks Sam."

He nodded to her as he left them.

Leith turned to Buchanan. "Is anyone looking into Honeyweld's finances? Judy suggested in her journal her husband was buying these artefacts."

"Back at the office. Whitmere is on it."

"Good." She quickly filled him in on the journal and the papers found in the office.

"So there's a next of kin? Cabot is the tech guy, he's got the computer and the phone we found. Contact details for Malek Riskly are no doubt on one of the devices. That will make it easier to contact him." Buchanan left to track down Cabot.

Norcross and Leith wandered around the rest of the house, but no new information presented itself.

They returned outside as Inspector Pelly arrived. The inspector questioned Leith and Buchanan about the new evidence.

Norcross left them and wandered into the backyard and watched the forensic team inventory the north wall of the museum building for a moment. He blinked rapidly as the familiar feeling of some new piece of evidence was about to reveal itself to him. That was when he noticed the central display cases were on casters.

Since the four-person team was busy some five feet away, Norcross put his gloves back on and walked over to the first of six glass-top display cases. He checked the castors and found the brake tabs were not engaged. With little effort he pushed the case over to the south wall.

"Hey, what do you think you're doing?" The shortest member of the team called over to him. The vocal man stood on a ladder. He was in the process of taking down a mammoth tusk from the wall.

Norcross decided to ignore him and pushed a second case over beside the first.

"Didn't you hear me? Stop touching things. You have no authority–" The forensics tech jumped down from his perch and handed off the tusk to a female co-worker. He then strode over to Norcross, irritation plain on his face.

For his part, Norcross glanced up from where he squatted in the middle of the floor and gave the irritated individual a level stare. Without a word, he leaned down and grasped a metal ring recessed in the floor and pulled.

A four-foot door smoothly opened on hinges on the right side. Florescent lights automatically flickered on. These illuminated a set of metal steps descending into the basement.

"Oh." The shorter man sounded nonplussed, but that didn't stop him. He walked forward and looked down into the basement room.

Norcross waved a gloved hand at the other man. "After you."

Chapter Twenty-Two

Twenty minutes later, Adam crossed the lawn to find on Beth. The light was fading. He wanted to see if she was interested in getting something to eat.

As he approached, Pelly shifted her gaze to him. Norcross could not mistake the tightening of her mouth as she watched him. The inspector either didn't like him or didn't trust him, possibly both.

"We can talk more about this later," Pelly was saying to Leith.

"Sure." She responded, but to Norcross, it didn't sound like she was happy about it. "If you like." She turned to him. "What have you been up to?"

"Exploring." Then he addressed Pelly. "I think you'll need to call in Digital Forensics Services."

"And why would I need to do that?" The inspector spread her feet into a wide stance.

"You may want DFS to examine the computer room bunker we found under the outbuilding museum in the backyard. It appears to be where Honeyweld stored his black-market merchandise and did his sales over the dark web. There is enough tech equipment down there to run Twitter." Norcross gestured over his shoulder at Marty Cheadle, the lead hand inside the backyard museum.

Pelly bit back a curse and finally noticed a male forensic tech waving at her to get her attention. She gave Norcross a dry look then she made her way over to the man.

"There are servers under that shed?" Leith raised her dark eyebrows at him.

"There is, along with shelves and shelves of other artefacts. Inspector Pelly is going to need a bigger truck." He smiled at his lame joke.

Leith rolled her eyes.

"Okay, so don't laugh at my sad humour." He pretended to be perturbed and then Beth did chuckle.

"How about I buy you dinner, or supper as the case may be." Norcross tipped his chin toward her SUV.

Beth did not get a chance to answer.

"Sergeant Leith, where is Inspector Pelly?" Buchanan called as he came striding out of the front door.

"What's going on Glen?" Leith moved forward to meet the constable halfway up the walk.

"You need to see what Sam's people have found in the laundry room."

"Pelly is in the basement server room in the shed out back." Leith strode by him. "She'll need an update."

"There's a server room in the shed?" Glen sounded astonished as he entered the garage and headed for the back door.

Leith entered the house and Norcross turned to follow. The change from cool breeze and fading sunshine to dim smelly house was dramatic. What disturbed Norcross the most was the weird taste in the back of his throat, no doubt from breathing in the chewy air.

"Where's the laundry room?" Leith asked a coveralled tech pushing a dolly loaded with clear plastic totes to the front door.

"Through the kitchen, take a left."

"Thanks." They ducked around her and walked to the kitchen again following the floor mat trail.

The kitchen was a shambles, much like the bulk of the house. Dishes were piled up on the counters. There were flies and bugs crawling over everything. Leith did not comment as they did a fast walk through the room. Norcross wanted to hold his breath, even though the windows were open. He settled for breathing shallowly.

"What did you find, Sam? A body?"

Sam snorted. "No, but we've found more on the ammonium nitrate mentioned in those papers. It's all through this freezer."

He and Jason continued to stack glass containers covered with plastic lids from a huge deep freeze into another tote. The badge on the open freezer door said General Motors. The appliance was monstrous and old.

"And?" Leith prodded.

Sam pointed at a separate smaller plastic tote. "Over there are the remains of a cooler cold packs, in that box. The pack originated from in here." He gestured to the giant deep freeze. "At some point, they became damaged and broke open."

"The things leaked all over the contents of the freezer," Jason added, receiving a stack of three containers from Sam.

Cabbage rolls, perogies, and pork chops in gravy, if Norcross was any judge. The glass held a blueish tinge. "For spillage to happen, the pack must have thawed. Was the freezer not working?"

"No, no, it's working. However, there might have been a power outage at some point earlier on." Sam looked over at Leith. "It's possible our victim looked up the effects of the broken cold packs online, wondering if he could still eat these pre-made meals."

"Did any of the food become contaminated?"

"I don't know, they all appear to be well sealed, but we will find out with testing." Sam continued to hand out containers to Jason.

"Honeyweld must have come to the same conclusion. There are containers matching those in the kitchen. Empty," Norcross said.

"Yes, we'll have to take some samples to see if there is any residue in the used ones." Sam straightened and closed the freezer lid. "Well, that about does it. You should go for your dinner break, Jason. I'll continue here for a bit."

* * *

The restaurant hostess showed them a booth table.

"Cory will be right over to look after you." And the hostess left them.

Beth tucked her phone into her coat pocket and then slid into the booth seat. Norcross had removed his coat and she proceeded to do the same. "He didn't say it, but I think Sam suspects the freezer is the source of the contamination which poisoned our victim."

"I agree. I'm sure it is, but one question remains."

"Which is?" Beth lifted one dark eyebrow at him.

"Was the contamination an accident or done on purpose?"

"Mm, true."

305

"Tilly Key told me even as ill as Judy Honeyweld was from her cancer treatments she cooked up and froze numerous meals for her husband. Apparently so he could eat hot food while she was in hospital."

"Yeah, I'm sure the meals were all made by Judy, too. Who else would do that for Honeyweld? Still, would she actually poison her husband?"

Norcross opened his hands. "It is a valid line of inquiry. Sam's tests will tell us one way or another. We just have to be patient."

Their server popped up at the table with menus under his arm and ice water in tall glasses on a tray.

"Hi Beth." The young man smiled at her. "How've you been?"

"I'm good, Cory, and you?"

"Busy as ever. Can I offer you a drink from the bar?" They both chose to stay with water instead. "I'll give you a few minutes then."

After Cory left, Beth opened her menu. "My mother will be disappointed she can't grill you during supper tonight."

"Ah. I wondered why I got off so lightly yesterday."

"She was taking the measure of you last evening. I think she was planning her strategy."

"Do you think I will pass her scrutiny?"

"Who knows?" Beth lifted one shoulder. "She can be a tough customer."

"No doubt. What about your father?"

The left side of Beth's mouth quirked up. "Dad doesn't get involved. He told me once if the RCMP trusts my judgement enough to give me a Smith & Wesson to carry on my hip, he trusts my judgement when it comes to my dates."

"Saying he knows you can take care of yourself." Adam nodded.

"Pretty much." She tipped her head slightly in the affirmative. "And to forestall any of my brothers from over protectiveness or worse, trying pranks on my dates. When you have four male siblings, guys asking to date you need to be very careful."

"Good to know. So is this a date?" He gave her his most charming smile.

"Norcross, you know me better than that."

"Do I?" He changed his tone to sound innocent as he opened his menu.

She lifted her chin to give him a steady look. "One would hope so."

He glanced up at her, a touch serious now. "You're the job."

She opened her mouth to shoot an answer back but paused. She blinked and said, "I used to be."

Norcross looked over at Beth, something shadowed her good mood. Her trust in her own organization had been shaken. He knew how she felt.

Beth hadn't said much after they left the Honeyweld residence. Nor during the drive to the neighbouring town for a break and some food. The two cafes in Lone Spruce were doing a booming business with the cops and techs all over the place and were a bit overwhelmed.

"Are you all right?" He said this carefully. He wanted her to know he was concerned for her, although he was not crossing the line between personal and professional. Not if she didn't want him to. Norcross knew he wasn't good at determining what Beth thought about him. This surprised him somewhat, usually he was decent at sussing out how people felt about him. If not, he could rely on his talent to give him a hint as to how to handle them. With Beth, his ability deserted him completely.

She took a breath and cleared her expression. "Pelly warned me to watch my back."

"In what context?" His eyes narrowed slightly. "Did she mention anyone by name?"

"The top brass, but more specifically you."

"Ah." He smiled.

"Yeah, so I'm not sure where the inspector stands." Beth sounded annoyed and a touch confused. "Or if there's any pressure from above or outside the Force on her."

"You could take it at face value. Why would she warn you if she was running interference for Thrust or someone else?"

Beth gave a head waggle. "I guess."

"And you knew already I'm not to be trusted."

She snorted a laugh. "Not hardly, not with what I know about you."

His eyes crinkled at the corners. "You've been doing some digging on me, haven't you?"

"What makes you say that?" Her tone was all wrong. It was more teasing than sarcasm.

"Because it's exactly what I'd do."

"I think we've already established that fact." Her tone turned dry as the summer prairie.

"True, so?"

"I may have gotten a more in depth look into who you are."

"How did you do that, whom did you speak to?"

"I cannot divulge my sources. I called in a few favours though."

"I thought as much." Norcross was feeling pleased Beth had gone to the trouble. "Did you find out anything interesting?" He had to ask.

She shrugged. "Maybe."

Norcross wanted to ask what information she'd found. From her tone he suspected the data could not have been negative. She was speaking with him, wasn't she?

Finally she turned to him and lifted her dark eyebrows in a lofty fashion. "How was your walkabout in Iran?"

That he did not expect. "You have a long reach if you can pull out information like that." No one outside his office knew about the trip to Iran. This was something he should mention to departmental security, but of course he would leave out how he found out about the security loophole. Beth had enough things to deal with.

Again, Leith shrugged. "I know a few people. I also have lots of time on my hands. Or I did." She corrected.

He could tell she was uncomfortable about the whole administrative leave issue, so before she turned pensive again, he changed the subject to lighten the mood. "This was a school at one time?" He was looking around at the western décor of red brick walls and wood finishes. There was a jail cell door next to the dining area and their table. He could see beyond the metal bars where video lottery machines were located. The door and the sign attested to this fact and to keep out minors.

"Yep," Beth said and straightened her posture coming back to herself. "Enrollment has dropped in smaller communities. And it's more efficient, cheaper, and offers the kids more activities if they are aggregated into one school. Although more kids have to ride a bus longer as a result of that aggregation." She shrugged in a 'what can you do?' outlook and pushed her long braid over her shoulder. "If a small town loses its school, it usually signals a death knell for the community."

"But not here in Stene?"

"No, some residents got together and bought the old school. They converted the building, added this restaurant, a campground, hairdresser, barber shop, and in the old playground, there's a collection of picnic tables with a stage for stand-up comedians and music acts."

At that point their server returned. "Can I take your order, or do you need another couple of minutes?"

"No, I'm ready. I'll start with a Caesar salad, followed by a half rack of rib with fries and gravy on the side." Beth handed him back her menu.

"I'll have the same." Adam handed over his menu as well and the waiter tucked them under his arm.

"Thanks Cory." Beth said as the young man added ice water to their glasses. "How's Becky?"

"Good, she's got one more year of residency than she can write her own ticket." Wavy brown hair slipped over the young man's forehead and he did an unconscious flip to get it out of his eyes.

"Where does she want to practice?"

"Here, that was her whole plan right from the beginning. People from small towns get what the life is like and she can't wait to get out of the city."

"Too much concrete." Beth nodded.

"Exactly. I'll go put your order in." Cory gave them a dimpled smile and left.

They sipped their water in the silence that followed. Norcross thought Beth was becoming lost in her thoughts again when she surprised him.

Leaning forward, forearms on the table, she gave him a penetrating look. "Norcross, do you think everyone has a price?"

He did not hesitate. "Yes." He studied her. "You're thinking about Pelly?"

She shook her head. "Even you?"

Adam gave her a sad smile and nodded. "Even me."

"You surprise me, Norcross. I thought you had higher ethics, higher even than me."

He still held her eyes. "Sorry to disappoint you."

His tone made Beth narrow her gaze at him. She watched him for a moment. "Has anyone ever reached your price?"

"Not yet, no." He picked up his glass for a sip.

Her eyebrows lifted. "You work with politicians, how is that possible?"

He gave her his full smile as he placed his glass down on the thick wooden table. "My price is astronomically high. It's out of everyone's reach."

Beth smiled at this too.

Chapter Twenty-Three

Leith and Norcross refused the offer of cheesecake, and he paid the bill. They got into her SUV for the drive back to the Honeyweld residence after an excellent supper.

Again Leith was quiet as they traveled down the access road to the highway.

"Have you had an update on your review?" He thought her silence had to be something to do with the events from August.

"No, but Collin called to give me an update. Carrie Belter's case, Winslow Thrust's girlfriend, is moving through the system. She made bail and the Crown Counsel is going ahead with the case against her. It looks as though Carrie has been charged with assault, not Winslow."

"How is that possible?"

She shook her head as she slowed the vehicle to a stop at the intersection. "I don't know. It is true she attacked me from behind, but it was her boyfriend who had deadly intent. If I hadn't had my Taser out of its holster, I'd have just flipped her onto the ground." Leith rolled her bottom lip over her teeth as she made the right turn onto the highway. "Collin said her defense lawyers are not refuting the charge. He thinks she's going to take a dive for Winslow if she has to."

"Who is funding her team?"

She lifted one shoulder. "I can make a guess."

"Did Winslow Thrust make bail?"

She snorted a derisive laugh. "He wasn't in custody for more than four hours. Thrust might get the theft charges reduced, he's pleading mental issues. Apparently, a doctor is scheduled to file a report later this month on whether or not Mr. Thrust is competent."

"And yet he sits in the Legislature."

"Yep, his party is backing him so he stays on the job, innocent until proven guilty, except that they aren't denying he's guilty, merely troubled."

Unconsciously, Beth's right hand rubbed her left arm below her elbow. Adam wondered just how trivial the knife wound had actually been. He'd seen the scar.

"His party currently has a provincial government majority."

She shifted her hand back to the steering wheel. "I know, it's odd. Either Thrust has mental issues that should be addressed or he's a criminal and should pay for his crimes. The result is the same either way. He should not be in a position of authority." She waved this away. "But I can't change any of it. I can only defend myself and my ethics."

Twenty minutes later they were back on site. The pair found the forensic team was back loading totes, evidence bags, and computers into a new truck. This one was forty feet. The vehicle sported a rental company's name on both sides.

The driver watched as his truck was loaded with no little trepidation. This was when Norcross realized the man with his arms folded over his chest was Bruce Sangster from Lone Tree Towing.

"Bruce's business is also the local U-Haul franchise," Beth explained, and then walked over to the driver. Norcross followed.

"Can you believe what Honeyweld had hidden under his shed?" Bruce didn't wait for a greeting.

"Surprising isn't it?" Beth cocked one hip as she watched the loading. "Norcross found the hidden basement room."

"Marty was the lead," Norcross said.

Leith turned her head to give him a lifted eyebrow. "That's not what Pelly said."

"That's what's going into Marty's report," Norcross said this on the low side for her hearing alone.

"We should give them a hand so Bruce can get on the road," she suggested.

In the end, Sam snagged Beth to help him and Jason. Perforce, Norcross became a beast of burden too, although he chose to assist the crew in the garage loading Bruce's truck. He was more curious about the high-end items Honeyweld had stored in the basement. He assumed they were costly or at least more exclusive in any case. Why else would Honeyweld store the articles out of sight and so securely?

Besides, he'd rather catalogue and handle stone tools, weapon points, and pictograms on stones stolen from their sites than dirty dishes with food and chemical residue.

An hour and a half later, full dark had settled in. Beth switched from kitchen duty.

She was back with him and the shed. They finished clearing out the last of the evidence and packed up the small artefacts to be hauled to Bruce's truck.

"Where did Honeyweld obtain all of this stuff?" Beth picked up a pink quartz arrowhead and flipped it over on her palm. "It can't all have come from Saskatchewan museums."

"I suspect various museums and collections across Canada are missing artefacts. Most museums have vast storage areas and have a tiny fraction of items on display at any one time. Some they loan out. I'm betting unless someone goes looking, no one would have known these are missing artifacts."

"Someone, or possibly a team of people, will have to identify each item and try to return it to its rightful owner. Either to the museums they were stolen from, or the First Nations communities they were taken from." Beth turned the stone point to catch the available light. "It'll be a big job to handle the investigation. Probably it's going to be expensive too."

"No question. I suggest it's best to start with Dr. Orlinsky and the University of Saskatchewan, also local and municipal museums. The rest, well, someone will have to foot the bill."

"I think Honeyweld's estate should cover it. Rupert was the one who caused this mess." She placed the arrowhead back with the white and black ones on their bed of foam.

Later, Beth joined Norcross outside on the driveway and handed him one last container to load in the truck.

Norcross handed the box up to the waiting hands of Marty, the same short forensic tech who had bristled at his presence earlier on. "That's the last one."

"Thanks for your help, Adam."

"No problem." He and Beth stripped off their gloves.

"Sergeant." Buchanan waved at them as he re-entered the yard. Sweat stained his under arms and his face was shiny from exertion. The young constable looked knackered.

"You've covered some miles," Norcross said to him.

"I've been doing the door-to-door. I called Pelly, but she's back in the office. The inspector has scheduled a briefing for this evening."

"For all of us?" Beth asked.

Buchanan's eyes slid sideways to Norcross. "Not...all of us, sorry." He shifted his gaze back to the sergeant. "Be in Canora for six o'clock."

"Will do."

Buchanan nodded and headed over to his truck.

She tipped her head toward her SUV. "Well, what's she going to do if you do come with me? Take away your birthday?"

"I appreciate the thought, but I really should return some phone calls anyway." Shapiro had called him over an hour ago and he'd not taken the call.

"All right." She gave him a guarded look.

He knew she thought he was referring to his directive to get her to drop the charges against Winslow Thrust.

"I sent a query off about ammonium nitrate poisoning to my office. I'd like to

319

understand other incidents where this type of thing has happened and the resulting outcomes." His words immediately changed her expression and for that, he was glad. "We can catch up later and exchange information."

"All right." She gave him a firm nod. "I'll take you back to your truck."

When they arrived at the Leith Farm, Norcross paused before closing the passenger door.

"Come to Sleepy Hollow for breakfast tomorrow, I'll let Tilly know you're coming."

"Yeah, okay. Around seven-thirty?" Her eyes shifted away from his.

"Yes, see you then." He closed the door to end the awkward moment they'd shared. He knew they had to do something about the situation, but first, the Honeyweld murder needed to be wound up.

He got in the black truck and followed Beth back into town. Then she turned right at the gas station while he headed left to make his way back to the bed and breakfast.

* * *

When Norcross returned to his room at the bed and breakfast, he found a bottle of red wine and a glass on his dresser. Pleasantly surprised, he picked up the bottle. The label told him it was Sour Cherry from Wolf Willow Winery south of

Saskatoon. Intrigued, he opened the red and poured a sample into his glass.

The fragrance was fruity, and tart on the tongue, yet tasty. He filled the glass and toed off his shoes. The armchair in the bay window with a small, fluted side table offered a relaxing spot to deal with his boss.

Before he could dial, Norcross' mobile pinged and he looked at the screen.

Zara wanted him to call her at his earliest convenience. He would, after he called his boss back.

Walter Shapiro answered on the second ring.

"Where the hell have you been?" There was annoyance, but no outright anger in his boss' tone. Norcross took this as a positive sign.

"I'm working a murder case in Saskatchewan."

"Yes, I know." Shapiro's tone said Norcross was testing him and to stop it. "I meant why didn't you take my call earlier?"

"Sorry, it couldn't be helped. I was assisting to build a case against the murderer." Technically true, up to a point. "We found a hidden room under a shed."

"Bodies?"

"No, merely stolen artefacts which the victim was selling on the black market. We also found his access to the black web."

"Sounds entertaining." There was a trace of wistfulness in his words. Was

Shapiro remembering his own time in the field?

"It was, I'll send Ops his IP addresses."

"Good, they need more to do." This was said dryly.

Norcross ignored the statement. This was just Shapiro's way. "Anyway, that's not important now. I want to move ahead on the Beth Leith task." He took a sip from his wine, liking the tart taste even more.

"What's your play?"

"I want to turn this thing on its head."

"All right, what do you have in mind?"

"Winslow Thrust's attitude is dangerous. If he doesn't learn a lesson soon, he will be completely out of control later and become an even bigger problem."

"Especially with his big brother's unconditional support."

"No doubt. Winslow should be suspended from his seat in Cabinet, if not his seat in the Legislature for the charges against him."

"He either has someone propping him up for some reason not yet clear to me. Could be his party, but it feels like it's more than that." Norcross could hear Shapiro typing as he spoke. It was spooky how the boss of Norcross' section could divide his brain to handle two tasks at once. Working his thoughts to speak, and his hands to carry out mundane chores like data queries in ultra-secret systems. "No one is this careless with their reputation and position unless they think they will never be caught out."

"Or think there will be no repercussions for their actions. The man is also a serious security risk."

"Yes." Shapiro drew the word out. Norcross assumed his boss was viewing some information he'd retrieved.

"Winslow has been a busy boy over the past few years. The more I dig, the more misconduct I'm finding with regard to ethics and lobbyists, however I'm not sure this would be enough to make him rethink the charges he's launched against your Sergeant Leith."

"I came to the same conclusion. Last evening, I researched an entire list of infractions. Someone like that always has skeletons in their closet. I can send you what I found."

"Worse than the doorbell video?" There was revulsion in his boss' tone.

"Much worse." Norcross flipped to his email app and sent the information to Shapiro, then returned to the call. "Did you tap into the secure cloud?"

"Of course." There was silence on the line for a moment. "Well, Winslow is ripe for some foreign influencer to use him for their own agenda." Shapiro sounded serious. Whatever he'd seen on the system caused him grave concern. "We may as well pay him a visit now and avoid a critical scandal if, or when he makes it to Ottawa. I'll send someone to have a conversation with him. Tonight."

Norcross heard the emphasis in the last word and didn't relish being Winslow Thrust. The minister would regret the day he made himself visible on Shapiro's radar. "To be blackmailed by an unfriendly foreign power would be worse. It's a nasty business." Norcross slowly turned the wineglass in a circle. He knew the type of information his boss had just reviewed, so he made a couple of further suggestions for the upcoming, pointed conversation.

"We could run him as a double agent, for leaking misinformation, but I doubt he's stable enough for that." His boss' words were cold.

"I'd say you are correct with that assessment," Norcross said and Shapiro ended the call.

Next, he dialed Zara.

"I've found out a few things for you," she said.

"I'm listening." Adam put his sock feet up on the end of the bed.

"First, from my sources, I couldn't find any negative mention of your Sergeant Leith inside the RCMP or anywhere else."

His lips twitched at the second reference to his connection to Beth. Was Beth *his?* Not really, not yet, maybe someday. He focused on his associate's words.

"Leith's performance reviews are solid, her commanders like her, and she works well with others. 'Firm but fair' or something similar was the most often mentioned comment. Her cases resolved statistics are very impressive. Did you know she's solved twelve murders?"

"Yes." Norcross took a sip of the wine. He wasn't sure why he felt pride on Beth's behalf, but he did. "This current case will make it lucky number thirteen."

"Nice! Other than the review panel looking at accusations brought against her by that BC politician, that's the only buzz I can find on her. From my sources, some people think the charges brought against her are without merit. She's had a stellar career up until now, and the general feeling is she will be reinstated in short order."

"With an official apology?"

"Probably not. You know how these things go." Zara's tone was dry with resignation. "This complaint will never go away unless it's withdrawn. It will stay on her record and follow the sergeant for the rest of her career. The balance of the panel is leaning toward disciplining her, possibly making her leave the Force."

"So even if she were judged to have done nothing wrong, there would still be doubt." It wasn't a question.

"That's about the size of it, and it sucks."

"That it does." He took a sip from his glass. "Any hint Geoffery Thrust has his hand in this anywhere? Such as holding up the review? It's been dragging on from what I can tell."

"His name came up once, but if he is involved, he's exceedingly subtle about it."

"There is nothing subtle about Geoffery Thrust."

"My sources did say there was another name they heard connected to both brothers."

"From the PMO?"

"No, not from the Prime Minister's Office, but routed through justice, Silas Rivers."

Norcross stilled as a puzzle piece dropped into place. The figure was dark and fuzzy, no clear flash of insight, not yet. "Ah." He slowly put his glass down on the side table. "Why would Chief Justice Rivers have anything to do with Winslow Thrust, a lowly BC MLA?"

"I believe it could be more his brother. The AG and the chief justice do move in the same circles. Apparently, they had a relationship before either got into politics. Same schools, same friends. Their law degrees are both from Simon Fraser. Then, a couple years after graduation, Geoffery was elected as a Minister of Parliament for

Bear Mountain, and the two went their separate ways." Zara's chair squeaked as she must have moved at her desk. "The question is, which one of them is interfering in a case they should steer well away from?"

"I'll let you know when I find that out."

"Next, what do you know about Neil Communications?" Zara asked.

Norcross lifted his chin and blinked. "Kenneth Neil, owner of two newspapers, offering both morning, and evening editions, both based in Victoria, with distribution over the whole island and lower mainland.

"He also owns three television stations, Victoria, Nanaimo, and Vancouver locations. The corporation is profitable, influential, and headquartered in Vancouver, but maintains a more substantial staff in the office in Victoria. No doubt because all government business is done in the provincial capital. There was no conflict-of-interest objections flagged at the time Neil put the company together when he bought out smaller players. His enterprise has the lion's share of the news and advertising market in BC, and yet he still managed to finagle government tax breaks. Possibly, there was some inside help there."

"Yes, the Thrust family take care of their friends too. Guess who is on the provincial board to award grants and tax incentives?"

"Winslow Thrust?"

"The same."

"So it's possible there might be some undue influence from Winslow with regard to the stories Neil's outlets released."

"Muddying Sergeant Leith's reputation with a smear campaign? I'd say there is a distinct possibility. It also didn't hurt Neil Communications when the current federal government afforded media companies across the country generous subsidies to the tune of half a billion dollars. The business incentive was framed as financial help to transition legacy media into a more digital format, online streaming, apps, and the like."

"So we have both brothers paying court to Neil Communications." To Norcross, this smelled like a payoff to do someone else's bidding. "That's not healthy for democracy or free speech. An independent media is necessary for impartial reporting on the government of the day."

"Especially when one considers that the Thrust family has members on the board of directors for several of the big four news organizations."

No wonder Winslow thought he'd never face the music when it came to his illicit and unethical actions. "Did you find any link between Neil Communications and the

RCMP?" Norcross drained his glass and put it aside.

"Just rumours, nothing I can confirm."

"What about the sergeant's review panel? What are your feelings about the holdup?"

"The panel had some personnel issues, but those are now resolved. I think the review will now run its course. If they really want to get rid of her, it will take some doing."

"Then you don't think the panel would scuttle Leith's reinstatement at the eleventh hour?"

"How, by citing confidential information redacted to the hilt?" Zara sounded cautious.

Norcross frowned. "We've seen it before when powers that be want to twist the system to do their bidding."

"I can't find any evidence of that practise inside the RCMP." She paused for a moment. "However, I've found something else disturbing."

"Oh?"

"Yes, two other cases where the offending party was released from custody after an assault on cops at a rally turned riot. Alvin Whitehead in Toronto, and another, Tiffany Mullen-Poisson in Montreal. In both cases, they drew a weapon on a cop, Whitehead used a bat, and Mullen-Poisson, pepper spray. Similar to Sergeant Leith's case, these other two perpetrators were released on bond hours after being arrested."

"The judge let them go?"

"Yup, neither was deemed a flight risk or a risk to the community even with weapons assault charges against them."

"Who are these people? Are they linked to Thrust or Rivers in some way?"

"I haven't found any links yet. Whitehead works for CINS Engineering, and Mullen-Poisson is a chemist for a pharmaceutical company, which has since gone bankrupt. So far, their cases have not made it through the judicial system, and it's been several months." CINS Engineering told Norcross all he needed to know about Whitehead. More investigation would need to be done on Mullen-Poisson. Still, Norcross suspected he knew what that connection was, but Zara was speaking again.

"If the limit to receiving a speedy trial is missed, these two cases can be thrown out."

"Exactly, and I don't like where this is going. Assault on an officer needs to be taken seriously."

"I hear you; I don't like it either."

There was a six-hour time difference between his location and Zara. "I appreciate this. I should let you go, you're still at home, I'm guessing."

"Yes, behind an MI6 firewall."

"I owe you."

"No more than we owe *you*. Things turned out well in Libya and for that, I thank you. This poking around in some databases is the least I can do."

His last call for the evening was to his assistant, Maisy Greenwich.

"Hi there, I have some information for you." Maisy sounded cheerful even at this late hour.

"Sorry to call so late." He could hear her moving items on her desk. Then the plop of a thick file folder as it was dropped on her blotter.

"No, no, it's fine. Okay, there is a file on Rupert P. Honeyweld in the CPIC database, just as you thought. He had a juvenile record for petty crime and car theft. He did some time before he was eighteen and the record sealed. After that, there are a couple of assault charges in his twenties, and then it all goes quiet. Nothing came up until last year's assault complaint against Nicholas S. Leith. That complaint was tossed out by the judge, he cited lack of evidence. Do you want more details from Honeyweld's juvy file?"

"No, that's fine. Honeyweld's sister told us his history when we interviewed her yesterday."

"Did she tell you about her scrapes with the law?"

Adam blinked. "No."

"Huh, well that's interesting. Anyway, she was never charged with anything, but I found notes on three investigations where Hilda Honeyweld, then later Hilda Barker, was questioned and released. The cases were pertaining to missing artefacts from three different museums. She was never formally charged. I'll send you the report I compiled. I hope the information helps with your investigation."

His phone vibrated with the received file notification. "I'm sure this will. Got it, thanks."

"Moving on, it appears Sergeant Leith's review was stalled due to one of the three-person panel assigned to the case stepping down. She had to go on maternity leave. The baby was six weeks early, but mother and son are fine."

Norcross smiled at this detail but said nothing to let Maisy continue. At least it proved nothing nefarious was going on.

"Last week another panel member was selected so things are proceeding again."

"Does this panel have a date to file their report or judgement?"

"Yes, the union rep pushed for October 31st and the panel agreed to file their judgment on or before that date." There was the sound of keys being tapped. "With your request on ammonium nitrate poisoning, domestically I found a few instances, none fatal since 1947. Internationally–"

"Beirut explosion."

"Yes, it's inconclusive whether or not that crisis was terrorism."

"True, however the explosion released the chemical into the air and affected the water supply. The results are still being felt." Adam pushed his drink away. "Nothing recent in Canada?"

"Some emergency room treatments in the past two years, nothing fatal."

"Okay, good to know. Is that everything?"

"On the work, yes. I have something else to ask, if I can?"

"Certainly."

"Is it okay if I take this coming Friday as a vacation day?"

Norcross smiled. No wonder Maisy was in a perky mood. "Of course, enjoy. And excellent work, thank you."

* * *

After his phone calls were complete, Adam remained in the chair by the window, thinking. The name Silas Rivers left a bad taste in his mouth.

Finally, he got to his feet and walked across the room to his suitcase lying on the luggage stand. He quickly unlocked it and extracted the letter from his mother.

Adam looked down at the cream envelope in his hands. He knew it was time.

He turned it over and broke the seal on the flap. Inside was a single sheet of paper, also his mother's stationary. As he removed the page, the faintest hint of his mother's signature perfume reached his nose. Or was it merely a figment of his imagination?

Slowly, he unfolded the letter and scanned it once quickly before going back to the top to absorb his mother's words.

Dearest Adam,

Please ignore anything Wu Abernathy said about who your father is. I fed him a story so he'd leave it alone. Honestly, the man is an incorrigible snoop.

You probably already know your father is Silas Rivers. Yes, the Right Honourable Silas Rivers, Chief Justice of Canada.

Back when I was a newly minted associate, I clerked for him for two years after I graduated from Simon Fraser University. Of course that was decades before Silas was elevated to the high court.

Later we had a brief mad fling and you were the result. When I told Silas I was pregnant after we ended our relationship, he gave me a financial settlement and asked me not to tell you about him.

I had no trouble agreeing to this, because I'd come to the conclusion he would not be a suitable father or role model for you by then. I'd made a horrible mistake getting involved with Silas. I can't even figure out why I did. My excuse, I suppose, is I was attracted to the potential power he carried like a mantle. Even back then he was a man of influence. Silas possesses an odd kind of charisma I can't explain.

Anyway, I don't completely understand what you do for a living, but I'm not stupid enough to think you would never look into who fathered you no matter what I said. So there you have it, my confirmation on the identity of your birth father. Do with it as you will.

Also, under pain of death DO NOT read any of the books I penned as Ivy Blackwood.

All my love,
Mom

Chapter Twenty-Four

Beth was early for breakfast the next morning, but Norcross anticipated this. He was seated in the breakfast room with a carafe of coffee at the ready when she strolled in. She wore a tailored black jacket over a white button down shirt, jeans and black shoes. Beth removed a red scarf as she arrived at the table. Her long dark hair was subdued into an intricate design at the nape of her neck.

Tilly popped out of the kitchen to greet her as she delivered the yoghurt and fruit to the table for them.

Beth nudged the yoghurt away with one index finger but picked up her utensil to enjoy the cubes of melon, cantaloupe, grapes, and strawberries. It didn't take them long to get back into the case discussion.

"We got Knighly's complete pathology report yesterday. Pelly presented the findings at the briefing last night."

"Any surprises?"

She shook her head as she ate a chunk of melon.

"You and I have been at ground zero. Pelly just had to bring the rest of the team up to speed."

When she picked up her mug of coffee to take a sip, he added his opinion. "If Honeyweld was poisoned from the broken cooler pack, he was probably extremely ill. I'm surprised he could function, let alone drive himself to the property or dig around in a ditch. Something doesn't feel right."

"I agree." Beth nodded as she chased the last piece of fruit in the bottom of the bowl. "From what I could see, all those meal containers were sealed. How did the chemical get into Honeyweld's system? Was it a case of poisoning, even accidentally?"

Norcross release a long sigh as he stacked his empty bowls together.

"What?" She frowned and then her expression cleared. "You know something."

"It's murder. I suspect each of those homemade frozen dinners carries a traces of ammonium nitrate mixed in the food."

"Judy Honeyweld?" Leith kept her voice low.

Norcross' mouth twisted. "Forensics will probably find only Judy's fingerprints on the unopened containers. Sam's report is what I'm waiting for."

"You think we found the killer." It was not a question.

337

"I do." He folded his arms over his chest. "By the way, is Pelly charging Hilda Barker with anything?"

"Not until we know if smacking our victim with a rock had any adverse effect on him. Pelly told me the pathologist doesn't think so, but Knighly is looking into it."

"Doesn't intent come into the equation?" Norcross asked.

"It does to a certain extent. The inspector will have to meet with the Crown prosecutor to determine next steps. She's already given them Hilda Barker's statement and the phone recordings." She slowly turned her water glass in a circle. "I've asked to be allowed to view her questioning. Did you want to be there too?"

"I've always found the human mind fascinating. What is it that triggers normal people to do something criminal? So yes, I would."

Tilly pushed the kitchen door open with her hip and brought in the hot portion of their breakfast. This morning it was sausages, pancakes and a side of fried tomatoes. She also left four-ounce glasses of orange juice. They waited to continue their conversation until Tilly returned to the kitchen.

"Why do you think Judy did it?" Norcross asked and speared a chunk of sausage.

Leith drizzled maple syrup onto her pancakes. "I got another look at Judy's journal entries after the briefing. Glen had them printed out. If her words are to be believed, she wanted her husband to stop spending money."

Norcross raised one hand. "Why wouldn't you believe what Judy wrote in her diary?"

Leith shook her head. "It feels weird is the best way I can describe it. Life with Rupert Honeyweld couldn't have been easy. It sounds like he was depleting their savings with no regard for her needs. Her hopes to look into alternative cancer treatments were crushed after an argument with Rupert. She wrote in her journal she thought he was merely buying artefacts with the money, but from what you found for us in the shed lower level of that outbuilding, Rupert had gone through a lot of their savings in an effort to setup his black-market site. Cabot found receipts for the gear in the shed basement. Most of it is only a couple of months old."

Norcross speared another piece of pancake with his fork but paused. "Did Judy mention anything in her journal about the site in the basement?"

"No, she was in the midst of her cancer treatment and wrote mostly about that. Not much about her husband, except to say he hardly spent any time with her." Beth looked

339

up at Norcross. "She said things like how selfish Rupert could be and how angry she should be, except she didn't have the energy."

"Stage-four liver cancer might not be something you can get alternative treatments for and live. Was she thinking Mexico or something?"

"No," Beth swallowed. "Vancouver, they do specialized work-ups on each case and customize a treatment plan for each patient, but the living costs and travel were off the table, they couldn't afford it."

"Rupert took their savings. So maybe to her, he took her last chance."

"She had to depend on other people for everything. To help her get to Yorkton for her cancer treatment, clean the house, buy groceries, you name it. One of her last statements has stuck with me. 'Rupert is just waiting for me to die.' I'm guessing Judy realized in the end she was living with a sociopath."

"I think Rupert was a bit more than a sociopath."

"He was incredibly self-centered." Beth picked up her glass for a drink.

"Not all psychopaths are serial killers. Some go into politics."

Beth snorted the contents of her glass when she laughed and had to use a napkin.

"Sorry." Norcross winked at her.

"We should go." Beth finished off her coffee.

"Where are we off to?"

"Pelly okayed you to attend Hilda Barker's interrogation this morning. We have to be there before nine."

Norcross smiled at her. "Let's burn my gas this time."

Beth shrugged and got up to put on her coat. "Fine by me."

They got into the Tacoma with Beth in the passenger seat. Five minutes into the drive, Norcross knew this was a mistake. The woman wasn't good at being idle.

Beth launched into an analysis of the case as she tapped her fingers against her thigh. "You remember Hilda said, 'people don't change, they just get better at hiding what they are.' I believe that's true, up to a certain point. Then as people age, they no longer care what anyone thinks, and we get to see their character in living colour." She rubbed her thumbnail along the seam of her jeans as she narrowed her eyes at the highway ahead.

He gave a nod. "I agree."

"Then when Judy realized she was going to die, she decided to make a plan."

Norcross nodded. "So it would seem."

"I've been living at home the last couple of months and witnessed our victim trying to wreck more than just my dad's reputation and livelihood. The assault

341

charges were devastating for Dad. He was incredibly relieved when the judge tossed them out. My father has never been a physical person." She chewed her thumbnail for a moment. A faint smile flashed briefly. "In our family, discipline was dealt out by my mother. Dad was too much of a softy. One or other of the boys was always doing extra chores for something they got caught doing wrong."

"You never got into trouble?"

She grinned at him. "I had four examples of 'what not to do.'" Beth pushed a stray strand of dark hair off her cheek. She tucked it behind her ear with her left hand. "Why Honeyweld chose my family to pick on, I don't know, but I doubt his bullying stopped with Dad."

"Buchanan said he canvased the neighbourhood. Did he bring back any other reports of people having problems with Honeyweld?"

"I don't know, we'll have to ask him."

"Rupert must have done or said something over the top to trigger your dad to punch him."

She nodded. "Yep, but he won't talk about it. Mom said something about Honeyweld accusing dad of incompetence, funds mismanagement, with regard to the Historical Society. It was during the Christmas party and there was an open bar that didn't help. Dad should have walked away."

"We can't always do that."

"I know, a bully has to be faced down."

Norcross glanced sideways and noted the set of Beth's jaw.

* * *

Norcross followed Beth's directions through the small city of Canora and parked the Tacoma in a visitor's slot at the RCMP detachment where Inspector Pelly had her office.

They were early for the interrogation, but it took some time to clear the way for Beth and Norcross to enter the building. A call to the inspector sped things along.

Both she and Norcross wore visitor ID tags when they'd entered the office area. Looking around at the office area made Beth blink. The layout, furniture, and equipment were similar to the Duncan BC detachment. The sameness and time elapsed since she'd been in her own office caught up with her for a brief moment. Then she adjusted her black blazer down over her jeans and looked around properly.

Glen Buchanan greeted them. "Looks like we might wrap this case up in the next day or so." The constable was much more cheerful this morning. Beth suppressed a smile as Buchanan all but bounced on the toes of his feet.

"We can only hope," Norcross said. "Have you received Sam Malcolm's report yet?"

"Not yet, his analysis should be here sometime this afternoon."

Pelly stepped out of her office and frowned when she saw Norcross. It was clear to Beth the inspector didn't trust him.

Not that it appeared to bother Norcross at all. "Ah, Inspector," he said when he spied her. "If I could have a moment of your time, please?"

The inspector gave him a considering look. It was apparent to Beth, Pelly wanted to refuse, but then she nodded. "Come in." And waved him into her office.

Beth lifted one eyebrow as she wondered what Norcross was up to. What could they be talking about that he didn't bother to include her in the conversation? For one moment, Beth wondered if this private conversation had anything to do with her work situation. She hoped not.

Well, she'd find out later. That was a certainty. In the meantime, she turned to address the constable.

"Glen, did you get many neighbours reporting they'd had interactions with Rupert Honeyweld in the day preceding his death?"

In answer, Buchanan reached over and picked up a file folder approximately an inch thick. He did a quick fanning motion through the papers. "Only a few, and all negative." His tone was derisive. "Honeyweld was a thorn in many people's backside."

"Interesting turn of phrase." She allowed a small smile. He was so young.

"If we didn't have Hilda Barker as our main suspect, I'd be reviewing these statements again and narrowing down the field."

"Is this the biggest case you've been involved in so far, since you left the Depot?"

"Yeah, it is. I know you've worked murders before." His look said he knew exactly how many she'd worked on.

"One or two." She shifted her feet. It was an odd tally to keep in her head, but she did none the less. "Who says Barker is our main suspect?"

"Pelly."

Beth nodded without comment and wished they had Sam's report.

Then Norcross and Pelly emerged from her office. The inspector gave Norcross a stiff nod, but she didn't appear to be annoyed by him, so maybe they had settled their power struggle.

Norcross walked back over to join her and Buchanan. The man was comfortable anywhere. That thought was a touch disturbing.

His face was bland as always, approachable, but gave nothing away. A lot of the time she could read him, but not always. Probably only when he let her.

"Come on, I'll take you to the observation room." The constable waved a hand toward the back of the large central room. "Coffee area is over there, help yourself. Whitmere brought in a blueberry crumble cake. It's pretty good." Buchanan led the way down a hallway.

Chapter Twenty-Five

They stood behind another pair of constables in the back of a bare room. Buchanan was already seated in the small box like interrogation space on the other side of the one-way window. Pelly would join him when Hilda Barker was brought in.

This would be a learning moment for Buchanan. He would take notes, listen, and only speak if Pelly wanted him to. There was nothing like a live interview with a real suspect to teach a rookie how things were done.

One or two more people would be keeping tabs on the interview from the electronics room. All interviews were videotaped with audio recorded as standard practise.

It felt odd to Beth to be out of the action, but then she reminded herself she wasn't in charge of the investigation.

Norcross glance down at her but did not comment, for that she was glad. Sympathy was not helpful.

Movement in the hallway signaled Hilda Barker's arrival. She entered the room looking freshly scrubbed, no makeup today, although she wore the same clothes as yesterday. Her long ash-blonde hair was pulled back off her pale face, tied back in a ponytail.

Her lips were compressed and her eyes downcast as the cuffs were removed and took a seat kitty corner from Buchanan. She folded her hands in her lap. The male officer who brought her in retreated and slipped the handcuffs back into the case on his belt.

"Do we know if Hilda has lawyered up?" Beth asked Norcross in a low voice.

"I don't know, Pelly didn't say."

Five beats after the suspect was seated, the inspector entered the room.

Hilda watched Pelly with narrowed eyes.

The inspector carried a file folder under her arm, which she placed on the table and took the chair across from the older woman. Pelly smiled at Hilda and introduced herself.

Hilda huffed a dry laugh. "I don't know why I'm here."

"You assaulted your brother with a rock. We have your confession." Pelly tapped the folder. "Would you like me to read you the transcript?"

"I didn't kill my brother."

"We don't know that. Why did you assault Rupert? And why with a rock?"

Beth folded her arms across her chest, making her jacket rustle. She wasn't sure what Pelly expected to get out of Hilda with this line of questioning, possibly more background on their victim.

"I told the other cop what happened."

"Yes, but I'd like to understand your side. Let's talk about Rupert."

Hilda lifted one shoulder. "What do you want to know?"

"I understand you and your brother didn't get along. You were estranged for years."

Hilda laid her hands flat on the table, rubbing one index finger into a dent in the table top. "That's true, but when Judy got sick, I rethought how I felt. It all didn't seem to mean as much anymore."

"When was the last time you saw your brother? Was it before your confrontation on the Leith's property?"

Pelly waited. This was the lie Hilda had been caught in yesterday.

The blonde woman sighed dramatically and waved one hand in a resigned gesture.

"I saw Rupert at Judy's funeral a little over two weeks ago."

"Was the funeral well attended?"

"There were tons of people there. Judy was very well liked. Four different women

349

stood up to tell different stories about her. Judy was a good, giving person."

The inspector turned to the younger cop. "Is that what you found, Constable Buchanan?"

"Absolutely, Judy Honeyweld was community minded. She was involved in several projects and organizations in Lone Spruce. By all accounts she was also generous with her time and money."

Hilda frowned at this last part of the assessment.

"Do you think Rupert's marriage was a happy one?" Pelly tipped her head like she was listening intently.

"I don't know, do I?" Hilda's tone was flat. "How can anyone know what goes on in someone else's relationship?"

"Did you and Judy stay in contact while you were estranged from your brother?"

"Christmas cards and such, that's about it."

"That's odd." Pelly pulled a sheet of paper out of her file folder. Even from where they were located, it was easy for Beth to see the yellow highlighted lines of a telephone bill. "These are calls from you to Judy's mobile phone. Unless of course you were trying to call your brother?"

Hilda shook her head. "I was returning Judy's calls. She needed someone to talk to. She was scared about her cancer and angry with Rupert's disregard for her condition."

"I see." Pelly pulled out another sheet. "There are over a dozen calls recorded here over the past three months." She added two more sheets to the pile. "Were you helping Judy?"

"What would I help Judy with?" Hilda shook her head.

"Yes, you're right why would you help your sister-in-law? Were you trying to get Judy to help you instead?"

Hilda rolled her eyes. "With what? Judy was very nice, but not much of an intellect. I talked to her to support her because Rupert had abandoned her. She was alone and frightened."

"That doesn't stack up with what their neighbours told us," Buchanan interjected.

"No, it doesn't, does it?" Pelly nodded to the constable. He handed her a stapled, typewritten statement. "Tilly Key told us she would take Judy to her medical appointments, she and another lady from the Auxiliary they all belonged to. I have a whole list of names. People who helped Judy in many ways during her illness. That's the thing about small towns; everyone pulls together when there is a crisis." She handed the statement back to Buchanan. "Judy wasn't really alone even if what you say is true and Rupert was negligent in her care."

"After someone has died, everyone says they helped out in some way. Judy needed a confidant, she needed me."

The inspector continued to look at Hilda as she put her hand out again and Buchanan dropped another spreadsheet into it. The inspector laid the report on the table in front of Hilda. "This is the amount of video chats Judy had with her brother in Australia. It seems she spoke to him quite often. And Mr. Riskly confirmed that assumption. So Judy had a confidant, I doubt very much you entered into it."

There was a tightening around Hilda's mouth as she narrowed her eyes.

Pelly tried again. "So, why all the phone calls? What did you talk about with your sister-in-law?"

"I don't remember." Hilda dropped her eyes again. "I don't want to do this anymore."

"You really don't have much of a choice."

"I'm done talking. I want my lawyer."

"He's on his way from Saskatoon. Your boss, Doctor Orlinsky, made arrangements."

Hilda sat back in her chair, folded her arms over her chest, and glared at Pelly. For the next fifteen minutes, Hilda did not say one word, no matter how Pelly asked her questions.

352

"Take her back to her cell." Pelly closed her folder and studied Hilda as she was handcuffed and taken away, still silent and defiant.

Beth tipped her chin at Norcross. "Come on." She led the way next door.

"I don't want to play that card yet. I'm not sure how she'd take it." Pelly was saying to Buchanan when they entered the room.

"You think Hilda helped Judy murder Rupert?" Leith just came right out with her supposition. In her mind it was a waste of time to beat around the bush.

"I think that's a likely scenario." Pelly stood and picked up her folder.

Buchanan's phone pinged and he took out the device.

"Have you looked at Judy's journal?" Beth asked Pelly.

"I've read the pages from the past two months." Pelly edged toward the door.

The constable stood. "Sam's report is ready. He's sent it to you and wants you to call him."

"Let's move this to my office." Pelly led the way out of interrogation and back to the office area with the other three trooping behind her.

In her office she gestured for them all to grab a chair. Pelly picked up her handset and began to dial. "I'll put it on speaker."

Beth took the chair to the left of the desk, Norcross the one next to her, and finally Buchanan. He paused to push the door shut.

She felt Norcross' eyes on her and looked over at him. His black eyebrows disappeared into his silver hair. "What is it?"

The phone set to speaker rang. "Sam's morgue, you stab 'em, we slab 'em."

"The journal. It's been bugging me since yesterday–" She stopped talking when Pelly held up one finger.

"Not funny, Sam."

"Sorry Inspector, I didn't realize it was you."

"Sure. I'm here with Norcross, Sergeant Leith and Constable Buchanan, you're on speaker. What have you found?"

"Okay," Sam drew out the word. Some shuffling could be heard on the line. "First, the food in the containers, all the food we brought back with us, was contaminated with ammonium nitrate. I suspect the rest in storage will be the same."

"A lethal amount of the chemical?" Pelly leaned toward the phone.

"Yes. Secondly, I spoke with Knighly about the percentages we found in the food, and he agrees our victim was poisoned with the homemade frozen dinners. He must have been consuming them since his wife died over the past couple of weeks. From the amount of discarded containers in the kitchen, Knightly postulates the toxins built up in our victim's system over time and that is what eventually killed him. The crack on the head wouldn't have mattered one way or another. The blow would have only done superficial damage as Knightly told us."

"Fingerprints?" Pelly interjected.

"Yep, the prints on all the items belonged to Judy Honeyweld. We took samples from other things in the house. Items which we determined she would have touched. We are reasonably certain the prints on the containers are hers. The rest of the fingerprints in the kitchen and laundry room were Rupert Honeyweld's."

The inspector slowly dropped into her office chair behind the desk. She narrowed her eyes at the phone. "Have you eliminated any other prints found in the house?"

"You mean the ones you sent me from Hilda Barker? None of the prints in the residence match hers."

Pelly's expression turned annoyed.

"If I may?" Norcross spoke up, and Pelly waved at him to continue. "Did you find any disposable gloves in the residence, Sam?"

"Yes, we found a box of the standard blue ones you can buy at any pharmacy. These were found in the main floor bathroom under the sink."

"Any used gloves found?"

Pelly focused on Norcross more intently.

"Yes." Sam said, over some background noise of shuffling items on his desk. "However, we were unable to extract any prints from those gloves. Here it is. The team in the garage found a pair of partially burned disposable gloves, again blue, in the woodstove. The heat from a fire made it impossible to determine who used them. The material was damaged beyond extracting any DNA or prints from the two fingertips left, I'm afraid."

"Someone lit the gloves on fire?" Buchannan interjected.

"Well, they started a fire in the wood stove. I couldn't say if it was done on purpose. Still, it does look hinky."

"I hate that word. I want solid evidence," Pelly muttered, then raised her voice. "Thanks for this Sam, I'll read the full report as soon as I can."

"No worries." Sam hung up.

Norcross shifted his gaze to Leith. It was her turn.

Beth leaned forward. "The journal is bugging me."

"Yes, you said that. What about the journal?" Pelly shifted her focus to the sergeant.

"The change in attitude in the wording along with the changes in writing style, it doesn't add up."

"What's your theory, Sergeant?" Pelly asked.

"I think, Hilda Barker framed Judy for the death of her husband." She looked back at Pelly, and from the corner of her eye, she saw Norcross give a shallow nod. "Hilda set it up to make it look like the dying wife took revenge on her husband. I think she put those entries into the journal. I also think Hilda added the ammonium nitrate to the food Judy prepared for Rupert. She would know what Judy was doing, as far as the food was concerned from their phone calls. Hilda just had to get in the house, probably before or after the funeral and poison the food. Who would think it odd a sister consoling her widowed brother?"

"That makes more sense than thinking Judy Honeyweld murdered her husband. I couldn't find one person who would say anything negative about the woman. What I don't get is why Hilda would want to kill her brother?" Buchanan looked around at the other three for the answer.

"I can tell you the reason." Norcross leaned forward, resting his elbows on his thighs.

He was enjoying solving the puzzle. This realization made Beth blink. Was it like a game to him?

"Go ahead, Mr. Norcross, don't stop now." Pelly's tone held more than a slice of irony. She rested her chin on her fist.

"Do you have the Honeywelds' financial statements yet?" For his part, Norcross kept his tone even. Still, Beth sensed he was toying with Pelly. Probably because the inspector gritted her teeth whenever he spoke, and he'd noticed.

"As it happens, we do." Pelly gestured to Buchanan.

The constable was already getting out of his chair and heading for the door. He left them but almost immediately returned with a sheaf of papers in hand, reading as he walked to the inspector's desk. "This is interesting."

"What is?" Pelly reached for the report.

"There's nothing remarkable in the joint accounts at the credit union, government pension deposits going in and daily living expenses going out." Buchanan handed the document over. "But look at the next page. The Honeywelds had accounts in a couple of banks in Yorkton, in both their names."

Pelly pursed her lips as she flipped to the second page. "That's... a significant amount."

Norcross nodded. "Four hundred and seventy-six thousand dollars. You will find the cash deposits are from online sales. Mr. Honeyweld was not employed and hasn't been for decades. He made a tidy sum on the dark web selling antiquities." Norcross leaned back in his chair. "A Clovis artefact can go from two hundred to twelve hundred dollars apiece. I'm sure his wife knew how he provided for them. Possibly she thought he gained the artefacts by honest means, who can say now? However, it remains Rupert was in no way cash strapped. And neither was Judy."

"Hilda told us in her interview yesterday, Rupert stole artefacts from her office." Pelly closed her eyes briefly. "How did I miss that?"

"Do you really think he stole the items?" Beth lifted dark eyebrows at the inspector.

Pelly opened her eyes and now focused on Leith.

"They were a partnership together," Beth explained. "Hilda procured the artefacts and Rupert sold them. Hence the courier boxes in the garage."

"That makes sense." Pelly was on the same page.

The inspector shifted her gaze to Buchanan. "Did you have Whitmere trace the origin of the shipments? We will no doubt find they came from his sister."

"I did, I'll check with him," Buchanan said.

Norcross dug out his mobile phone from his inside coat pocket. "Inspector, I received a report on Hilda Barker. It won't be admissible as evidence, but the document makes for informative reading about her past and shady character. It may help with the interrogation."

Pelly tipped an index finger at him. "Send it to me." She rubbed her forehead with her other hand. "You think Rupert was ripping his sister off?"

"I am persuaded to think so, yes." Norcross tapped and swiped his phone screen as he spoke. "As his closest relative, Hilda would end up inheriting Rupert's estate in any case. I suspect she lost her temper with him since he was using the artefacts as props in his personal war with Nick Leith. I suspect the argument was real and when Rupert would not get with the plan, Hilda assaulted him."

"Possibly, she was checking on the progress of her ammonium nitrate effectiveness and found it wasn't going as fast as she wanted." Pelly straightened in her chair.

"I wonder if she was also worried about running the sales side of the business on her own with him gone. That's added stress," Beth suggested, and Norcross nodded.

"No doubt." Pelly used her mouse to click open the report Norcross sent her. She quickly scanned the document.

Finally, Pelly lifted her eyes and looked at Leith and Norcross. "You've shortened the investigation time on this case considerably. Thank you both." She shifted her eyes to look at Buchanan. "Well, I think it's time to get Hilda Barker back into the interrogation room, Glen."

"Will do." The constable popped to his feet again and left.

"You need an admission of some kind to link Barker to the ammonium nitrate." Beth pointed out.

"I do. Good thing I love a challenge." The inspector rose to her feet.

Chapter Twenty-Six

This time Leith and Norcross rolled a couple of office chairs into the observation room to sit in comfort while they watched Pelly take Hilda Barker down.

The inspector was speaking when they turned their attention to the exchange. "We found your disposable gloves in the wood stove," Pelly remarked.

"I don't know what you're talking about." Hilda frowned and placed her hands flat on the table. Her left index finger found the dent again. "I don't know why I'm still here. Where is my lawyer?"

"As I told you half an hour ago, driving down from Saskatoon." Pelly picked up her pen and tapped the closed folder in front of her. "You did set fire to the gloves. However, they did not completely burn."

She gestured a finger at Buchanan, and he extracted a photograph from his folder and it placed on the table.

"Did you know?" The inspector pushed the photograph forward. "The inside of disposable gloves will take a fingerprint?"

This made Hilda pull her hands back as if she might be burned.

Pelly turned to Buchanan. "Which fingers were still intact, Constable?"

He consulted the papers in his file folder and extracted one photo. "The left thumb and the right index finger."

Inspector Pelly tapped the photo in front of Hilda. "We have the capability of extracting fingerprint evidence from discarded gloves."

"Nice," Beth said. "Pelly told Hilda a solid fact and left the rest to Hilda's imagination."

Norcross nodded in satisfaction.

The inspector changed her body language, leaning forward with one elbow on the table. This said to Norcross she would now change tactics and appeal to Hilda's vanity.

"It would take someone very organized and exceedingly brilliant to not get caught funneling stolen property to Rupert Honeyweld. The archeological world can't be terribly large. Someone might have noticed missing items coming up for sale periodically, even if it was over the dark web, where the majority of the population never goes."

The suspect merely lifted her chin, though there was the hint of a smug smile.

"How long had this game been going on? Five months?"

"Years." Hilda let this slip. She covered her lapse with an arrogant expression and looked away to study the clock on the wall across from them.

"Really?" Pelly sounded impressed. "Like from when you both were kids? It must have been a hard life living with parents who cared more for ancient artefacts and dead things than you and your brother."

Hilda glanced at Pelly and probably only finding sincere empathy, shrugged one shoulder. "They dragged us all over the world chasing their bits of junk."

It took time and perseverance, but finally Inspector Pelly had stroked the suspect's ego enough. "Was that T-Rex your first theft?"

Their suspect had dropped her guard. "It was supposed to be, but it went wrong. We learned from that experience and got smarter."

"You played the long game, didn't you? Clever that. Ammonium nitrate isn't lethal in small doses. All you had to do was wait it out." Pelly leaned forward a touch. "How did you find out what Rupert was up to? Was he pocketing part of your share? He wasn't honest with you, was he?"

"Rupert, honest? Please." Hilda swiped a stray strand of hair back toward her ponytail. "I knew something was up even before Orlinsky told me about Rupert's 'discovery.'" Hilda used air quotes as she spoke. "He was supposed to be selling the artefacts, not planting them, the idiot."

Pelly, chin in hand, appeared fascinated by every word out of Hilda's mouth. "What did you do?"

"When I came down for the funeral, I searched the house and shed for all the artefacts I'd sent him. The most valuable ones were missing. He'd taken th."

"Did you know about the room under the shed?"

Hilda's head snapped up. "What room?"

Pelly gestured to Buchanan. He handed her three photographs.

The pictures were placed one after the other in front of Hilda. She snatched these up to stare at them hungrily. "There's the rest of the collection of flint points." She moved on to the next picture. "The Cameroon monoliths," she breathed in apparent relief.

Jaw clenched, Hilda turned her glare on Pelly. "He had a whole room full of things. He kept them to himself and the money he made. I knew he was cheating me."

"When did you poison those food containers Judy stored in the deep freeze with ammonium nitrate?"

"Over six weeks ago, after Judy went into the hospital. He deserved it, the little bastard."

Beth released a snort. "Sociopaths always want to show everyone else how smart they are."

"Mm." Norcross agreed. "Psychopaths are much the same, probably more so." He tipped his head at the Inspector. "Pelly is very good at this type of questioning, almost as good as you." Norcross knew Beth turned to look at him, but he kept focused on the interrogation.

"The nitrate was taking too long, wasn't it?" Pelly asked this gently.

Hilda nodded. "Rupert took some of the best artefacts and buried them on that stupid pit. I had to stop him before he lost something. Or we were discovered. Orlinsky isn't very bright, but he would eventually figure out what Rupert was doing. Then Orlinsky would know I was involved. So I suggested to my brother he could make it look like he'd made the find of the decade or even the century, right here in his own backyard. I played him like he played me." She lifted her chin defiantly, pleased with herself.

"Please, go on. I'd love to hear the details."

Hilda snorted as she leaned forward. "I told him, 'Wouldn't it be wonderful if we could prove he'd found some evidence of a pre-Clovis settlement adjacent to the first set of finds by the river?' He was hooked." She dropped back in her chair with a self-

366

satisfied expression. "I was at the camp, as part of the dig. All I had to do was ensure I kept an eye out for him."

"You took on all the errand trips into town?"

"Of course I did. No one would wonder where I'd gone. This way I would know the right road Rupert took and in which area he decided to plant the evidence for the pre-Clovis settlement. I still find it unbelievable he went for it, genius my eye." She shook her head. "It was too easy. What was worse, Rupert had no plans to stop. I mean, really, a stone circle? As if."

Hilda took a swallow of water from the disposable plastic cup to her left and then took a new breath. When she looked up, it was easy to see she had become lost in the retelling. "I found the dirt road where Rupert was working. His machine was parked beside the ditch and I watched him drive off that evening. The next morning, I went back. This time I hiked there before sunup to get ahead of him and waited."

Buchanan made a note. Norcross presumed it was something about lying in wait.

"He left a shovel by his ATV and picked up a cardboard box. I followed him down into the ditch. He carried the box of artefacts over to his trench. He began placing them in one at a time. I recognized

367

some of the items. The ones I'd sent him in the last shipment."

"Was the stone mallet among the items?"

Hilda was calmer now and barely reacted to Pelly's question. "I saw it in the cardboard box. All the artefacts were tossed in it like they were nothing, Rupert never respected the science." Her lip curled in disgust. "He got to his feet for some reason. I let him take a couple of steps toward the road. I decided right then I wanted it to be over. I didn't want to deal with him for one more second or wait for the ammonium nitrate to finish him. I grabbed a rock from the spoils heap beside the trench. I never said a word to him. I walked up behind him and struck him on the head and he fell." She relaxed back into her chair. "That's when I noticed his skin had turned blue."

On the drive back to Lone Spruce, Norcross told Beth about his conversation with Zara Dare. He left out his associate's name, only referring to her as a trusted source. After he concluded, he waited through Beth's silence.

Finally, after several minutes h asked, "What are you going to do now?" Adam felt he knew but needed to hear Beth say it.

"Someone at a high level is behind my suspension. I could put this all behind me and hope it doesn't come back to bite me in the butt if I do what they want. I'd have to keep my head down afterward and not make waves. And hope it's not Geoffery Thrust, even if he did get you involved." Beth heaved a huge sigh and rubbed her left eyelid tiredly. "The problem is, once I comply to their demands, now I'm compromised." She dropped her hands to her lap, defeated.

"That is the danger." He didn't add that once someone thought they could use you once, they'd always come back to try it again. "Typically, politicians claim some kind of mental breakdown in these situations. A lapse in judgment of some kind or beg the family pressure excuse, or rehab. The person in question can usually find an out, and the prosecution has the option to let him off."

She nodded. "No doubt. I still think Winslow should be brought before the court in a timely manner. He shouldn't be allowed to drag out the case with pricy lawyers hoping the whole thing gets tossed out because the Crown didn't get him to court quick enough."

"Winslow is hoping the voters will forget about his involvement with the riots." Norcross slowed the truck for a coyote to scurry across the highway.

"His political career should be over with everything he's done, with only himself to blame." Her hands flexed where they

369

gripped her thighs. "Why do I get the feeling he's going to come out of this with nothing sticking to him?"

"If things progress the way he wants them to," Norcross agreed and glanced over at her set expression. "What's your plan?"

"I don't know. What bothers me is the fact that every time he got away scot free, he did something progressively worse. The way he intimidated his female neighbour is so disturbing. It's like he's ramping up to something. I can feel it, but no one is paying attention. Well, except me and Collin." She sat up and straightened her posture. "I'm not dropping the charges. Doing so would set a bad precedent. I can't let him get away with assault. What will he try next?"

"You'll wait for the review panel to run its course then?"

"What else can I do? My hands are tied. Until the review panel comes back with their judgement, my life is in limbo."

"Are you opposed to me giving you some assistance?"

She glanced sideways at him and their eyes met. "Two months ago I might have refused your help. Now I need all the assistance I can get and I'm guessing you bring some serious weight to the argument. So, no, I wouldn't mind your help, not at all."

Norcross nodded and then turned his eyes back to the road and waited. Twenty minutes later, Beth's phone rang.

She frowned at the display. "It's Taggard." She accepted the call. "Yes, sir."

"Beth, I wanted to be the first to tell you the review panel just contacted me. All charges of harassment, assault, etcetera, have been withdrawn by Winslow Thrust's legal counsel at the MLA's behest. This means the panel has dropped the inquiry into your conduct. You've been re-instated in full."

Leith took a breath and moistened dry lips. "Thank you, sir. That is great news. What about the charges of assault against Thrust?"

"The Crown prosecutor is going ahead with the case. There is a scheduled court date now too. This could be the result of his psych exam. Collin heard Thrust is going to step down from his seat in the Legislature."

"That's something anyway."

"It is. Now, I don't expect you to jump on the next plane back here, but we could use your help as soon as possible. You know how understaffed we are."

"I can be back at work on Monday, Boss."

"Do you have a place to live? I didn't think you kept your apartment. Do you want us to setup accommodations in a hotel until you get situated?"

"That won't be necessary." Beth looked over at Norcross. "I have a friend who needs someone to house sit for him."

Norcross gave her a nod as a smile curved his lips.

After her conversation with Inspector Taggard concluded, Beth narrowed her eyes at Norcross. "What did you do?"

He tipped his head slightly in acknowledgment. "You did say you'd take my help."

"How did you get Winslow Thrust to back down?"

"Oh, I merely found out what his politics are."

"And what are his politics?"

Norcross shook his head. "That, I'm afraid, is above your pay grade."

Beth looked like she was going to argue for a moment. Then she nodded, lips pursed. "AG Thrust will not be happy with you."

Norcross gave her an edged smile. "I hope not."

Chapter Twenty-Seven

Doctor Robert Orlinsky sat in his Jeep with the engine running. After the Tacoma pulled in beside him, he waited for Beth and Adam to walk over to his vehicle. He powered down the window. "Is it all wrapped up, then? Is Hilda going to be getting out soon?"

"No, Robert, she isn't," Beth said gently. "I can't give you the details, but she's been charged with the murder of her brother."

Orlinsky closed his eyes briefly and shook his head. "I had a feeling something wasn't right with her." He looked back at the pair and lifted his chin. "That's too bad. She was a good curator." He sighed. "I asked the legal firm for the museum to speak to her. See if they can recommend a criminal lawyer but Hilda may want to get her own counsel." He shrugged.

"I believe someone contacted her just before we left the detachment," Norcross said.

"Can I help you with something?" Beth lifted one dark eyebrow at the archeologist.

"No, no. The GPR team will be back tomorrow to finish the areas they couldn't reach today. I contacted Inspector Pelly already but felt I should keep Nick informed."

"Did you find any other caches of artefacts?" Adam asked.

"No new ones, no. However, the one in the pit went down another metre. I think I recognize some of the finds." Orlinsky cleared his throat. "Hilda was in charge of those items." He shifted his sad eyes to Leith.

"She confessed to being involved with her brother. They were both profiting from the sale of stolen artefacts. It would be helpful if you can give Inspector Pelly a statement with regard to the evidence you found."

The archaeologist nodded. "I'll delay going home until tomorrow, then. I'll call the inspector and make arrangements."

"What brings you to the farm?"

"I dropped in on your father to thank him and say goodbye. Mike and Selma have already packed up and left. You will have your land back by end of day tomorrow. I was just bringing Nick up to speed on what I'll be putting in my report. Which is there is no credible evidence, of any type, this particular section of land is heritage sensitive. That means the land can be classified as having a low potential for ancient First Nations camp sites, burial places or ceremonial sites. That includes ancient Paleo-Indian sites. I'll make sure Nick gets a copy of the report when I file at the end of next month with the Heritage Conservation Branch."

"That's good news, thank you." Leith smiled at Robert, which he returned.

"You even included the stone circle?" Norcross asked evenly. Leith nudged his foot with the toe of her shoe. He gave her an innocent look.

"Even the stone circle." Robert nodded. "However, if you dig up anything interesting, the Heritage Property Act of 1980 states all artefacts belong to the provincial government," the archaeologist reminded them.

"Mm." Leith nodded. "The artefacts found on our new parcel of land, possibly including the stone circle, are more than likely stolen, along with everything else found on the Honeyweld property in town. Each item will need to be catalogued and the rightful owners identified. Inspector Pelly asked us who would be the best person to speak to, and we gave her your name."

"Oh," Robert said, his tone hesitant. "Thank you."

"You would be able to apply for several grad students to help you with the work." Adam suggested.

Orlinsky brightened at this suggestion. "Yes, I bet we could. It would be a wonderful learning experience for students and good doctorate material."

"Here's Pelly's contact information." Leith handed the older man a business card.

"Thank you." He tucked it away. "Well, I must get moving. Rachel is back and it will be home cooking tonight." He smiled. "My wife is roasting a chicken."

After exchanging farewells, the pair stepped away from the vehicle and Robert waved at them as he drove away.

"What was that about the stone circle?" Beth turned toward the house and Adam fell into step with her.

"You'll probably get to keep that feature. Those stones are no doubt from a local quarry."

* * *

"I have to say, I'm a bit disappointed we don't have an important archaeological site here somewhere." Maria walked around the table filling everyone's tea mugs after supper.

"Who says?" Nick's tone was mildly disgruntled. "Just because Honeyweld was a fraud and a thief, doesn't mean we don't have something historically noteworthy."

Beth lifted one shoulder as she looked at her father. "All the artefacts found were placed here by Rupert Honeyweld. None of them were legitimately discovered on our property."

"That's not strictly true. Back when I was a young man, we used to walk the fields picking rocks. Everyone did, that's how people found arrowheads and stone hammers. Now a days, farmers use mechanical means. We sit up on a tractor and pull a rock picker behind it. That means you're too high off the ground to notice something as small as those quartz arrowheads." Nick took a sip of his black tea and grabbed a homemade oatmeal cookie off the plate Maria placed within reach.

Adam leaned forward, resting his elbows on the table as he looked at Nick. "Tilly Key told me people check their rock piles after they dump the pickers."

"I've done that once or twice when I was a teenager." Beth took a cookie off the plate too. "Just to see what was in there. I never thought I'd find anything good."

"That doesn't mean we've never found anything." Abruptly Nick stood and, without another word, left the farmhouse kitchen. The door closed behind him.

Adam stirred a dash of milk into his tea as he looked at Beth. "So, you've got some travel arrangements to make."

"I'm so pleased everything got sorted out for you, Beth. You were right to be patient." Maria placed a hand on her daughter's shoulder and gave it a squeeze.

"Thanks, Mom." Beth smiled up at her mother.

"Now, I have a request." Maria walked over to her kitchen bookshelf and extracted a novel. She briskly returned and dropped the paperback volume in front of Adam just as he was reaching for another cookie. "Tell me about this."

Adam froze and lifted his eyes to Mrs. Leith's narrowed gaze. "What would you like to know?"

"Is it true?"

"What are you talking about, Mom?" Beth lifted one dark eyebrow at her mother.

Adam nudged *Steamy Nights, A Dark Scandal Novel,* away from his cookie with one index finger. He cleared his throat and gave Maria a tight smile. "Yes, my mother wrote those books."

"I knew it as soon as I heard your name. Beth said you were from Vancouver Island. I thought you had to be related to Evelyn Norcross." She chuckled and picked up the novel and ran one hand over the cover.

"If I may ask, how did you connect my mother to Ivy Blackwood? That's her pen name."

Maria slid the novel back into the opening between books. She turned to look at him. "When you find an amazing new author it's like getting a surprise Christmas gift. I've read all her mysteries, they are great stories, and I re-read them periodically. So I researched her to see what else she'd written. There are websites that will give an author's complete background and writing resume. Now I have these books to look forward to." Maria's happy expression turned serious. "I'm only sorry I never got a chance to meet your mother. I'm sure she was a wonderful lady."

Adam gave Beth's mother a nod. "She was. My mother was one of a kind."

Maria put one hand on his shoulder and gave it a pat. "Even so, we have her books to remind us of who she was." Her smile was back in place.

"Those novels aren't–" Adam began, but Beth frowned at him and shook her head. He got her hint it was time to change the subject. His mouth twisted as he came up with a new topic. "Do you think your father is disappointed? No historic or remarkable finds were uncovered. As a member of the Historical Society, no doubt he must have hoped for at least some new artefacts for the museum."

Beth's frown cleared. "I expect you're right." She wrapped her long fingers around her mug of tea. "Dad has such a love of history he would have enjoyed some kind of revealing discovery, even if it would delay the cattle expansion and the bin yard." She took a sip of her tea. "On the bright side, he can now run for the LTHS president's chair again. I doubt after everything that's happened over the past couple of days, anyone would challenge him."

A moment later, they heard the door open and the screen door bang.

Beth's father strolled back into the kitchen carting a medium-sized cardboard box.

Maria looked up from loading the dishwasher. "Lay out some newspaper first, please, Nick." She tossed this over her shoulder.

Unceremoniously he placed the box on the kitchen table.

"Nick really, newspaper!" Maria said, annoyed. "The dirt will get everywhere." With a sigh he dutifully picked up the dusty cardboard box.

Beth jumped up and grabbed a wet dishcloth to wipe the table.

Adam retrieved yesterday's edition of the Lone Spruce community newspaper from the recycle bin and spread the pages out on the cleaned tabletop.

Nick placed the box on the newspaper and opened the flaps. He paused to give Beth and Adam a smile, his eyes sparkling. "Normally I have these all wrapped up, but Robert was just here."

Adam, still on his feet, lifted dark eyebrows as his gaze snagged on the contents of the box. "Those aren't Clovis projectile points, are they?"

"No, they're not." Nick's tone was sombre. He reached into the box and extracted one item. "These are much older. From 50,000 years ago. Pre-Clovis so I'm told."

"Dad, you said you haven't made any finds on the property across the road." Beth lifted one dark eyebrow at him.

"I haven't. These are from the seventeen acres on the other side of Conjuring Creek. Robert will be back in the spring to start the dig."

The End

Readers we need you.

Please leave a review, even a one liner counts, and has a big influence on our future sales.

Published by BWL Publishing Inc.

Musgrave Landing Mysteries
Death and Cupcakes
Fun With Funerals
Condo Crazy

Adam Norcross Mysteries
The Wrong Words

Yvonne Rediger was born in southern Saskatchewan. She lived and worked in northern Manitoba, New Brunswick, Alberta, and Vancouver Island. She now resides in central Saskatchewan with her husband. She has two grown children.

Facebook   -
https://www.facebook.com/YvonneRediger
Author
Twitter   -
http://www.twitter.com/blackyvy
Instagram - @blackyvy50

bwlpublishing.ca

Ingram Content Group UK Ltd.
Milton Keynes UK
UKHW020652050623
422889UK00016B/1644

9 780228 625308